ALINA
A Song for the Telling

Malve von Hassell

ALINA
A Song for the Telling

bhc
press™

Livonia, Michigan

Edited by Rebecca Fischer

Published by BHC Press

Library of Congress Control Number:
2020933340

ISBN: 978-1-64397-072-1 (Hardcover)
ISBN: 978-1-64397-104-9 (Softcover)
ISBN: 978-1-64397-105-6 (Ebook)

For information, write:
BHC Press
885 Penniman #5505
Plymouth, MI 48170

Visit the publisher:
www.bhcpress.com

TABLE OF CONTENTS

PRINCIPAL CHARACTERS

FICTIONAL CHARACTERS

Alina de Florac

Milos de Florac, brother of Alina

Garsanc de Florac, uncle of Alina

Marci de Florac, aunt of Alina

Beatriou de Florac, mother of Alina (deceased)

Guy de Florac, father of Alina (deceased)

Maria de Florac, sister of Alina (deceased)

Meir ben Eleazar, assistant to Benjamin of Tudela

Sarah, wife of Meir ben Eleazar

Beryl, servant in the citadel

Baltasar de Aurignac, knight from Provence

Ralph, squire of Count Raymond of Tripoli

HISTORICAL CHARACTERS

Agnes of Courtenay (c. 1136 – c. 1184), Countess of Sidon, mother of King Baldwin IV of Jerusalem and Queen Sibylla of Jerusalem (mention only)

Amalric I of Jerusalem (1136 – 11 July 1174), King of Jerusalem 1163–1174

Benjamin of Tudela (1130 – 1173), medieval Jewish scholar and writer (mention only)

Baldwin IV of Jerusalem (1161 – 16 March 1185), called the Leper, son of Amalric I of Jerusalem and his first wife, Agnes of Courtenay

Baldwin of Ibelin (c. 1130 – c. 1187), noble of the Crusader Kingdom of Jerusalem in the 12th century (mention only)

Balian of Ibelin (ca. 1143 – 1193), noble of the Crusader Kingdom of Jerusalem in the 12th Century, brother of Baldwin of Ibelin, married Maria Comnena, widow of King Amalric I in 1177 (mention only)

Henry de Milly (also known as Henry the Buffalo), (ca. 1107-1165) Lord of Arabia Petra (mention only), father of Baudoin (mention only) and Stephanie, Agnes, and Sibille de Milly.

Hugh III of Burgundy (1142 – August 25, 1192), Duke of Burgundy

Isabella I of Jerusalem (1172 – 5 April 1205), half-sister of Sibylla, daughter of Maria Comnena

Maria Comnena (c. 1154 – 1208/1217), second wife of King Amalric I of Jerusalem and mother of Queen Isabella of Jerusalem; a second child was stillborn in 1173

Melisende of Jerusalem (1105 – September 11, 1161), Queen of Jerusalem from 1131 to 1153, and regent for her son between 1153 and 1161 while he was on campaign (mention only)

Miles of Plancy (d. 1174), Seneschal of Jerusalem (mention only). After King Amalric's death, he briefly sought to act as unofficial regent for King Amalric's son and successor Baldwin IV, however, was displaced by Count Raymond of Tripoli, with the support of other powerful barons in the kingdom

Raymond III of Tripoli (1140 – September/October 1187), Count of Tripoli from 1152 to 1187, regent after the death of Amalric I in 1174

Shawar ibn Mujir al-Sa'di (died January 18, 1169), de facto ruler of Fatimid Egypt, as vizier, from December 1162 until his assassination in 1169 (mention only)

Sibylla of Jerusalem (c. 1160–1190), Countess of Jaffa and Ascalon from 1176 and Queen of Jerusalem from 1186 to 1190, married William Longsword of Montferrat in 1176, and Guy de Lusignan in 1180

Soběslav II, Duke of Bohemia (ca. 1128 – 1180), Duke of Bohemia, 1173 to 1178 (mention only)

Stephen I (1133–1190), first Count of Sancerre (1151–1190)

William Longsword of Montferrat (c. 1140 – 1177), Count of Jaffa and Ascalon

William of Tyre (c. 1130 – 29 September 1186), Archbishop of Tyre, medieval prelate and chronicler at the court of the Kingdom of Jerusalem, tutor to King Amalric's son Baldwin IV.

A chantar m'er de so qu'eu non volria
I must sing to tell my tale though I'd rather keep silent.

— *Countess Beatriz de Dia*

(c. 1140 – active 1175)

ALINA
A Song for the Telling

CHAPTER ONE

A FUNERAL

THE DAY of my father's funeral, the snow began to melt.

The path from the church to the cemetery had turned into a sea of slush, and Father Otho's feet and the hem of his hooded cloak were spattered and heavy with mud. With grim satisfaction, I kept my eyes on the blue toes and cracked nails poking out of his worn sandals.

Just two days ago he was in the great hall, drinking the last of my father's wine.

"This will do for the priest," Uncle Garsanc declared with a sniff as he brought the bottle up from the cellar.

My father was proud of that wine, but now it was deemed merely good enough for an inconsequential guest. My uncle already behaved as if he owned the manor.

Uncle Garsanc arrived within days after the lake ice melted enough for the reeds to loosen their grip on my father's sodden limbs. When my uncle rode into the courtyard, followed by his wife and several servants, my brother and I went out to welcome him.

Milos was silent, his arms folded over his chest, so I had to say something—even though, as a daughter, it was not my place. "Thank you, Uncle, for coming." I sank into a curtsey.

"It is high time for someone to take this place in hand." He shook his head as he handed his reins to a flustered stable hand and frowned at the boy's dirty tunic and bare feet.

Mutely we followed our uncle into the great hall. Aunt Marci, my uncle's wife, took a kerchief out of her satchel and spread it on a chair before sitting down. To welcome them, I had placed a tray on the table with beakers and a jug of ale, but was unable to do anything about the state of neglect and confusion.

Aunt Marci glanced at the beakers and beckoned her servant. "Take these to the scullery and scrub them clean before you bring them back."

I flushed. I had cleaned the beakers myself earlier, but I stayed silent. It was as if I could hear my mother's voice, admonishing me for my quick tongue. "You are a lady. Learn to act like one." Sometimes she would add with a smile, "Remember, Alina, as a woman you can accomplish more if your manners are always impeccable." I bit my lip. Be grateful, I kept repeating to myself. We need their help.

The priest arrived at the manor that same afternoon.

"Thank you, Alina," my uncle said when I carried in a tray with a flagon, beakers, and a platter of biscuits. In front of company, his tone of voice was kind and courteous. "Would you pour Father Otho some wine?"

The priest took the beaker from me and sipped. He pointed at the platter on the sideboard as if I were a servant. I resisted the urge to toss it in his lap and silently offered it to him. He took a biscuit and stuffed it into his mouth, washing it down with another swallow of wine.

My uncle watched him impassively. "As I explained earlier, we hope to lay my brother to rest on Saturday."

With an expression of sympathy pasted onto his jowly face, Father Otho avoided my uncle's eyes as he spoke. "Good sir, I am sure you will understand that I hesitate to offer your departed brother a place in our cemetery. There is serious doubt about the manner of his death." He put down the beaker. "But I am grieved for your loss and will be sure to include your brother in my prayers."

I stared at him in dismay. People in the village whispered, but none could say definitively that my father had killed himself. Of course, I knew—that is, I believed—he simply gave up and escaped into the void.

But I wanted him to be able to rest there, under the yew trees in the cemetery, with my mother and my sister, not outside the wall in the little wood.

Ivy had just begun to crawl over the edges of their mound, but there was nothing to mark their passing other than the entry in the family bible in my father's shaky hand—Beatriou de Florac, beloved wife of Guy de Florac, 1139-1172, and Maria de Florac, beloved daughter, 1156-1172.

Uncle Garsanc sat quietly, glancing at the priest's grimy cassock with remnants of scrambled egg and breadcrumbs stuck in its folds, before raising his eyes to Father Otho's face. "Thank you. We are all grieved. Indeed, these are troubling times." He stood up and gestured politely toward the door.

Father Otho first looked around to see whether my aunt had come back into the hall, then quickly stuffed several biscuits into his sleeve as he passed by the board.

"On another matter..." My uncle lowered his voice as he followed the priest outside, so I could barely make out what he said. "I visited the church earlier today. The roof is showing signs of age." The door closed on Father Otho, who was clutching his cassock and turning his face toward my uncle.

When Uncle Garsanc came back inside, he smirked at Aunt Marci, who had returned to the hall and now sat on my mother's favorite chair. "The funeral will be the day after tomorrow," my uncle announced. "A new roof seems a small price to pay to protect the family's name."

Now we stood at the open grave, the muddy bottom around the pine coffin already a dark pool from the persistent sleet and rain. Water dripped off the eaves of the church onto icy patches below. I shivered, and my head ached as I listened to the disjointed pitter-patter, wishing I could force it into a comforting rhythm. None of the servants attended the small service. In fact, only a couple of old women from the village were there, and they came to every single funeral. Studying their dark gowns and shawls, I remembered my brother's tutor telling us about the chorus in a Greek play, with their gloomy commentary on the tragedy of a son murdering his father or a girl dying alone in a tomb.

I caught myself grinning—my parents would have appreciated the irony. At that thought, I was flooded with grief. I would never again see my mother's gentle smile or the detached amusement on my father's face, smiling at me as if sharing a secret.

Uncle Garsanc and sour-faced Aunt Marci presided over the grave, glancing about with identical proprietary expressions. With a pang, I realized that I could hardly argue the point. They now controlled everything that had belonged to my father, and for the time being my brother Milos and I were powerless to do anything about it.

Shivering in my threadbare gown, I thought about the past year. Just nine months ago, we were all together. Sitting in the great hall, we made music while my mother listened, her head bent over her work. Occasionally she looked up and smiled at my father. His dark eyes always responded while he continued playing melodies on his lute, nodding to Milos and me to make sure we didn't miss a beat. That was the last time I saw my father content and at ease.

A few days later my mother and my sister Maria fell ill. A monk came over from the nearby monastery and spent a short time in my mother's chamber before he came out again. "It is the sweating sickness. I have heard that others have also succumbed to it." He did not look at me, busying himself with closing the straps on his scrip, the leather pouch monks used.

"But you can help her, can't you?" My hands shook, and water from the pitcher in my hands slopped onto the flagstones.

"I did what I could." The monk shrugged. "God sends illnesses to punish us."

"And my sister?"

"I am sorry." The monk lifted his hands and let them drop.

"Please stay," I begged, grabbing his cassock. "Please help them."

He pulled the coarse brown cloth out of my grasp, sketched the sign of the cross, and walked away quickly, his sandals flapping and his scrip bouncing on his back.

The monk had, indeed, spread sweet-smelling herbs all around the room where we were caring for Maria and my mother, but I couldn't imagine what good it would do.

I could not give up. There had to be something else. I shouted for the servant to bring more water and started bathing their faces again. I tried to get them to drink something, but it was no good. My mother turned her head away, and when I spooned ale into Maria's mouth, the pale liquid dribbled down her chin and onto the pallet.

At least they had both stopped flinging off their blankets. I took a comb and began to untangle my sister's long hair, brushing it until it lay straight around her shoulders. For a moment she clutched my hand, and I hoped she might speak to me, but she only sighed.

Maria died that night.

I gazed at her face, stunned and bewildered. It was already that of a stranger, with her lips cracked and the skin slack, devoid of all life. My mother lay unmoving under her blanket, although I could still hear her breathing.

I had to get out of the room or I would suffocate, so I walked outside to find the apple trees in the orchard covered with exuberant, sweet-scented clouds of white blossoms.

I could hardly bear to look at them. It was as if their beauty was mocking me. If God sent illnesses to punish people like my mother and my sister, who never hurt anyone in their entire lives, I didn't want to have anything else to do with Him.

My mother died while I was outside.

I returned to the room to find my father kneeling next to her pallet, his head on the blanket and his arms flung out as if trying to hold onto her. I watched helplessly from the doorway, heartsick over his racking sobs.

Finally my brother gently pulled him up and led him away. For days my father sat mute in his dark study, aimlessly plucking the lute strings. On the day of the funeral, he walked to the cemetery, like an obedient child, holding on to Milos's arm. With a blank expression on his face, he watched as we put my mother and Maria to rest. Then he returned to his study and shut the door in our faces. From that day on, my father ignored everything relating to the land or the manor. Instead he spent all his time in his study where, in better days, he used to take care of business and meet with his tenants. Now he did nothing but stare into the fire.

With no one to oversee them, the servants neglected their work, the cook developed a mysterious illness and frequently was nowhere to be found, and tenants were late with their rents.

My father said nothing when Milos disappeared for days on end. He said nothing when I tried to prepare our meals, burning things half of the time, wishing I had paid more attention to my mother's housekeeping advice and examples.

Peire, our old steward, well-meaning and loyal to a fault, tried to jar my father into action. I happened to be in the hall when he knocked on my father's door. There was no response. The steward hesitated, then pushed it open and stuck his head inside.

Peering over his shoulder, I could see my father at his desk. His blood-shot eyes vacant, he gazed at the steward without saying a word. His face was drawn and pale, his hair disheveled.

"My lord, you need to know something—so you can take steps to protect Master Milos and Mistress Alina." Peire looked uncomfortable but determined. "There are rumors of witchcraft in the village. They are saying that my lady and Mistress Maria must have done something wicked for God to punish them so."

My father said nothing. After a moment, he shook his head, walked over to the door, and closed it, shutting us out. Peire glanced at me, shrugging helplessly.

My father's silence wound itself around my head, tightening and tightening until I felt it would explode.

The night before he disappeared, I yelled at him. He never moved, never looked at me, his face turned toward the fireplace. Apparently he hadn't bothered to put on more wood, because the fire was out.

Of course I wasn't pleasing to look at—an awkward, bony girl, scruffy and grimy, with dark, curly, unkempt hair, and ill-fitting clothes in need of mending.

In truth, I had never cared about my looks, and my mother finally gave up trying to get me to be more concerned with my appearance. I could not compete with the memory of my lovely mother and sister, or even with the lanky charm and grace of my brother.

But it hadn't mattered to me until that moment. My father had never before made me feel invisible.

Enraged beyond words, I picked up a pewter pitcher and threw it at the fireplace. It clattered against the stones, rolled onto the floorboards, and lay still. I got an odd satisfaction when I saw I'd managed to dent it.

My father turned toward me as if waking up from a dream. For the first time in months he looked me full in the face. His scraggly beard emphasized the hollows under his eyes, and his pasty skin had begun to sag. With a sad smile, he said, "You are a good girl, Alina. Now go, my dear, and leave me be."

I stared at him, overwhelmed by the raw desolation in his voice, and I backed slowly out of the room. He had already forgotten me. Staring at the ashes in the fireplace, he continued to play his lute, the random notes organizing themselves into a familiar melody. When he began to sing, his voice scratchy from lack of use, I realized he had changed the words.

My soul wants to fly out to sea.
My soul wants to fly over the mountains
To find my love who has gone from me.
My soul is lost in the darkness
And has forgotten how to be.
My songs are gone like wisps of clouds.
I pluck the strings, but no one can hear me.
So I wrap myself in my lover's shrouds.
May they carry me home to the sea.

I fled up the stairs and huddled on my pallet, trying to block out the anguish in the words and the sad, dead sound of my father's voice. Frightened and ashamed for having screamed at him, I could not sleep for a long time.

That same night he disappeared.

"Mistress Alina, I don't know where your father is. He didn't sleep in his bed the night." The young servant girl, one of the few who continued to do her work diligently, watched me with a frown.

The servants, Milos, and I searched everywhere. We looked in all the rooms and outbuildings. No horses were missing from the stable.

After a while I couldn't bear it. My father was gone. Forever. I was sure of it. I went to the hall where I left him the night before. His lute lay on his desk, wrapped in an old shawl my mother had often worn. I picked it up and breathed in my mother's scent.

This was my fault. I kept hearing myself shouting at him. I had abandoned him. I should have forced that monk to stay and give my sister and my mother some medicine. Instead I walked away and let my mother die alone, just as last night I walked away from my father's misery.

I went back outside. In the courtyard, Milos wandered around aimlessly. "Alina, what are we going to do?"

"I don't know."

At that moment, the steward came over to us, his back bent forward as if trying to shoulder a burden. His face was pale, and he seemed to have aged overnight.

"Master Milos, Mistress Alina, we found tracks in the snow leading to the lake. We are afraid there has been an accident."

I followed Peire and Milos out of the courtyard, numb.

"Shouldn't we call for help?" Milos said urgently as he trotted alongside the steward. "We could use this." He held up a coil of rope he had grabbed from the stable.

The steward was silent.

Squinting against the glare from the thin layer of fresh snow glittering on the ice, I tried to follow the uneven tracks down the hill to the edge of the ice. I rubbed my hand over my eyes. For a moment I imagined the tracks were made by a child skipping and shouting and laughing for joy as it scampered through the snow.

But these footprints had not been left by a child.

They were made by a grown man stumbling around in the dark. I stared across the ice at the spot where it had broken up and water seeped to the surface. In the pale winter sunlight, the water looked oily, black, and still.

I pictured my father rushing blindly out onto the surface—running away from his grief. Deafened by the roar of his thoughts, he would not have heard the ice cracking or paid attention to the dark patches where thaw had set in.

I wondered whether, for a moment before sinking, he relished the sharp pain as he cut his hands on the ice—a moment of clarity. Perhaps he felt nothing but relief, finally joining his beloved wife in death.

A grip on my arm dragged me back to the present.

Startled out of my dark reverie, I glanced at my brother.

"You looked like you were about to fall in," Milos whispered, nodding toward the open grave.

"Thank you," I murmured, taking his hand.

His dark eyes met mine. His face was leached of all color, and he looked confused, as if unsure about what he was supposed to do. He gripped my hand so hard it hurt, and leaned toward me, abandoning his customary pose of being superior because he was fifteen, just a year older than I was, and the only son. Then he straightened up, and both of us returned our attention to the priest.

Father Otho had reached the end of the ceremony, mumbling the final petition so quickly that I could barely make it out. He sprinkled the coffin with holy water and perfunctorily waved incense over it, his cloak fluttering in the wind. "Rest in peace," I whispered, praying that it might be so.

Uncle Garsanc murmured his thanks to the priest, and we turned to walk back to the manor while the gravediggers picked up their shovels. The sleet had turned to snow, but it did not muffle the thump and clatter of the dirt hitting the top of my father's coffin as we trudged along.

"What's going to happen now?" Milos whispered. His shoulders were hunched, as if to keep warm, and his tunic was getting too short for his lanky frame. He was almost as tall as our father had been.

"I have no idea," I said weakly, wishing I could reassure him. Helplessly, I reached out to grab his hand. It was cold and clammy. "Something tells me we will find out soon enough. But at least we're together."

CHAPTER TWO

TRAPPED

OTHER THAN his lute, my father left nothing but debts and an estate complete with a damp, musty-smelling mansion, forests, fields, vineyards, and disgruntled serfs.

Uncle Garsanc was my father's younger brother and his only living relative, and my uncle didn't have to travel far to reach us. His small estate was in the same county in Provence, stuck between Savoy and Lombardy to the east and the Kingdom of France to the west. I suspected our uncle was elated at the opportunity to get his hands on my father's land at last.

His own estate, as befitted the younger son, was smaller, but he had kept it in good order through constant hard work. During his visits over the years, my uncle had never neglected to point out that my father was not a good steward of the family land. He ridiculed my father for having married late in life to a woman without much of a dowry. Uncle Garsanc looked at us with disdain, proud of the fact that his daughters were already grown and, moreover, settled in life, with wealthy husbands.

And so, starting on the day they arrived, my aunt and uncle took over. Admittedly, Uncle Garsanc worked hard. Traveling back and forth between his manor and ours, he settled my father's debts, repaired the mansion, and reestablished the family's position in the region. He could rightfully claim what was left as compensation for helping us.

He felt compelled to give us room and board but had no interest in doing anything else. My brother and I were little more than objects of his charity. Of course, in theory, Milos would inherit eventually. However, for the time being he had little choice but to stand by and gratefully accept whatever Uncle Garsanc was willing to provide. I had even less choice, as I soon found out.

A few days after my father's funeral, my aunt cornered me and bade me join her in my mother's little workroom. To my dismay, I noticed that she had already packed away my mother's things.

"Now, Alina, we need to do something about you." She wrinkled her nose, looking with distaste at my old gown and unkempt appearance. "Clearly there has been a lot of neglect since your mother died."

"We managed," I retorted.

"Don't take that tone with me, girl. You're in no position. We will do our best to get you settled properly. Of course, without a dowry, and given all the questionable learning you have been exposed to, you won't have the opportunities my daughters have." With a satisfied smirk, she ran her hands over the velvet ribbons on her gown. "You can have some of Miranda's old gowns. I get the impression your mother was sadly remiss in preparing you for married life. And your father—well," she coughed delicately, "let me not speak ill of the dead, but your father did you no favors by letting you play the lute to the detriment of everything else."

"He told me I could become a trobairitz, and I will," I burst out. For years, I had dreamed of following in my father's footsteps and becoming a trobairitz, a woman troubadour, performing and composing my own music and verses.

"How unfortunate that he encouraged you in this foolish dream." My aunt pursed her lips. "Perhaps if you were a wealthy lady, properly established in a marriage and at a court, you might be able to indulge in some music. But that's not very likely, is it?"

I shook my head mutely.

"Come, child, you have to see that this is impossible."

"But why can't I make music? My father told me of many women who are doing just that."

"And exactly how did he imagine you would manage it? He can't have intended for you to wander about, singing and entertaining like a minstrel—hardly an appropriate activity for a respectable young woman. Surely you know that whatever you do reflects on all of us. You owe it to your name and your position in life."

"But that's silly," I snapped. I hated how Aunt Marci talked about my father. "First you tell me I don't have enough of a position to make music, and now you say I have too high a position to do the same thing."

"I am shocked by your attitude and your lack of respect. I am sure your mother would not have approved."

That stumped me, because it was true. In fact, this subject was one of the few areas my parents ever argued about.

"Don't confuse the child," my mother would say in her gentle voice, one of the few reproofs she ever voiced to my father. As long as I could remember, she had managed the household, quietly and discreetly setting things to right.

My father didn't have a practical disposition, but my mother never openly criticized him or blamed him for the problems he was having with the estate. Instead she would quietly adjust the budget and cut back where needed.

Only when my father talked about my musical ability would she chide him. "You know she won't have much of a dowry. It is not likely she will be in a position to indulge in music as if she were a lady at court. It is better that she learns to accept her lot in life."

My father was undeterred. Often he would sit with me, showing me new songs, teaching me how to modulate my voice, and insisting that I learn different styles.

Remembering, I was once again close to tears. I did not dare look at my aunt.

She took my silence for agreement. "But first we need to get this house in order. You will have to help me with that. Consider it part of your education. And then we will see what to do about your future."

So she put me to work. Like a servant, I scrubbed and washed and sewed. I resented it bitterly. In between, she insisted on giving me lessons in ladylike comportment and proper dress.

"I don't know what your mother was about to let you get so wild," she would say in frustration, as she poked and prodded and pulled me into her idea of a proper lady.

I was tempted to point out that my mother had taught me well, that none of this was new to me. But I kept my silence. My aunt wouldn't understand that since my sister's and my mother's death, followed by my father's descent into desolation, my dress and my comportment as a lady had hardly mattered to me.

Meals in the great hall became torture for Milos and me. My mother had always managed to make even the blandest food taste interesting by adding herbs or wild greens. There would usually be flowers on the table, or a bowl with fruits. In winter she arranged fragrant pine cones and bunches of dried lavender in the center of the table like portable magical forests, and while we ate, my parents told stories, and we laughed. For my mother, the practice of frugality was a discipline and a skill rather than a reason to feel deprived.

Aunt Marci seemed to enjoy having her cook prepare unappetizing meals that always left me hungry. "Don't pick at your food, young lady," she scolded me. "Your uncle has been very generous about repairing the sorry state of affairs around this estate. I expect a bit more appreciation." I looked down at the grey mess of barley congealing in my bowl as I tried to block out Aunt Marci's strident voice. Sitting in my mother's place, she conducted an almost uninterrupted diatribe, going on about the frayed cushions, the worn floorboards, or the cracks and flaws in the plates.

Uncle Garsanc was often away attending to matters at his own estate. When he returned to our home and sat down for meals with us, he frequently laid into Milos. "Why your father did not have you taken on as a page is beyond me. At least then you would have learned something." He pursed his lips and shook his head. Never one to stop from saying the obvious, he insisted on answering his own question. "Of course, there were no funds because of your father's bad stewardship."

Milos looked away, his fists balled up in frustration. He had often asked our father for precisely this.

"I am sorry," Father always said, shrugging helplessly. "We just can't afford a proper horse or weapons and armor for you, which you would need to become a page."

However, to have Uncle Garsanc say this about our father just made Milos angry. It did not help that Uncle Garsanc had little interest in teaching Milos how to manage the estate.

"He won't let me do anything," Milos fumed one afternoon when we sat together in the schoolroom.

"I miss Brother Gervais," I said. The tutor had been dismissed within days after Uncle Garsanc's arrival.

"Odd, isn't it?" Milos raised his eyebrows and smirked. "Even I miss him."

Milos and the tutor had enjoyed a relationship of ongoing, small-scale warfare; Milos persistently avoiding his work, and Brother Gervais pushing him as much as he dared. Milos was not a good student.

"Your sister is learning more than you are, Master Milos," the tutor would say with a frown. When I first started sitting in during Milos's lessons, eager to learn history as well as French, Latin, and our native Provençal, the tutor had remonstrated with my father. "You hired me to teach your son. Besides, it's unbecoming for a young girl."

My father laughed at him. "If it aggravates you so much, let me augment your pay. I want all my children to learn as much as they can. Anyway, Alina's presence might motivate Milos to work harder."

Milos picked up the wax tablet and put it down again, looking almost wistful. "I asked Uncle Garsanc about work at the mill, and he brushed me off. I asked him about letting me help with the accounts. He said I was too young and too immature. In truth, I think he just wants to have complete control."

Frustrated and at loose ends, Milos rode all over the neighborhood and spent a lot of time chatting up travelers who came through our region. After vanishing for days on end, he would return and tell me tales of the port of Marseille, where spices and silks arrived from the east while ships loaded with cloth from Flanders, woolens, salt, oil, and wine set out for the return journey. He even managed to pick up some Arabic.

"Why would you want to learn Arabic?" I asked, surprised.

Milos shrugged. "Oh, you never know. It might come in handy one day." He picked up the lute and ran his hands over its pear-shaped wood. "In Arabic, this would be called an 'oud.' Funny word, isn't it?"

"I wish I could come with you sometimes," I muttered. I took the lute back and began to play, wandering through the many songs my father taught me.

Milos had started a train of thought that was hard to stop. There was an entire world out there, but I might as well stop thinking about it right now. I could not get away from Aunt Marci unless I accepted one of the suitors she kept forcing on me—or entered a convent.

CHAPTER THREE

TURNING POINT

ONE DAY Milos returned from one of his excursions brimming with excitement, trotting over to where I sat in the shade of a willow tree near the river. Aunt Marci had sent me outside with a pile of linen she wanted me to scrub and bleach in the sun.

"What a lot of laundry." Milos laughed as he squatted down next to me. "You're going to look all wrinkled and bleached yourself if you aren't careful, Froggie."

Hearing the old nickname made me feel warm and sad at the same time.

"You look like a frog," my sister Maria once told me, "especially when you sulk," and pushed out her lips while making her eyes bulge. Then she grinned at me, crouching as if about to hop, and swaying from one side to the other, she chanted the ditty about frogs our father had taught us, "Sunt sub aqua, sub aqua malidicere temptant," which meant "they sit underwater, and underwater they chatter maliciously." I tried to grab her, but she ran off laughing.

I would give anything now to hear her teasing me again.

Even my father used that nickname with me. "Ah, Froggie," he'd say when I sought him out in his study. "I missed you today. Come, let me play you a new song."

Milos fingered one of the linen cloths restlessly. Then he dug in his satchel and took out a pair of dice. "You said you wished you could come with me. Well, I have a plan. I talked to a knight who recently returned from Jerusalem. That's how I thought of it. I think we should go there."

"Go to Jerusalem?" I gaped at him. "You know that's impossible. We couldn't even pay for the journey. You realize, don't you, that it takes at least four months to get there by the overland route if you travel on horseback? That's assuming you have a horse."

Bracing the wooden washboard with one hand, I scrubbed away at the linen cloth. "Milos, just picture it—can you see us walking all the way to Jerusalem, hand in hand, clutching our staffs? We'd be frozen to death or starved or eaten by wolves before we ever got there."

Sometimes pilgrims passed through our village on their way to Santiago de Compostela, and my mother would give them food and shelter for the night. To me, they looked pathetic—with their long tunics, broad-brimmed hats, staffs, and leather scrips carrying their few possessions, and most were unkempt, lice-ridden, and self-righteously bragging about being attacked or robbed on the road.

Milos was undeterred. "Look, that's just details. We could figure it out."

"But why should we go to Jerusalem in the first place? People die there. You can't tell me you accept everything Father Otho says about the crusades when you don't believe anything else he says."

We both had heard Father Otho exhort the young men to go fight for Christendom and defend the holy sites in Jerusalem. The priest used to get quite heated when he went on and on about the infidel and all the horrible things they did. The last crusade had taken place ten years before I was born, and my father told me thousands had died. Of course we were taught that to give one's life as a soldier for Christ would provide spiritual immunity, but spiritual immunity hardly seemed to be adequate compensation for dying on a pile of sand far away from home.

"Sure, some die. But we won't. Really, Alina, think about it. Perhaps I can become a squire. I have heard so many tales of endless riches to be made and great deeds to be done in Jerusalem. When we come home, I might have the means to dislodge Uncle Garsanc and reclaim my heritage. I might even have enough for a decent dowry for you. What can we do here, with our uncle hoping we will vanish so he can take control of the manor permanently?"

His eyes sparkled, and he looked puffed up the way he always did when he was about to win an argument. "Besides, just imagine not having to deal with Aunt Marci and her pinched face." Milos grinned at me. He knew how many times in the past months I had run afoul of our aunt.

Out of the corner of my eye I watched him roll the dice, his long, slender hands mesmerizing in their speed and grace. He had gotten the dice from someone who returned from the Holy Land.

Over the years I had learned to be wary whenever Milos tried to convince me to go along with one of his harebrained schemes. Once, when we were much younger, he talked me into running away. "You'll gather berries, and I'll set traps, and I'll cut rushes so you can weave a basket we'll use for fishing."

I was enthusiastic, even if something about the division of labor did not seem quite right to me. It took two days for our parents to find us. Damp, cold, and hungry by that point, Milos and I were secretly relieved and completed the extra chores our parents set us as a punishment without a single word of complaint.

Another time he talked me into trying to sell mushrooms in the village. Fortunately, the cook encountered us when we were sneaking out of the manor, armed with a basket full of mushrooms we had collected. She took one look at our harvest and immediately took it away from us, flinging it as far away into a thorny thicket as she could. "You could have poisoned someone," she screeched. "Don't you have any sense?"

That little escapade cost us several long weeks spent confined to the manor.

As always, when I listened to Milos, I was torn between doubting everything that came out of his mouth and being charmed by the warm timbre of his voice, the voice of a singer.

"We have no way to fight Uncle Garsanc for control over the mansion or the land, and certainly no money to pay him back for taking care of Father's debts. We have nothing—unless you count Father's lute, that is." He tossed the dice onto the ground.

Perplexed, I saw that they had come up a zero.

"Uncle Garsanc won't let me do anything. He won't even let me work with the young horses. What can I do here but live on charity? I might as well accept some charity on the road." Restlessly he palmed the dice again.

"And you? You know Aunt Marci won't stop trying to palm you off on just about any man still breathing." Milos pulled his face into a perfect copy of Aunt Marci's sour expression, primly pursing his mouth. "You should be grateful, my girl. You have no dowry, and I am doing everything I can to get you settled. You are hardly any man's dream." He got her querulous tone just right.

I pinched my lips together, trying not to laugh. But it was true; Aunt Marci had already introduced me to several suitors. One was a pimply youth, the second son from a neighboring estate, who had stood in my father's hall, twisting his cap in his hands and looking frightened at the very idea that I might say yes. Two were widowers with small children who had studied me appraisingly, as if to determine whether I was strong enough for the work they had in mind. So far I had managed to decline their suits politely, referring to my state of mourning as an excuse.

Of course I knew I would eventually have to accept someone. But right now, just the notion of entering a stranger's house as a bride was more than I could bear. I would have to give up all control over my life. I might as well be in jail.

"She does have a point, you know, Froggie." Milos retrieved one of the dice that had slipped inside his sleeve and then looked at me as if to apologize for Aunt Marci's harsh words. "You are too tall and too clever with your words. And you don't have even a small dowry."

Aunt Marci had said this so many times that I had become inured to it. Still, to hear it from Milos stung. Ruefully I eyed the pile of unfinished washing, the white linen shifts grey and dingy even though I had already scrubbed them repeatedly.

I supposed I had outgrown the frog phase, but I knew full well that I had little to recommend me to suitors. I was tall for a woman, with thick curls I could never manage to arrange becomingly, plus ruddy skin and a nose that stood out like a beak. At least I had begun to fill out a bit, and now, at fourteen, could no longer be mistaken for a boy. Of course, none of that would matter if I had a dowry.

Aunt Marci waxed on about this topic ad nauseam. "Your mother must have failed to impress upon you the appropriate comportment for a woman and wife. You must always be modest, courteous, and dignified, whatever the situation. You must serve your lord and husband faithfully, and you must be diligent in the business of his house. Above all, you must not give anyone cause to slander you, so you must always be discreet and virtuous in all your dealings." She stabbed her needle into her work and glared at me. "Of course, since you have no land or wealth to bring to a marriage, you have to be especially careful not to offend." After hearing repeated lectures of this sort, I hardly listened anymore, but the essential lesson was unavoidable. I had little choice about how my life was going to turn out.

"Anyway, is this the life you want?" Milos waved his hands, dismissing my current life like a speck of dust. Then he went on with renewed intensity. "Come with me. We could join a troop of knights on their way to Jerusalem. How could they not like having a few musicians in their ranks? Father taught both of us enough to be creditable performers. Besides, we sing well together. You know that."

"That sounds a lot like Aunt Marci's worst dream." I grimaced. "You should have heard her warn me about what would happen to a 'respectable young woman' who would do something like this. We'd be like joglars."

"Dear me." Milos smirked. "Mere joglars, minstrels of the common class!"

"That's not what I meant," I protested weakly. I looked down, feeling in the wrong all of a sudden. It was true, a part of me was appalled at the notion of being little better than a street entertainer.

"Well, let me tell you one thing. I have heard some joglars, and I think we could do much better than most. Anyway, if you keep listening to Aunt Marci, you'll soon be wedded to some greasy old fellow and living in a drafty mansion somewhere. In Jerusalem, nobody will care that we're the children of an impoverished troubadour who took his own life, or that his wife was falsely accused of witchery."

"Nobody ever actually said that about Mother."

"They didn't have to. Just the facts alone are enough to raise eyebrows. Anyway, it's all in the past. Who is to say we can't do things differently?"

With an elegant flourish, Milos rolled a set of clay marbles, cheerfully painted in red, blue, and white, onto the linen I had spread out in the sun for bleaching.

"Hey, stop that. I'll have to wash this all over again!"

"Oh, sorry." He chuckled, not sounding sorry at all, then swept up the marbles, making them disappear so fast that I couldn't see where he put them. Then he reached over, stuck his fingers under my cap, and pulled one out.

"You wretch!" I laughed. "Show me how you did that."

"Tricks of the trade, dear sister!" He stood up and grinned at me. "Anyway, think it over." He sauntered off, whistling.

Dispiritedly, I ran my hands through the soapy water. I thought about my father's lute. Handling it filled me with a mixture of such grief and joy that it was hard to bear.

It was the only one of his things that my aunt and uncle did not want. I wanted it passionately, and yet the very thought of it was painful. To touch it was to see his fingers on the strings, slender and strong. When I closed my eyes, I could remember the rough skin of the inside of his palm when he patted my cheek during his rare shows of affection, and his scent—a comforting mix of wood and resin that clung to his clothes and his skin.

I used to sit in his workroom for hours, watching him carve out and sand thin pieces of wood, shape them on a wooden mold for the bowl-shaped body of a new lute, and carefully fit them together so none of the joints showed. Mostly he was silent while he worked, only occasionally pointing out details like the pear wood he planned to use for the bridge or the construction of the fingerboard.

My mother sometimes tried to recall him to his duties. "I thought you had a meeting with the steward?"

He would smile at her, oblivious to the hint. "I'll be right there."

But a few moments later, he had forgotten all about it. "Look at the pattern for the rose," he said, showing me a drawing of a floral-like pattern, austerely geometric and flamboyant at the same time. "Do you like it?" Eventually he would carve it out for the sound-hole, also known as the rose in the body of the lute. "The rose is like a window into the soul of the lute," he told me. "You have to make it your own through your music." I didn't understand what he meant, but it didn't matter. I loved sitting there and watching him work. It was all I needed.

When I played the songs he taught me, my heart ached. My eyes blurred at the memory of his white, wasted face on the night before he disappeared. I wished I could forget, and yet it hurt that even the last image I had of him was fading from my mind.

I made music whenever I could escape from my aunt's incessant complaints and commands. The lute had become a part of me, to the point where I even missed my father chiding me. "You will never get anywhere with this if you don't work at it. You need to practice." It used to irritate me when he said it. I got bored with playing the same piece over and over. I liked to go on to something new.

Right now I would have given everything to hear his frustrated voice. "You could be so good if you kept at it," he complained. I missed our evenings together, with Milos playing the flute and my father and I taking turns with the lute and singing. I tried to talk to Milos about him, but I quickly gave up. There was something in Milos that could not face thinking or talking about our father and mother—as if he was afraid he would shatter into pieces if he slowed down and allowed the sorrow to catch up with him.

If we went to Jerusalem, I would take the lute with me. I stopped in my thoughts, amazed at where they were leading me. Something tugged at me—a dream of seeing distant lands and hearing other voices, away from the strident, nasal tones of my aunt and the brittle abruptness of my uncle, the suspicious and unfriendly stares of the villagers, and the three graves behind the church.

Still, it was an absurd idea. We had no way to support ourselves. Besides, for all that I resented my aunt's harping about my being a lady, I also didn't want to become a traveling minstrel, forced to live off whatever pittance we might earn during a performance.

Then two things happened that changed everything.

First, Aunt Marci gave me an ultimatum. She cornered me when I was folding linens into the oak trunk on the upstairs landing. I knew what was coming even before she opened her thin lips, her arms crossed over her flat chest as if to ward off intruders. "I have just about had it with you, my girl. That was a perfectly respectable man you turned down yesterday."

I kept my eyes on the linen sheet in my hand. There was a yellow stain in one corner. I sighed. I would have to take it back out and bleach it in the sun yet again.

The middle-aged man standing in the great hall yesterday had smelled bad, his hand hot and clammy, holding mine far too long. Licking his lips, he ran his eyes over me as if he wanted to undress me on the spot.

I pleaded that I had some mysterious illness. It worked. The unlucky suitor departed in a hurry, leaving Aunt Marci fuming over the latest failure to marry me off.

"The next one you will accept, or it's off to the convent with you, young lady."

Going to a convent might not be so bad. At least I would be left alone there. That notion lasted as long as it took me to get out of the manor and walk out into the orchard to get away from Aunt Marci. Once the convent gate closed behind me, I would rarely be able to play the lute or sing the songs I wanted to sing. There had to be more for me. I wanted to have what my father and mother had had. It was as if I had a secret voice inside me, raging at the punishments God had inflicted on our family for no reason I could understand.

I kicked some pebbles as I walked along. No, I could not imagine a life devoted to prayer. I couldn't go to a convent. Not now. Certainly not yet.

But then Milos got caught stealing. I was sure he hadn't meant to do that—it just looked that way—but he didn't think, as usual, a habit that got him in trouble over and over again.

Uncle Garsanc had decided to sell off some of the remaining silver to help pay off outstanding debts. He had the maids polish platters, candle-sticks, and other silverware until everything sparkled, and had it all arrayed on the big table in the great hall. A merchant was supposed to look at them later that day. That was when Milos had hit on the bright idea of taking one of our father's silver chalices.

I found it hard to blame him. Our father had loved those chalices. He had often admonished the maids to polish them, and frequently described the meaning of the coat of arms his father had engraved on them. We remembered this all the more since our father had not cared much for any of his other possessions—aside from his lute.

I never was able to figure out what Milos had intended to do with the chalice. I suspected he just wanted to have it as one of the last remaining links to our parents. But he didn't get far. He had wrapped his cloak over its awkward, bulky shape and walked across the courtyard, whistling and sauntering as if he did not have a care in the world when Uncle Garsanc noticed him and recognized the signs of deceit.

He dragged Milos back into the great hall. My aunt and I looked up from our work when they came in to see Uncle Garsanc carrying the chalice. I thought he was about to knock Milos over the head with it, but he restrained himself. He waved it at Aunt Marci. "Your nephew was about to make off with this."

Aunt Marci pursed her lips, glaring at Milos.

Uncle Garsanc turned back to Milos. "How dare you? Is that how you repay me for all I have been doing? I am working very hard to try to keep the estate for you. You don't work. You run all over the county when you aren't juggling out there under the oak tree. Juggling? Is that what you intend to do in the future?" Red splotches stood out on his cheeks.

Milos was white-faced and silent. With a curious dignity, he held himself up straight. "You don't let me do anything," he finally said in a low voice.

"I told you. You haven't learned anything, and you are too young. There has been so much damage done over the last years, it takes a man of experience to repair it. Now I know you are just as irresponsible as my brother always was."

At that, both Milos and I flushed with anger. Milos clenched his fists. Frightened for him, I grabbed his tunic and pulled on it. He looked at me. I shook my head at him in warning. I knew what we were going to do.

I set aside my sewing and stood up. "Uncle Garsanc," I said, raising my voice.

My uncle glanced at me as if I was an annoying fly on the windowsill.

"Alina, it's not your place to speak," my aunt snapped.

I ignored her. "Uncle Garsanc, we both appreciate what you are doing. We are truly grateful." I could feel Milos fuming next to me, but I went on, holding on to his arm. "Milos and I would like to ask your permission to go on a pilgrimage to Jerusalem to pray for our father's soul. We would like to leave as soon as possible."

Milos pulled his arm out of my grasp. He had not expected me to do this.

"You want to do wh-what?" Uncle Garsanc sputtered. "That is the most ridiculous plan I have ever heard. How exactly do you propose to do this?"

Milos had recovered from his surprise. "We hope to join a group of merchants and knights traveling to Jerusalem."

"It sounds very unsuitable." Uncle Garsanc frowned and shook his head. Aunt Marci looked stunned.

"I think it might be good for the family name if we did this." It occurred to me that this was, indeed, the only thing Uncle Garsanc cared about.

"It would hardly do the family name any good if you bandied about the circumstances of your father's death, not to mention the deplorable state he left things in," he said slowly. Then he glanced at Aunt Marci, and I knew we had won. He would get rid of both of us in one stroke. "Let me think about this. I suggest you both remove yourselves while we discuss it."

When we had reached the hallway, Milos grabbed my arm. "You really want to do this?"

"It was your idea."

"Yes, but I didn't think it was possible."

"Well, maybe it is. Anyway, it has to be a lot better than more scenes like that. At least it would buy us some time."

As it turned out, Uncle Garsanc knew someone who was leading a group of knights and pilgrims about to set out for the Holy Land. Muttering and sighing, he wrote us a letter of reference. In flowery language, courtly and polite, he told Baltasar de Aurignac that his nephew and niece wanted to go to Jerusalem to pray for their recently deceased father's soul. "There is no need to say anything else," he said. Evidently he was afraid that we would talk about it, and it would reflect badly on the family and on him.

He even provided us each with a horse, and augmented our funds so we would be able to support ourselves throughout the journey.

Gathering what we would need on the journey was easy, since there was little we could take with us. Aside from a few stained gowns my aunt had grudgingly passed on to me from her daughter, my only possession was my father's lute.

Baltasar de Aurignac's response arrived quickly. He addressed it to Uncle Garsanc and assured him he would be delighted to have us join him and his group of knights and pilgrims.

"Have you thought about what we will do once we get there?" I asked Milos when we went for a walk in the orchard a few days before our departure.

"Don't worry," Milos said lightly. "It will all work out." After his initial surprise at the news that Uncle Garsanc would support our venture, he had abandoned all doubts.

I shook my head. Milos was turning out to be as much of a dreamer as our father was.

Meanwhile, something had shifted inside me. I couldn't wait to leave. It was as if a trap had snapped shut behind me, just missing my foot, letting me run free for a while longer. Eventually I would have to come back and face all this, but I quickly dismissed the thought. Any apprehension I had was swallowed up by my excitement. At least we would be doing something rather than remaining stuck here at the mercy of our reluctant uncle and aunt, waiting for them to dispose of us.

So finally, in the spring of 1173, we set out to travel north and east to join the knights on their journey to the Holy Land. My uncle and aunt stood outside the manor and made a show of wishing us well, piously claiming they would pray for our father's soul and for us.

I found the sight of my aunt's mournful face ridiculous, and at least it distracted me from the pain of leaving behind the last link to my parents and sister as Milos and I rode across the courtyard paving stones to the road beyond.

CHAPTER FOUR

ON THE ROAD

"YOU SHOULD listen to me, Alina." Milos craned his neck as he turned around in his saddle and glared back at me disapprovingly. "You can't behave as if you were still at Florac Manor."

I pulled off my scarf and shook it out, glad to have my hair blow free in the wind. I was stiff and sore from riding for hours at a time. And it didn't help that I was famished, and we needed to keep going for at least another hour before finding a place to rest for the night.

We had been traveling for four days and would shortly reach Lyon, where we were supposed to meet Count Baltasar de Aurignac. While the nights were still chilly, it rained only once, for a few hours. The trees and bushes were beginning to leaf out, and I relished the fresh green shimmer that had enveloped the landscape almost overnight. After a mild winter, the roads from our home in Provence northward to Lyon were not badly rutted. Thus, we were able to cover about twenty-five to thirty kilometers a day without straining the horses too much. But in those four days, Milos annoyed me more than he ever had before.

"So who is being all strict and responsible now?" I snapped at Milos. "Stop acting like Uncle Garsanc. All I did back there was to talk to a family on their way to Rome."

"Well, at least don't tell everybody where we're going. They might be bandits in disguise, for all you know," Milos said huffily.

"I didn't tell anybody anything," I snapped at him. "I am just friendly. Anyway, if we keep going at this rate, we won't have much of anything left for bandits to steal. You're the one who insists on spending all our money on costly inns and expensive cheeses."

The truth was I found it fascinating to talk to other travelers, especially those claiming to be on a pilgrimage. To my amazement, the roads were busy, and at times we had to carefully maneuver our horses around horse-drawn carts and groups of people walking along. The last family I chatted with told us they wanted to pray for their departed mother's soul. But the husband proudly showed me a book they had purchased, called *Mirabilia Urbis Romae*, which apparently listed and described various sites of Rome they hoped to visit.

"I heard that there are fabulous baths in Rome, and the food is said to be delicious." His wife beamed in anticipation.

"Ah, women." Her husband smiled at her indulgently. "I am more interested in the aqueducts myself."

Perhaps we weren't the only ones whose motives for undertaking a pilgrimage didn't bear closer examination.

Because the roads were so well traveled on this early stretch of our journey, we weren't all that worried about bandits. Still, we tried to stay close to other groups for added safety.

I had thought it would be hard to find accommodations for the night, but I was wrong. In fact, in the larger towns we had to choose among competing offers. Often when we reached the outskirts of a settlement, we encountered boys on the road on the lookout for travelers. Hotel owners and innkeepers used the boys to lure in customers. I also saw a few road signs advertising an inn in the next town. Given our limited resources, we had to be careful with our spending.

"Let's stay here. I like the name."

Dubiously I looked up at the freshly painted inn sign saying Blue Bull. "No, let's go back up the road. The other one looked less expensive."

"Come on, a few pennies more or less won't make any difference," Milos complained.

"It will if we want to make it all the way to Jerusalem."

"Fine. Have it your way." Milos pulled his horse around. "I wager, though, that I can make some money on the way. You wait and see," he added with his usual grandiose assurance.

I shrugged and decided not to comment. I worried about Milos, but he could hardly get into a lot of trouble as long as we traveled with other noblemen and knights. Surely their presence would keep him in check.

After a lengthy argument, he agreed to split up the money Uncle Garsanc gave us, and I carried my half in my scrip. One more reason why I was glad I had found the large leather pouch among my father's things. My few personal belongings fit in easily, and I could stash my half in the folds of my clothes. If one of us was robbed, we would at least have some money left.

Initially I found it hard to sleep in the common room of the inns where we spent the night. Even when I pulled my shawl over my head, I could still hear the groans and snores of the other sleepers. The air was always stuffy, too, and I kept imagining fingers groping toward me, which was why I took care to put my scrip under the pallet. Still, it was warm and dry and safer than sleeping in a barn or an abandoned hut somewhere. By the third night, I was so tired that the shared surroundings no longer bothered me.

The closer we got to Lyon, the busier the roads. Some of the travelers made me sad—apparently homeless—old people, men and women, bedraggled and weak, stumbling along, children without parents. Some held out their hands and called to me, "Please, Miss, can you help?"

I had to learn to shake my head and avoid meeting their eyes, although I was ashamed. At least I had my brother and wasn't starving by the roadside.

We found Count Baltasar at an inn just outside Lyon.

"Welcome, Mistress Alina." The nobleman bowed courteously when my brother introduced me. "I regret that there are no other noblewomen to keep you company on our long journey. Some merchants will join us in Venice, however, and I believe several will travel with their wives. So you will have company during the second half of our journey. Meanwhile, we will do our best to assure your safety."

"Thank you, Count Baltasar." I smiled at him. "I am sure I will manage very well."

The count was not much taller than I was and about thirty years old. A mop of brown curls framed his chubby face, giving him the appearance of an overgrown cherub. He seemed gentle and kind, and I had a hard time imagining how he could manage a large group of knights and pilgrims on the long journey ahead, much less serve as a defender of Christendom in battle.

However, after a few days I began to appreciate his experience. He knew the route well, having journeyed this way three times already, and I was struck by his ability to get along with everyone. Quiet and soft-footed, he missed nothing, and appeared immediately at the slightest sign of conflict among the travelers, and yet he remained invariably polite and attentive throughout.

Every morning began with a briefing about the day's route. Count Baltasar willingly shared what he knew about the places we passed through, and he never forgot to remind us to "stay together...remember robbers prefer easy prey." When we rode through wooded regions, he reminded us to be especially careful. "Always be alert, and call out if you notice something unexpected. In isolated spots like this, bandits like to hide in the undergrowth or behind rocks and trees. Pay attention, no matter how tired you are."

Our first port of call in the Holy Land would be Acre. We would travel overland, east via the Republic of Venice, and from there east and south to Constantinople. In a short journey by boat, we would cross the Bosporus to the eastern portion of the Byzantine Empire and from there continue overland via Antioch to Acre.

During the first weeks on the road, I struggled with exhaustion, but slowly it got easier. I adjusted to being on horseback for hours at a time. Of course, when we passed travelers who walked to their destination, I realized that we were among the fortunate ones. On most days we covered about twenty kilometers.

I quickly learned the routines of travel. More importantly, I learned to lower my expectations about food, or places where we stayed overnight. It allowed me to be pleasantly surprised by comfortable straw pallets, clean water, or a tasty meal at an inn. On cold days I found it easy to ignore the smells and dirty conditions, grateful for getting out of the rain and wind. When we stayed in a village, we sought shelter in a barn or a stable, and larger settlements often had alehouses that could accommodate us.

There were three older men in the entourage, pilgrims to the Holy Land. They never smiled, and they avoided talking to anyone else. They were wealthier than most pilgrims and had their own horses, but traveled with us for protection.

Count Baltasar had brought along five knights who wanted to help defend the Kingdom of Jerusalem. There also were a few young men without rank or property who, like Milos, hoped to find opportunities in a foreign land, as well as three Templar knights, members of a Catholic military order whose task it was to help protect us on the journey.

The young knights in Count Baltasar's retinue irked me with their smug conviction that they were on a godly mission, but were nonetheless happy to indulge in any pleasures that caught their fancy. I thought they were ill-informed and hasty, careless of the places and people we met on the road, and full of pride and vanity.

The Templars, wearing their distinctive white tunics with a large red cross down the center, stayed aloof from the others, although occasionally I saw them go off to one of the churches we passed on the way. They spoke to Count Baltasar and his knights, but the other others in our group were beneath their notice.

Nonetheless, I found their presence comforting, though I was troubled by their notion of provisioning. As we traveled farther and farther east, the Templars often conveyed what they wanted by gestures since they didn't speak the language of every group we encountered.

They seemed to believe it right and proper to ask local people for food. I knew they had taken vows of poverty, chastity, and humility, and upon joining the Templars had surrendered their wealth to the order. But this mantle of poverty had not changed their air of entitlement. Their every gesture and movement conveyed disdain for others, announcing to the world that they were men of position who had a perfect right to demand that frightened villagers surrender some of their food stores.

Then one day Count Baltasar put a stop to the most egregious form of foraging. In disgust, I watched one of the Templars return for the night from an excursion to a farm in a valley below our resting place, a makeshift shelter for sheep in a mountainous region in the Kingdom of Italy. He carried two birds on a string, their once-lovely feathers dragging in the dust.

"Where did these chickens come from?" Count Baltasar demanded sharply.

The Templar looked at him arrogantly and pointed toward the farm in a nonchalant manner.

"I assume you compensated the farmer."

The Templar sniffed. "They should be grateful to us for defending the faith."

"Indeed." Count Baltasar glared at him. "They will appreciate your actions all the more if you treat them fairly. I know for a fact that you are not short of funds. Undoubtedly you are planning to place your wealth at the disposal of the church when we get to Jerusalem. Before you do that, let me accompany you to ensure you generously compensate the farmer for the loss of these birds—they look like fine laying hens. He might even spare a prayer or two for your soul."

"I am glad you protected that farmer," I said to Count Baltasar the next time he happened to be near me.

"Trust me, I didn't do that for altruistic reasons." Count Baltasar laughed. "We have to travel back through this region, and people remember. Besides, it was a good opportunity to remind the Templars of who's in charge on this journey."

I gazed at Count Baltasar's amiable, round face, surprised by the calculating ruthlessness.

But who was I to judge? Anyway, Count Baltasar clearly knew what he was about. After that scene, provisioning was more restrained, and he made sure the farmers were fairly paid for meat and anything else they were asked to surrender.

One afternoon, somewhere to the north of Venice, Count Baltasar called for an early stop. "It's going to be a long day tomorrow. We'll push all the way to Venice."

Sore and stiff, I stood in the yard in front of the alehouse where we would spend the night and gazed around at the activity in the yard. Milos was busy brushing the horses. Several knights walked about in the yard, while the others had already disappeared inside the alehouse. Count Baltasar sat on a stone ledge, with a tankard of ale next to him, and wrote into a small ledger. I took a look at the small building and the smoke coming out of the chimney and decided that I couldn't face the dormitory just yet.

So I walked out of the yard toward a grove on the bottom of the hill, listening to the swishing and gurgling of the stream next to the road. It was peaceful. I relished the solitude, and yet at the same time, I felt lonely, rest-less, and filled with doubt. I worried about what we would do once we got to Jerusalem and how we would find the funds to travel back home. I missed the easy fun I used to have with Maria and with Milos. I missed making music. Due to the rapid pace of travel, there had been no opportunity to do so, and moreover I was embarrassed in front of all these men.

I picked up a branch and tossed it into the stream. It was swept away quickly. I could see the multi-colored pebbles in the clear water. It was lovely, and yet I felt hemmed in at all sides by the mountains. I missed the open hills of Provence.

When I returned to the yard, one of the Templar knights in the yard raised his eyebrows disapprovingly.

Count Baltasar got up from his stone ledge, followed me toward the inn, and held the door for me. "Mistress Alina, you really shouldn't wander about by yourself. It's not safe."

"Thank you," I muttered ungraciously. "I won't do it again."

I went straight to the women's dormitory in the back and sat down on my pallet, annoyed and angry at myself. Of course, it was stupid of me to go off like that, but I felt as if I had traded Aunt Marci for a lot of sanctimonious knights. I envied Milos his freedom.

I didn't sleep much that night. In the morning I felt more settled again. What had I expected? Of course, I could not leave behind all the restrictions that came with being a girl and my status in life. "You need to work with what you got," my mother used to tell me when I rebelled against the interminable rules. I had made a choice when I told Uncle Garsanc we wanted to go to Jerusalem. Now, I had to work with what I got.

It took us about four weeks to get to the Republic of Venice.

Just north of Venice, Count Baltasar called a halt. "We'll rest here for a few days. Some of you will want to go into the city to pray at St. Mark's Basilica. If you do, beware of thieves and pickpockets. Stick together at all times."

I glanced at Milos. His cheeks had two red spots. He looked the way he always did when he was excited. He dismounted and immediately walked over to one of the younger knights he had spent a great deal of time with lately. After whispering for a few moments, he came over to me and said, "Alina, I will go into the city with Filipot and the others. Maybe tomorrow I will take you to the Basilica."

"Just be careful," I admonished him.

"You don't need to remind me." Milos scowled.

In fact, I was glad of the rest. It had recently become hot, my eyes were irritated and gritty from road dust, and my gown and overcoat seemed to have absorbed pounds of dirt. The gown was becoming threadbare. Much as I hated doing it, I needed to mend some of the tears.

The inn had a clean common room, and, even better, there was a public bath close by. Originally constructed by the Romans, it was a beautiful, spacious complex. Curiously, I studied the intricate mosaics on the walls of the entrance. I had never seen anything like them, so rich and vibrant, and this was merely a bath.

"You like?" asked the attendant in an oddly accented Latin.

I smiled at him. "Yes, I like."

"Come from Byzantium." He pointed at the mosaics. "All new." He handed me a towel and pointed me toward the changing rooms set aside for women.

Inside I found a hot-water pool and a cold-water basin as well as an exercise area. There even was a steam room. And I had the place almost to myself.

Just a few older women were soaking in the warm water. On a bench on the side of the cold-water basin, an old woman lay face down on a pillow, and an attendant massaged her back, which was exposed all the way down to her waist. Embarrassed, I looked away, and chose to make do with the hot-water pool. It was wonderful. Hours later, relaxed and content, even if my skin had shriveled from the long immersion, I returned to the inn.

Milos and the other knights had not yet returned from their excursion, but I wasn't worried. He wasn't alone, and the older knights would watch out for him. I sat on my straw pallet to mend my gown. The dormitory was so quiet, I found myself nodding off, so I put aside my work and stretched out. I fell asleep easily.

"Wake up, Mistress Alina."

A hand grabbed my shoulder and shook me gently. Groggily, I opened my eyes and looked into the face of Count Baltasar, round-cheeked and jovial as always—except for a frown. "I am sorry to wake you. Your brother and one of the knights are still in Venice. The others came back last night."

I sat up and rubbed my eyes, startled to see sunlight streaming through one of the narrow windows. I had slept through the night.

"I just wanted to let you know that I'm taking one of the Templars with me to look for them. Don't worry too much."

By now I was fully awake. I stared at Count Baltasar, fear tightening my throat. The instruction not to worry had the opposite effect.

"They are young men, and I should have kept a closer eye on them." The count smiled at me reassuringly. "But we'll find them. Anyway, the merchants have arrived. Before I leave, I want to introduce you to their wives, who will be traveling with their husbands all the way to Acre."

Eagerly I followed him outside, quickly adjusting my gown and rubbing the sleep out of my eyes. It would be nice to have some women to talk to in the weeks ahead.

The two women standing in the courtyard turned out to be stately, expensively dressed matrons.

"Mistress Lavinia and Mistress Antonia, allow me to introduce Mistress Alina."

Flustered, aware of my tousled hair, I curtsied as I smiled at them.

"Well, I will leave you now." Count Baltasar bowed and walked off.

"Where are you traveling, Mistress Alina?" Mistress Antonia asked. Not a wisp of hair showed underneath her tight cap. Her high collar, richly embroidered, did not disguise the beginnings of a double chin. Mistress Lavinia, also with her hair modestly tucked away under her headdress, had pale features and thin lips, the lines around her mouth making her seem older than the other one.

They both smiled approvingly when I explained about our pilgrimage. "But are you alone?" Mistress Lavinia asked.

"No, my brother is with me."

"Oh, a young woman...a mere child...traveling all the way to Jerusalem with just a brother to look out for her?" Mistress Antonia sniffed. "What is your family thinking?"

"It was the only way." I felt my face grow rigid. I was getting angry at their assumption that I needed to explain myself at all. They seemed like another version of Aunt Marci.

"Well," Mistress Lavinia said, "we must excuse ourselves. We have a lot to attend to."

With identical haughty expressions, they minced into the inn, fastidiously holding up the hems of their long gowns.

I was torn between disappointment and irritation, but then I remembered about Milos and put Mistress Antonia and Mistress Lavinia out of my mind. The next hours I spent in increasing agony as I tried to imagine what could have happened. Mostly I paced back and forth outside. Finally, in the late afternoon, I watched Count Baltasar trudge along the path to the inn. He and a knight were shepherding Milos between them, while Filipot followed behind.

Milos looked bedraggled. His tunic was ripped, and he had a bruise on his forehead. Filipot's right arm was in a sling.

Count Baltasar glanced at me. He stepped back, dropping Milos's arm.

"What happened?" I asked, shocked by his appearance. His eyes were red, and he looked as if he had a crashing headache. He shook his head mutely.

I moved closer to get a look at the bruise and wrinkled my nose at the smell of stale ale. My sympathy vanished, and I felt like slapping him. "What have you done?"

"I..." Milos faltered. "Let me sleep for a bit. I'll tell you tomorrow."

"No, tell me now."

"We had something to drink." Milos looked down.

"I can smell that. Well?"

"Some other fellows challenged us, and we gambled for a while."

"With what?" I got butterflies in my stomach. "Don't tell me you gambled away our money."

"Not exactly. Actually, I won some." For a moment, Milos looked pleased with himself. "It's just..." He stopped again. "Look, Alina, I don't remember what happened. I got into a fight, and the next thing I know I was in the town lockup."

I remained silent as I took this in.

"That's where I found them." Count Baltasar said, sounding apologetic. "Apparently the local guard noticed the fight. By the time he came on the scene, Milos had been knocked unconscious, and Filipot wasn't in much better shape. The Republic of Venice doesn't have much patience with brawling in the city limits, so they locked them up. But it's over now. I paid their fine."

"Mistress Alina, I am so sorry," Filipot said. He sounded as if he had a cold, and his nose was swollen. "We were attacked. There were too many of them."

I ignored him. "Why did you pay the fine?" I asked Count Baltasar. Then I realized that this sounded rude. "I mean, thank you, truly, but shouldn't Milos have paid his fine himself?"

"That's the thing." Milos coughed. "We were robbed. My scrip is gone."

"Oh." I was appalled. I wanted to scream and shake him, but it would hardly help. I shook my head. There was nothing I could do. "Just go to sleep," I snapped. "We're leaving early tomorrow."

Now we had only what I carried in my own scrip. At least we had divided what Uncle Garsanc had given us, so we weren't destitute, but by the time we reached Jerusalem we would be. By some strange irony, God had seen to it that we would enter the Holy Land as proper pilgrims—without a penny to our names.

The next morning Milos's eye was swollen and bruised-looking. However, to my irritation, he appeared cheerful and apparently oblivious to our predicament. I was so frustrated that I ignored him for the rest of the day.

It turned out that three merchants had joined our group of travelers. Two of them had brought their wives, the less less-than-cordial Mistresses Lavinia and Antonia, who took a long time to get ready on the first morning. Amused, I watched servants run in and out of the inn while raised voices came through the window. A harassed-looking merchant berated his servant for something.

It reminded me of the time my father caught me being rude to the servant maid. He pulled me into his study, closing the door behind him. "I do not ever want to see you behave like that with people who cannot defend themselves." He spoke in a tone of voice I had never heard from him before. "I expect you to go back to her and apologize for your behavior."

I never forgot the lesson. Now, watching the servant's averted eyes and hunched shoulders, my eyes stung. I would give anything to have my father here to berate me again.

Count Baltasar walked around, checking on the progress of the various members of his group. He stopped next to me and smiled. "Mistress Alina, I'm glad to see at least you are ready." He shook his head in irritation. "I hope we will be on the road before the morning is gone." He bowed smoothly in the direction of one of the merchants, who glanced in our direction.

"What are they trading with?" I asked Count Baltasar, flattered that he did not hide his frustration from me.

"Oh, the usual," he said dismissively. "I believe that the bulk of their trade goods consists of wool, but they also carry wax and some bars of precious metals."

"And what will they get for it?"

Count Baltasar looked surprised at my interest. "I think they usually bring back small items of value that are easier to transport, such as spices, pearls, and perfumes."

Just then Mistress Antonia swept into the courtyard, her cheekbones splotched and her wimple askew. I stepped aside since she evidently wanted to speak to Count Baltasar.

"Count Baltasar," she said in a voice that carried across the yard. "I hope our accommodations will be better from here on. I saw several rats in the sleeping quarters."

"Good morning, Mistress Antonia." Count Baltasar smiled at her. "We will do everything in our power to keep you safe on the journey. Regrettably the quality of the accommodations is not something I can control, but we will do our best." His calm and self-effacing demeanor seemed to mollify Mistress Antonia. At least she tipped her head graciously and walked away.

Count Baltasar winked at me. "It's going to be a long journey," he whispered. He took my arm and led me a few steps away from the commotion. "Mistress Alina," he said. "I have a small request. As you see, our group has increased substantially." He gestured toward the bustle of servants and merchants grappling with mules, knights getting their horses ready, the Templars strutting around, and two young knights who had joined us in Venice engaging in mock swordplay.

"This is not the first time I've escorted pilgrims and other travelers to the Holy Land," the count continued. "And I have learned that providing regular, light entertainment in the evenings is enormously beneficial for the entourage's overall mood. Milos told me you are an accomplished lute player, and that you and he have often made music together. I wonder whether you would honor us with some music in the evenings. I would provide you with a small stipend in recognition of your work."

Embarrassed, I hung my head, speechless. I hadn't slept all night, worried about our funds. Never mind how much I enjoyed Byzantine mosaics and warm baths, I almost wished us back at home. Having to listen to Aunt Marci's strident voice might not be such a steep price to pay for food and shelter after all. Meanwhile, this offer seemed uncomfortably close to charity.

"You haven't even heard us play," I demurred. We had been moving along at a steady clip, and most evenings everybody retired after supper in order to get up early the next morning. There had been no time for music.

Anyway, I would have felt awkward in front of these men. I could just imagine my aunt hissing at me. "A lady should never put herself forward."

"I have no doubt that you and your brother will acquit yourselves well." Count Baltasar smiled at me. "Anyway, we'll be taking it more slowly from now on, partly because the merchants' cart horses slow us down, and because there are fewer inns along the way until we reach Constantinople. This means longer periods of rest for the horses. Fortunately, it gets warmer as we go farther south, and being able to relax and listen to music will be a delight. There will be plenty of opportunities for you to entertain us. Trust me. It would be an enormous help."

"Thank you," I said. "I will talk to Milos." Then a thought occurred to me, and I almost burst out laughing. Milos and I would be entertainers, making music for money while traveling on rough roads toward a foreign country. This was exactly the sort of scenario Aunt Marci had envisioned, and, to be honest, what I had feared for myself. Well, Aunt Marci was far away, and I was tired of being afraid. I beamed at Count Baltasar.

He raised his eyebrows in a query.

I shook my head. I couldn't possibly explain it to him. "Thank you," I said gratefully. "We will be happy to entertain the travelers with our music."

CHAPTER FIVE

CAMP FOLLOWERS, SLAVES, AND HERMITS

"WHO ARE they?" I asked.

It was late morning by the time we set out for Constantinople, and even though we had been trotting along for just a short while, the horses' necks were already damp with sweat. I pulled the top of my gown away from my body as discreetly as I could, to let some air in, and dreaded the thought of how hot it would get once we turned south.

Milos glanced around. Three women, coming along the road that led to Venice, rode toward us. One of them waved as they came closer.

Count Baltasar pulled up his horse. He greeted them like he knew them. After a short exchange, he returned to the head of the group, giving the signal to keep moving. The three women waited for us to pass and then fell in behind the merchants' carts.

"Who are they?" I asked.

"I'm not sure." Milos shrugged. "I think they're camp followers."

"What are camp followers?"

I was surprised to see a flush creep over Milos's neck and cheeks.

"They are...well, you know. They aren't married, and travel along with soldiers, and..." Milos fumbled. "Aunt Marci would say they have loose morals."

"Oh." I had heard of such women. "How did *you* know what they are?"

"I saw some when I went to Marseilles." My brother's face turned a deeper shade of red.

I studied the women. They looked confident and self-sufficient, with their bedrolls tied on the backs of their mules and an additional mule carrying their baggage. Their clothes were colorful, with glittering bangles and necklaces of beads.

I tried to get a closer look by pulling up my horse and pretending to check my saddle, waiting for them to reach me as we rode along. They chatted among themselves cheerfully in what sounded like a version of the Latin I had already heard in this region.

The oldest of them wore face paint, with a bright red stain on her lips and her eyes outlined in black. She wore large silver rings in her ears that bounced with every step of her mule. She smiled at me as she rode past, giving me an unobstructed view of the large gap in her teeth. Embarrassed to be caught staring, I turned back to my saddle, pulling on the leather girth as if it had been the only reason for me to stop.

Later that day, when we stopped, I approached Count Baltasar, pretending that Milos had not said anything to me about those women. "Are they also on a pilgrimage?"

"Well, not exactly." He glanced at me sideways, and I thought his lips twitched. "But I suspect they will travel with us until Acre. They asked me whether I was willing to offer them protection on the road. Meanwhile, excuse me, Mistress Alina. I need to see to our arrangements for the night." He bowed politely and turned away.

I grinned as I watched him walk away. The journey had just gotten much more interesting. Count Baltasar didn't seem to be willing to share what he knew with me. Little did he know that this made me even more determined to find out more.

One evening, a few days after we left Venice, I went to the little stream behind the barn where we were staying for the night. I was not worried about marauders, since the others were just up the hill, so for a few moments, I was able to relish the solitude.

Then I noticed a young woman I hadn't seen before. Her head was wrapped in a scarf, and she sat at the edge of the stream next to a bucket, resting her feet in the water. She looked tired.

"Hello," I said. "It's pleasant here, isn't it? My name is Alina."

Her head jerked up, and she stared at me like a startled deer. Then she scrambled to her feet and grabbed the bucket. Before I could say anything else, she hurried back up the trail toward the barn, water slopping out of the bucket as she went. Intrigued, I followed and watched her climb inside the cart that belonged to Master Tibaut, who was the unmarried one among the three merchants traveling with us.

When I turned around to go back to the barn, I ran into Milos's friend, Filipot. Since Venice, he had been much friendlier to me. Perhaps he was ashamed to have dragged Milos into such a stupid adventure. Maybe he would know about that girl.

"Filipot, I just saw a girl I haven't seen before," I blurted, blushing as I realized how awkward that sounded.

"Indeed." He smiled at me. "And who might that be?"

I described the young woman.

"Oh, that's Aissa, Master Tibaut's slave."

"A slave?" I stared at him.

"Yes, I think he bought her in Acre several years ago."

"*Crusaders* sell slaves?"

"Well, yes, among other things. Acre has a slave market."

"That's permitted?" I gaped at him. It had never occurred to me that crusaders might be engaging in trade, much less selling slaves.

"Yes. Of course, no Christian, whether Western or Eastern, can be sold into slavery, and any slaves who convert to Christianity must be freed. But Muslim prisoners of war can be sold, just as Christian prisoners can be sold as slaves by Muslims."

"So why doesn't she convert to Christianity?"

"Why are you concerned about this girl? Maybe she doesn't want to become a Christian," Filipot said. "Anyway, excuse me, Mistress Alina. I have some things I need to take care of." He hurried away.

I looked at the cart. Probably that's where the girl slept at night. Later I told Milos about her.

"So she's a slave." He shrugged. "Why is that so important? Did you forget that we have serfs at home?"

"But our serfs have always been on our land. It's their home. They can have a family. This girl is being dragged all over the world. She looked scared, Milos."

"What do you want me to do about it? We have enough problems."

I supposed he was right, but it was upsetting. I looked at the Templars and their haughty expressions, then at the young knights, so smug and brash, and also at Count Baltasar with his friendly smile and chubby cheeks. These were men of God, and yet they condoned a girl being sold as a slave, and didn't appear troubled by camp followers traveling with them.

Meanwhile, here I was, trying to get away from my aunt's attempts to marry me off—not as helpless as a slave, but now, thanks to Milos's carelessness, obliged to make music to pay for our way. According to Aunt Marci's standards, it was probably not much better than what these women did. And yet, I was happy at the thought of making music again.

Just as Count Baltasar had hoped, Milos and I made music on many evenings. Now that we had the count's sanction, I no longer felt embarrassed at the idea of performing in front of an audience. Sometimes Milos performed some of his tricks while I played the lute in the background. Often we sang together. I remembered my aunt's warning, but I quickly shrugged it off. She was far away, and her disapproval couldn't touch me now.

Besides, Count Baltasar, true to his word, had discreetly augmented our funds, and I held on to the scrip for dear life.

"No, Milos, let me keep it for now," I would always say, clutching the leather pouch when he pleaded with me for some coins whenever we reached a town. I had not yet forgiven him for being so careless before.

"You're a fine one to talk to me about being careful," Milos said spitefully. "You are the one who befriends camp followers. I can just imagine what Aunt Marci would say about that."

His taunt didn't bother me. "Aunt Marci won't know, so she won't have any reason to get upset," I said lightly. "Anyway, let's practice some more."

It got hillier as we continued moving east and south, farther and farther into the Byzantine Empire.

I loved the juniper and stunted holm oaks and the scrubland awash with swaths of lavender, sage, wild thyme, and rosemary of my childhood, reminding me of how I used to rub the silvery wormwood leaves between my fingers and relishing their spicy fragrance.

At home, our sandy loam didn't permit much variety in what the peasants could grow. Here, in the fragrant, dark soil, everything seemed to flourish. The villagers willingly traded apples, pears, plums, and vegetables, and we could buy all sorts of pungent sheep and goat cheeses. The peasants also raised grapes and made wine.

Some of this wine ended up with the knights.

Milos had taken to regularly drinking with a few of the younger knights. "Give me some coins, Alina," he cajoled when we arrived at a village.

"You know perfectly well we have to watch our funds." I clutched my scrip tightly.

"Now you're the one who sounds like Uncle Garsanc," Milos grumbled. "Fine. Have it your way."

It turned out that he had found another way to get coins for wine. He got the soldiers to bet on what tricks he could do. I worried about him, but there was nothing I could do or say. He had to know that as an impoverished young nobleman without training or skills to speak of, and without a knight to support him or take him on as a squire, his chances of doing anything more than acting as a foot soldier in battle were limited.

At least he was able to perfect his juggling skills and master numerous tricks to perform with dice during those months on the road.

I finally gave up on the slave girl, Aissa. She was so uncomfortable whenever I tried to start a conversation that I decided to let her be. It wasn't as if I could do anything to help her anyway.

But I was able to get her to relax just once, and only briefly, when I managed to buy two jars of honey from a beekeeper. On an impulse, when the merchant happened to be elsewhere, I went to the cart where Aissa spent most of her time.

"Aissa, this is for you," I called into the opening.

She stuck out her head uncertainly.

"It's honey." I held out one of the jars. "The beekeeper told me it's from linden tree blossoms."

She took it quickly. I heard a soft "thank you" before she disappeared inside. After that she sometimes smiled at me when nobody was looking.

Meanwhile, I did not do much better with the three women who joined us outside of Venice. They usually stayed at the tail end of our group when we were on the road. I let my horse fall back sometimes and tried to chat with them.

However, they rejected my overtures. They were polite but stiff.

"What do you want from them?" Milos asked me. "Anyway, if you keep this up, you'll soon be considered one of them."

"You think I care what those stuffy merchant wives think of me?" I frowned at him. "Anyway, I don't want anything from them. I just want to talk to them."

"Oh, be honest. You're burning with curiosity."

I didn't respond because Milos was right.

A few days later we rested for a few hours on a meadow. After eating my bread, I got tired of sitting by myself and decided to walk around for a while before we got underway again. It felt good to stretch my legs.

A small stream curved into the woods, away from our temporary campsite, and I followed along its bank. As long as I remained within calling distance of the others, I should be safe, but I halted when sounds from the bushes caught my attention.

A scuffle, a woman's voice hissing, "Get your hands off me, you oaf," followed by a man's muffled curse.

"Stop!" I shouted as I burst through the brambles. "You there, leave her alone."

A woman stood in the thicket, her gown in disarray, her face blank. It was the oldest of the three camp followers.

The man had his hand on the woman's shoulder, as if he had been trying to shake her. It was one of the young knights Milos spent much of his time with, although I hadn't spoken to this one at all so far. He glared at me. Then, with another curse, he dropped his arm and stalked off.

"Are you hurt?"

"No, not at all, young lady." The woman started to laugh. With a few deft moves, she adjusted her gown. "You just interrupted a commercial transaction." She laughed again. "It wasn't going too well, so maybe it's just as well that you interrupted."

"A commercial transaction?" Then I realized what she meant. My cheeks grew hot as I looked down. An image of Aunt Marci's distorted features floated in my mind. I could practically hear her screeching at me for associating with "loose women."

"Come now, don't take it to heart. I know you meant well. In fact, it was rather brave of you to rush in like that—although perhaps not the smartest thing to do."

That was the beginning of a strange friendship. It turned out that heavy-set Lana, with her shiny, dark hair and bright, laughing eyes, was as curious about me as I was about her. The other two women continued to keep me at arm's length, but Lana and I sometimes sat together for meals, and on the road we often rode side by side.

She laughed at my stories about Uncle Garsanc and Aunt Marci. "But they didn't treat you all that badly," she said when I complained about them too long. "Think about it. They fed you and took care of you, and even gave you money for this journey. It's more than anybody ever did for me."

I hadn't thought of it that way before. After a silence, I asked, "What will you do when you don't want to go traveling anymore?" I didn't know how else to put it. I wondered what would happen when she got older.

"I've been squirreling away some money here and there." Lana shrugged. "Perhaps, when the time comes, I will be able to manage on my own. On the other hand, I suspect I might not need to worry too much about getting very old." She pulled up her horse and dropped back, evidently tired of my questions.

Later it was as if the conversation never happened. Lana began to give me advice about how to handle some of the knights who apparently thought I was fair game—an unattached girl with no one but an unkempt sprig of a brother to look out for her.

"Mistress Alina, come sit with us," the knights would cajole me, and many weren't above trying to grab me when no one was looking.

"You have to learn how to laugh at them and not show them any fear," Lana told me. "Still, it's a better idea not to be caught alone in the first place."

She entertained me with her opinions about the men in our group. Some she viewed with tolerance and others with disdain.

"That one," she discreetly pointed at one of the older knights, "looks like he swallowed his own sword, so stiff and proper. He is actually funny, and quite decent. You just never know what someone is like until you spend time with him." Lifting her chin, she glanced at one of the younger ones. "Be careful with that one, Alina," she warned me. "He is a bad one. We can handle him, but he's not right for you." She had little to say about Count Baltasar. "I don't know anything about him, really."

"But you knew him already when you joined us," I said, surprised.

"Yes, he has escorted several groups of knights and pilgrims to the Holy Land. Still, I can't say I know much about him. He is polite. He does a good job of seeing to the success of the journey."

"And Milos?" I asked, trying to sound offhand about it.

"Oh, your brother is sweet." Lana glanced at me from the corner of her eye. "And he is very young. Don't worry too much about him."

"Oh." I didn't dare say anything else. I was terribly homesick just then, and tired of worrying about Milos and about what we would do once we got to Jerusalem.

"Soon we will get to the best *caravanserai* in this entire journey," Lana said, as if she hadn't noticed my abstraction. "Trust me, you'll like it." We were in a hilly region north of the city of Sofia, and the journey ahead seemed to stretch out endlessly in my mind.

Inns in the Byzantine Empire were called *caravanserais*. Located along busy merchant routes all across the Empire and south to the Holy Land, these *caravanserais* made me think of small fortress towns. Framing a large central courtyard, they supplied everything travelers might need—sleeping areas, kitchens, blacksmith services, doctors, and even people specializing in the care of animals. The rooms were clean and comfortable, and the braziers used to provide heat seemed a lot more efficient than open hearths.

"Wait till you see the marble in the bath."

"This place has a bath?"

"Yes, isn't it wonderful?" Lana laughed at me as we rode up the hill. "I have been here before. It's because of the traders—they like their creature comforts, and pay well to have the baths set up."

I looked at the elegantly gowned backs of Mistress Lavinia and Mistress Antonia, riding ahead of us. "It never occurred to me I might have to be grateful to those two—or rather, their merchant husbands, but the idea of a bath makes me want to kiss their feet."

Our next stop south of the city of Sofia was an inn near a small monastery in the Rilski River valley.

"Come with me, Milos, please," I begged. "Let's go to the church." I pointed at the wooden structure on the hill, the two onion-shaped domes dominating the landscape.

"Oh, there'll be enough churches when we get to the Holy Land. I want to play a game with Filipot."

I shook my head. I couldn't honestly blame him. It was not as if I had paid a lot of attention to the fact that we were on a pilgrimage. Perhaps it was just as well to go alone. Besides, I was glad to get away from the others for a while.

The church was surrounded by a rickety wooden fence, and the gate squealed when I pulled it aside. The roof almost touched the ground, and the roof shingles were dark, some covered with moss. Because the roof stuck out so far, it looked as if the entire structure floated in the air.

Other than a distant chirping of birds, there wasn't a sound anywhere when I stepped up onto the porch and opened the unlocked wooden door on the western side.

Inside it was cool and dark, with a musty smell of incense. It took a few moments before my eyes adjusted and I was able to make out a simple stone altar in the back, framed by golden images glowing softly in the perpetual light, while candles flickered on the sides.

I knelt on the floorboards. Feeling shy about making a sound in this holy place, I just mouthed the words of prayer for my father's soul, and for Maria's and my mother's as well. Although I rarely talked about them, I missed them acutely and thought about them every day. Finally, I prayed for Milos and myself.

Afterward I was calm and settled in a way I had not been in a long time.

When I got up and turned to go outside, I noticed a painting on a thick wooden base on the side wall of the church illuminated by a table covered with candles.

It showed two male figures, curiously elongated, with long, silvery beards, dark robes and slender, pale fingers. Each man held one hand over his heart and the other on a large scroll between them while above their heads floated an image of Mary and the Christ child. The edges of the painting were covered with gold leaf in an elaborate floral pattern.

I moved closer, trying to get a better look at the lettering on the scroll.

"That is Cyrillic," a deep voice behind me said.

Startled, I turned around and almost flattened my nose against the broad chest of a man clad in a black robe. He wore a dark cap, and his luxurious beard rivaled those in the painting.

"Who are they?" I pointed at the painting. "And what is Cyrillic?"

"Those figures are the saints Cyril and Methodius. They gave us this alphabet called Cyrillic for our language, which you call Slavonic. These saints are venerated everywhere in the region." He spoke in Latin, but he spoke an odd, stiff version of it. "You are alone here, my daughter?"

"Yes," I said. "But only right now," I added awkwardly. "I came with my brother. We are on our way to the Holy Land."

"Welcome." He studied me, his dark eyes kind. "My name is Brother Gregorius."

"My name is Alina."

"This is a remarkable icon," another voice spoke behind us.

"Oh, Count Baltasar." I hadn't heard him come in. Then again, I hadn't heard Brother Gregorius either, but he seemed to belong here, almost as if he had grown out of the wooden floorboards.

"Mistress Alina, I saw you go up the hill. It occurred to me that it might not be safe for you all by yourself."

Brother Gregorius frowned. "We are peaceful people."

"Certainly," Count Baltasar said smoothly. "But one never knows where strangers might be lurking. I notice you don't lock the door to this church. Are you not concerned that someone might steal this lovely icon?"

"No, the door is always open." Brother Gregorius's bushy eyebrows made me think of a fierce, bearded owl. "Of course, no one entering the church is ever truly alone." It was as if he spoke to *me* rather than to Count Baltasar. "Shall you sit on the porch with me? I can tell you the origin of the church. It might help you to understand our ways."

Count Baltasar sketched a bow, and we followed the monk outside to a bench along the wall. It was peaceful, sitting there in the shade, with the sun just reaching the tips of our toes.

"Allow me to tell you how this church came to be." Brother Gregorius turned his face to look over the fence into the valley, his silvery beard resting on his broad chest. "There once was a monk by the name of Ivan Rilski. He came here some two hundred years ago. First he lived all alone in the forest, without a roof and without food, just the beasts of the wild to keep him company. Soon others followed, inspired by his example of living a simple life devoted to prayer. That was the beginning of the monastery."

I could feel Count Baltasar fidget next to me, but Brother Gregorius ignored him and went on. "Soon his fame spread far and wide. Even King Peter of Bulgaria wanted to meet the hermit. He sent many wonderful presents and an invitation to the hermit to come to his palace. Ivan Rilski refused the invitation and sent back all the presents. When he died in 946, he was canonized, thus becoming a saint." The monk glanced at Count Baltasar from the side. "Perhaps now you understand why locking the door would have been anathema to him."

"Quite. Certainly admirable." Count Baltasar smiled. "Still, the prayer 'lead us not into temptation' comes to mind. One can never be too careful when it comes to safety." He stood up. "Mistress Alina, let me escort you back to the inn."

"Thank you, Brother Gregorius," I said to the monk. He gave me a small bow and made the sign of the cross. "Travel safely, my daughter."

"I thought he would never stop," Count Baltasar scoffed when we were out of earshot.

I was taken aback. I had liked the monk, and Count Baltasar sounded almost disrespectful.

As if he sensed my disapproval, he added, "It is a beautiful church. I am glad I saw it."

The low point of the journey was when we were holed up near Adrianople for several weeks. A powerful storm had forced us off the road, and it was followed by more wind and rain. The inn was small and cramped, and I quickly got tired of mending my gowns. The only thing that cheered me was my lute. I played as much as I could. Thinking of my father, I even began putting together new combinations of chords.

"Do you like this, Milos?" I asked as I played a melody for my brother one day.

"Not bad, little sister." He grinned. "But what about the lyrics?"

"I'm working on them," I said, annoyed at his dismissive reaction. "You try to write them if you think it's so easy."

"You know I'm not good at that. I like to play, but I can't come up with new music."

Mollified by his honesty, I bent over my lute and played some more.

"Father would have liked this," Milos said suddenly. This was the first time he had mentioned our father since his death.

I got better at gauging audience reactions, learning when to increase the speed or the drama of the music, when to play soft, gentle melodies, and when it was time to stop.

One of my favorite songs was *Quan lo rossinhol el follos* by Jaufre Rudel about a nightingale. It was perfect for two voices, and Milos and I sang it frequently while our father was still alive. Father played a recorder for the opening, then switched to the lute. I loved the song for its wistfulness and the dreams it evoked, and even more for its dancing, almost-teasing rhythms, full of promise and hidden laughter.

Deep among the trees, the nightingale
Sings its love, yearns for it, and receives it back,
Shaping the sound of its voice into a delight for the soul
When praising the beloved.
When water shimmers and ripples, and grasses sway like silk,
Filled with the serenity that rules the firmament,
My heart overflows.

Over time, we both expanded our repertoire to the point where the others in the group would often ask us to perform. One morning, shortly before we were to reach Acre, it occurred to me that I hadn't dreamed about my mother and Maria for quite a while, nor had I been haunted by my father's face. I still missed them deeply, but it was as if a fog had lifted and some of the bitter grief had stayed behind.

Sometimes I worried about what would happen to me in life. Without a proper position in a respectable household, either through marriage or as a lady of the court, I could hardly hope to continue performing music. What was acceptable for a noblewoman on the road would not be acceptable once we arrived in Jerusalem. Eventually I would have to return to my aunt and uncle and accept marriage or enter a convent.

But then I dismissed these thoughts about the future. For the time being, I gloried in a freedom I'd never experienced before.

CHAPTER SIX

HORSES, TRINKETS, AND SILVER BALLS

WHEN WE reached the main gate of Acre, I noticed that the camp followers had fallen back. I pulled up my horse and turned around. "Lana, what are you doing?"

Throughout the journey from Venice, Lana had been cheerful and uncomplaining, even though sometimes, when she thought nobody was watching her, she would sit with her shoulders slightly hunched and a sad, and tired expression on her face.

"It would not be right for us to stay in the Templar quarters." She sounded offhand. "We have to look for another place to stay."

"But we always stayed together before."

"Alina, you know how it is. On the road, nobody cares about morals, but now the knights act all holy," Lana said, smiling at me. "Anyway, we'll be glad to be off the road for a while before we head back."

"You are not going to Jerusalem?" I asked, dismayed that Lana and the other women weren't coming with us. They were certainly plain-spoken, but they had their own code of honor, and had been kind to me. "What will you do?"

"Don't worry about us, girl. We are hardly the type to go on a pilgrimage." Lana laughed. "Acre is a good town. We like it here. Eventually, we'll probably travel west when there's a group of merchants leaving Acre."

I thought about the fortitude of these women, with nothing to call their own, no one to look out for them, and living entirely by their wits. While my choices were limited, at least I had a home with my uncle and was not unprotected.

In Acre, we had lodgings in the Templar quarter, next to the Genovese quarter. The Hospitaller Knights of the Order of St. John had built a new center next to the northern wall, north of the Church of St. John, but Alaric belonged to the Templars, so we were housed there.

Shortly after our arrival, Count Baltasar gathered us in the great hall of the lodging. "Allow me to introduce Count Raymond, regent of Tripoli." He gestured toward an elegantly robed, gaunt-looking man standing next to him. "Acting on behalf of King Amalric, he has come to Acre to meet you. He exemplifies service to the Kingdom of Jerusalem, having spent the past nine years in prison in Aleppo after a disastrous loss suffered by his crusader army in 1164, and King Amalric was greatly grieved that he was unable to free him any sooner."

"You can measure the extent of the king's grief by the sacrifice he made to free Count Raymond," one of the Templars, standing behind Milos and myself, muttered to a knight next to him. "It cost him a pretty penny—as much as 80,000 pieces of gold."

The count pursed his lips, which had the effect of emphasizing the hollows under his cheekbones. His lined face had a grey tinge, which I supposed was hardly surprising, given where he'd spent the past nine years. He didn't look pleased with this introduction. Perhaps he disliked the mention of his years in prison. I tried to imagine 80,000 pieces of gold and failed. Count Raymond must be very important to the king.

Count Baltasar introduced the various knights to the count. He also presented Milos and me, explaining that we had come to the Holy Land to pray for our father's soul.

Count Raymond frowned as if we were an unsatisfactory consignment of sheep and, with a small, curt bow, turned away.

The next morning, delighted after the luxury of a bath, I went to the central plaza. Looking out at the sparkling harbor, I was relaxed and content that we would remain here for a few days before continuing to Jerusalem.

I lifted my face into the wind from the sea until my lips tasted tangy and salty. Of course the wind didn't cover the smells of raw waste washing up against the stone walls of the castle, and the slap and gurgle reminded me of the sucking noises when cows walk through waterlogged meadows, but it didn't bother me. My worries about the future had receded, and I was eager to see Jerusalem.

The plaza near the harbor was a beehive of activity. Merchants had set up tables with their wares—silver beakers, ceramic jars, oil lamps, glass, beads, spices, as well as silks and other woven cloths. Water carriers moved among the crowds, shouting, as they carefully balanced their loads on their shoulders. Fruit sellers sat on the ground with baskets full of oranges, lemons, and pomegranates, while knights wandered around, their swords banging against their legs as they walked. I could recognize the Templars from their distinctive tabards and long white cloaks, the red cross prominently displayed on the front and back, as well as on the shields hanging off their shoulders.

The Hospitallers looked more somber, with their dark robes and the Maltese cross emblazoned in white, but I didn't really know the difference between them and the Templars. They all appeared to be men of dedication, wrapped in the mantle of poverty and chastity. I had heard that many of them gave all their worldly possessions to the order when they entered it. Nonetheless, most of them carried themselves with an air of privilege and pride—no humble monks, these.

From the raised steps where I stood I had a good view of the plaza, and the activity at the dock as well. I could see the white marble mosque glinting in the sunlight, along with its domed roof and tall tower, and the ships from Genoa and Pisa and other points west crowding the harbor. I counted at least fifty before I gave up—flat-bottomed cogs with square-rigged sails, large galleys with fierce-looking rows of oars like porcupine quills, and smaller sailing vessels—all gently riding on the swell in the protected bay.

"Halt, thief!" a man shouted and jumped after a small boy. The boy tried to duck between the crowds, clutching oranges in his shirt, but the man grabbed the boy by the arm and dragged him back to the stall.

Immediately I remembered how Milos once was caught red-handed by one of the peasants, stolen apples spilling out of his tunic. My father had laughed at the time.

The boy struggled and kicked the man in the shins while throwing the oranges at his face. Momentarily stunned, the man dropped his hand, shouting angrily, and the boy ran off.

I sucked in a deep breath, but winced as I relaxed my hand to discover I had dug my nails into my palm.

Like a homing pigeon, I started to look for Milos. There he was—next to some servants, all staring up at a ship that had just arrived. Reassured, I glanced at his lanky frame, loose-fitting tunic, and leggings.

He needed a haircut. Then again, I hadn't done much about my own appearance for quite a while, and my curls escaped from under my cap like furry snakes, making me look vaguely Medusa-like.

The ship attracting my brother's attention must have had a rough journey, for its sails were tattered, and one of the masts was at a slant. A seaman lowered the landing ramp onto the dock, and the first to disembark were several knights. Considering that they had traveled for weeks in cramped quarters, they looked remarkably fresh and alert, making their way down the landing ramp and onto the plaza with a peculiar, rolling gait as they tried to adjust to solid ground beneath their feet.

More blustering knights, I thought, as I watched them chatting with each other and laughing. My journey with the retinue of Count Baltasar had not improved my impression of knights at all—most of them struck me as foolish, reckless, and naive. Watching over people dying from sweating sickness a few times would deflate their self-importance. I remembered my mother's quiet competence whenever a servant or one of us had fallen ill. Even my aunt had been effective in the sickroom, for all that she was stingy, ungracious, and essentially joyless.

These men could swing a sword. They could maim and kill, but as to any other skills, I doubted they had them.

Servants began unloading the horses. The first one, a bay, burst out of the hold and clattered down the ramp so quickly that the servant was dragged along. He only managed to slow down the horse once they arrived on the dock.

Another horse neighed as it came out of the hold. It reared up on top of the ramp, its dun-colored coat like a ray of light against the dark ship. A servant hung on to the lead and tried to pull the horse forward.

The neighing turned into a shrill scream, and the horse jerked up his head, its teeth bared, foam flecking its flanks. Other men shouted at the horse from all sides.

Poor horse. It must have had a miserable time, hobbled for weeks on end in the dark hold and terrified during storms at sea.

I turned to look for Milos. He was good with horses. But I couldn't find him.

Meanwhile, one of the knights who disembarked earlier detached himself from the group on the dock and swiftly moved back up the ramp. I couldn't hear what he said, but the impact was immediate. Silence descended.

The horse stood on his four feet once again, rigid, trembling, with his head held high. The man approached calmly and with a firm step. It looked as if he was talking. Then he pulled something out of his pocket and held it out to the horse, which slowly lowered its head toward the man's hand and then, snorting, took the offering and chomped on it, shaking its head. After a moment, the man put his hand on the horse's neck and picked up the lead. Without looking back, he turned and walked down the ramp.

The horse followed him, picking up its hooves as if unsure of its footing. A sigh went through the crowd. Once on the dock, the knight turned to a group of servants and beckoned one over. "Here, take him, and see to it that he gets a good rubbing down," he said curtly and then rejoined the group of knights at the dock.

"Who is that?" I asked one of the women next to me.

"You don't know?" She turned to me in disbelief, so I could see her pinched face and droopy nose in all their glory. Her wimple trembled as she shook her head in dismay over my ignorance. "That's Count Stephen of Sancerre. The King invited him in the hopes that he might marry Princess Sibylla."

This didn't convey much to me, but I nodded as if I had known it all along and turned back to examine the man. He was not tall, but sturdy, and with broad shoulders, and his plain tunic and simple leggings appeared clean. Something in his confident, calm stance reminded me of people at home in Provence who worked the land with patience and perseverance.

I tried to think where I had heard the name Sancerre. Then I remembered. It was north of our home, in the Loire Valley, the heart of France. My father had told me about the grapes that grew there along sloping hills.

But enough of gaping.

I needed to get down to the marketplace to buy cloth to repair my travel-worn gowns before we set out for Jerusalem. Weaving my way through the crowds toward the stalls, I pushed the cap off my forehead. It had gotten warm.

The scent of spices tickled my nostrils, and I stared at oranges and apricots, barley, sorghum, flax, and various vegetables I didn't recognize in piles on brown sacking. The clamor of voices in many languages surged around me, and I was filled with a sense of well-being I hadn't experienced in a long time.

At home the nearest town was Aix-en-Provence. As a young woman, I would never have been permitted to travel there, much less walk around its market by myself. Here nobody paid any attention to me or made snide comments about a young noblewoman going about unattended. When I reached the silk merchants' tables, I quickly rejected several silks and brocades, choosing instead a generous length of rough-spun linen that had been dyed a pleasing shade of dark blue. It would be enough for a new gown and a hooded mantle.

I stopped at a table covered with an odd assortment of figurines, pendants, and bottles.

"Here, this water was blessed at one of the holiest sites in the entire Kingdom of Jerusalem—Mary's Well in the town of Nazareth." A man in dark robe pointed to several small flasks.

I shook my head.

"How about a souvenir badge to show your family at home, proof that you visited the Holy Land?" He spread out flat disks, some with a silver sheen and others in a dull brown. I could make out images of tombs and saints, and several cross-shaped ones. "See? You could wear it on your gown." The man held up one of the discs and pointed at the pin in the back.

Intrigued I picked up what looked like small sandstone fragments. "What are these?"

"Oh, mistress, those are the holiest relics we have. They come from the tomb of Christ."

For a moment, I was awed. Then I almost laughed out loud. These "holy relics" looked just like the pebbles on the road to Acre. Come to think of it, I had removed a few from my horse's hooves when we stopped for a rest the day before. Nodding politely at the man, I walked off.

When I glanced back, I saw two other people standing at his table. With an unctuous smile, one of the men proceeded to display his wares again, and with the same enthusiasm.

Satisfied with my purchase, I looked around, again struck by the vivid colors and the brilliant sunlight, exhilarated by the roar of the seas and the pungent scents of this new land.

Milos stood at a table covered with silver spoons, pewter bowls, glass vials, and exquisitely carved little boxes decorated with precious stones. He fingered a set of small silver balls. Perhaps he liked them because they were perfect for juggling. I couldn't imagine what else they might be good for.

Just then, a dispute broke out between a richly dressed woman and the elderly merchant. "This is outrageous." The woman berated the merchant in a loud voice that carried straight across the plaza. "Real pearls you said! Ha! They crumbled and melted like candle wax."

"Lady, would you show me the pearls?" The merchant cowered behind his stall. "Perhaps I can make amends?"

"Would I stand here and waste my time talking to you if I could? I told you the pearls fell apart just days after I bought them from you." Her voice had become shrill. "I don't know where you buy your wares. Merchants like you shouldn't be permitted to do business."

Other people drifted closer to watch the fun. I craned my neck to look past a heavyset woman when I saw Milos's hand swiftly scoop up three of the little silver balls. I caught my breath. I was too far away to do anything. *Oh, Milos,* I thought desperately. Then other people stepped into my line of sight.

Clutching my gown, I tried to push my way through the crowd to get to Milos when I stumbled and dropped my new purchase.

"Permit me." A hand reached out and snatched up the bundle.

In my haste, I barely glanced at the hand holding out the blue linen. I whispered my thanks, took it, and tried to move away, but the same hand grabbed me by the arm.

"Mistress Alina, walk with me."

I looked into the dark eyes of the man Count Baltasar had introduced earlier, Count Raymond.

CHAPTER SEVEN

AN OFFER NOT TO BE REFUSED

WITH A firm grip on my arm, Count Raymond walked me across the plaza, nodding courteously at people along the way. Finally he pulled me into an arched gateway and down a few steps into a tunnel.

Our steps echoed in a cool, dank vaulted space. Only a few torches in recesses along the walls were lit.

As I stumbled along, I thought of the scene at the market. There had been so many people, and the count must have been standing behind me. He could not have seen Milos. Perhaps he thought that I, as an unattached young woman, shouldn't be traveling to Jerusalem, or he disapproved of our music. Maybe Count Baltasar told him something about my father.

I was sweating and breathing fast, my gown sticking to my back.

We reached the end of the tunnel and went up again into a long hallway. We must have crossed directly underneath a portion of the city and ended up in the Templars' fortress. Count Raymond pulled me into a room and pushed the door shut.

My heart thudded in my chest. I clutched the linen bundle like a shield as I glanced around. The room was sparsely furnished with two chairs, a rug, and a table covered with manuscripts. Sunlight came through two small, arched windows, picking out the dark red glass of a flagon of wine and several beakers on the table.

"Sit down, Mistress Alina."

Reluctantly I placed my bundle on the floor and perched on the chair he had pointed out, holding on to the rim of the seat to still my hands.

Then I remembered my brother's tutor, who always told us to sit straight and proud. "The worst enemy will become smaller if you hold yourself straight," he would say. I had tested it when passing the gauntlet of stares from women in the village after the rumors about witchcraft started, squaring my shoulders and holding up my head as I walked by. It did not stop the whispering, but it made me feel better. So now I straightened and tried to look calm and composed.

Count Raymond poured some wine into two beakers and, to my surprise, handed one of them to me. Then he sat down, pulled down the sleeves of his tunic, and crossed his legs.

"I knew your father."

It was the last thing I had expected to hear. I stared at him.

The count drank some wine and coughed before continuing in his soft hoarse voice. "In fact, he made quite a name for himself as a troubadour. I heard Guy de Florac sing at the court of Eleanor of Aquitaine when I was a young man. He had a gift for words and music. It is a pity that he died."

"Thank you." I was amazed, and suddenly close to tears. I didn't want to cry in front of this man. "You are very kind."

Count Raymond proceeded to ask me questions about my father. He was so skillful that I found myself telling him a lot more about my life than I meant to, about my love of music, the songs my father taught me, even my sitting in when Milos worked with his tutor. My voice caught when I talked about my mother's and my sister's deaths, and I just barely managed to stay silent about the accusations of witchcraft that had made the rounds in the village.

The count listened thoughtfully.

I had just begun to like him a little when his next remark put me on my guard again.

"It's too bad that your father's talents did not extend to the more mundane aspects of life. I gather that he left his estate sadly encumbered."

It seemed an elegant way to describe my father's inability to manage anything of a practical nature. I bit my lip in frustration, wondering how this man knew so much about our family. I fumbled for something to say, but Count Raymond didn't wait for my response.

"Well, no matter." He studied me with his dark eyes. "I understand from Count Baltasar that you hope to pray for your father's soul in Jerusalem." His eyebrows were raised in a query.

"Yes, that is true."

"We'd be delighted to support you in this worthy endeavor." Count Raymond smiled at me blandly. "Your stay in Jerusalem would be easier and safer if you were attached to the court. I would be happy to arrange this in memory of your father."

I was at a loss for words.

"Count Baltasar told me of your talent. Apparently you and your brother helped relieve the boredom of travel with your music. This is most fortuitous. I have a small proposition for you. As you know, as an advisor to King Amalric, I have many duties and responsibilities. The king's concerns for the present and future of the kingdom are my concerns. That includes his issue. In addition to his son Baldwin, who is sadly of a sickly disposition, the king has two daughters—Isabella, a child, and Sibylla, of marriageable age, although young and," he paused to sip his wine, "at times impulsive."

He raised his eyebrows as if to make sure I was listening. "Perhaps you have heard Count Stephen de Sancerre is a contender for her hand in marriage. However, there are others who might be as suitable if not more so. I want to keep her from making a decision that might be detrimental to the future of the kingdom. Needless to say, I have her best interests at heart. Since I have been absent for some time, I am not on such terms of confidence with her as I might wish to be in order to guide and support her." He sounded smug and confident. "Now, you are a musician, and wellborn, as well as close to Princess Sibylla in age. I want you to be a companion for her at this critical time in her life. You might also teach her how to play the lute—though I must admit I have heard she isn't musically inclined."

"Why?" As soon as the word came out of my mouth, I realized that this sort of abrupt question was hardly likely to endear me to Count Raymond. Or to anyone. "You have to learn to curb your tongue if you want to be a lady," my mother had often told me. My aunt had been less gentle in her reminders. I suppose they both were right.

Count Raymond appeared unfazed. Smoothly he said, "It would be helpful to have a young woman who can establish a relationship of trust with Sibylla."

"So you want me to spy for you?"

He studied the rich brocade of his tunic sleeve. "You speak bluntly. However, there is no need to blow this out of proportion. Trust me, I have many others I can call on for such duties. Let's just say that your presence might be beneficial for all concerned."

"What if I don't agree to do it?" I asked before I could stop myself.

Count Raymond pursed his lips and shrugged as if disdaining to answer me. He ran his eyes over my dusty sandals and the frayed hem of my gown before focusing on my face again. "I gather that you and your brother may be short of funds for your journey home at the conclusion of your pilgrimage."

I nodded reluctantly, inwardly fuming that Count Baltasar must have told him about our situation and angry all over again with Milos for creating this problem to begin with.

"Perhaps we might assist you with that when the time comes. On the other hand," he said, brushing a speck of his sleeve. "I hardly need to point out that in the Kingdom of Jerusalem all individuals, whether high born or not, must comport themselves appropriately. Petty theft cannot be tolerated, and anyone witnessing such incidents would be obliged to notify the authorities."

I felt heat spread over my face. So he had seen Milos in the market. What would happen if the count mentioned this to one of the senior knights in charge in Acre? We probably would have to leave the Holy Land—and might have to be grateful if nothing worse happened.

Count Raymond raised his eyebrows expectantly as if to see whether I had understood. "Meanwhile, your cooperation would encourage me to overlook certain irregularities regarding your brother," he added delicately.

To buy myself time to think, I sipped some of the wine. It seemed as if I had no choice. I had freed myself from Aunt Marci's sour looks to land in the clutches of this smooth-spoken courtier. Maybe there was a way to salvage something out of this disaster. "Would it be possible to give my brother a position as a squire to one of the knights at court?"

Count Raymond sniffed. Then he arranged his face into his bland courtier's smile. "Ah, I see I have chosen well. In fact, it already occurred to me that something would have to be done about your brother. We wouldn't want him to be at loose ends. It would merely distract you from your new duties. Perhaps one of the more senior knights who has just arrived might require the services of a young man like your brother. Come to think of it, you just gave me an idea. I might have the perfect arrangement." He looked pleased with himself.

My anxiety increased when I saw his little smirk. He probably had another trap in mind for Milos.

He sniffed again, bringing a small piece of linen to his nose.

"Needless to say, I expect you to refrain from telling anyone about our little chat. That includes your brother."

I couldn't think of any way out of this, and felt very much alone and furious with Milos for getting me into this situation. I nodded helplessly, and he dismissed me.

Milos came to me that evening after my conversation with Count Raymond. "Oh, Froggie, I have been so worried about what we would do in Jerusalem, blaming myself for bringing you here." He looked flushed and excited. "You can't imagine what happened!"

I had been itching to scream at him for stealing and putting me in an impossible position, but this frank apology took the wind out of my sails.

Then, when he continued, I realized that this wasn't about what happened in the marketplace. He didn't know I had seen him. No, he had just been worried in a general way. He told me Count Stephen had approached him and asked him to serve as a squire. Count Stephen had no squire, and mysteriously discovered the need for one now he had reached the Holy Land. Milos was elated. "Apparently he had heard from Count Baltasar that I'm good with horses and quick on my feet. See? I told you it would work out. Once we get to Jerusalem, I'll find something for you."

Clearly, Count Raymond worked fast.

I remembered my father's skeptical response to us whenever we told him about something exciting. "*Pourvu que* ça *dure*—long may it last," he would say in his tired voice, gently questioning and doubtful. It had always irritated me, effectively putting us down and squelching our enthusiasm with the mildest words imaginable.

Now I almost said it myself, but I held my tongue. Milos looked dazed with happiness. Maybe this *was* a chance for him. I would just have to figure out how to extract us from the trap. Perhaps now would be a good time to mention my little arrangement with Count Raymond, but it would make Milos feel bad to know that he was the reason this odious man had a hold over me.

I would wait for a while. Anyway, Count Raymond might change his mind.

A tiny voice in the back of my head admitted that there was another reason. I was proud that someone had noticed my musical abilities and flattered to have been asked to serve as a companion to the princess. Besides, without my suggestion, Milos might not have gotten such a great offer. I might even make friends with the princess. Perhaps I could become a court musician. I just would have to figure out a way to deal with Count Raymond. I didn't want to share any of these thoughts with Milos.

"You are not pleased?" Milos looked at me with an expression of puzzlement.

"Oh, yes, I am. You'll do well, Milos," I said impulsively.

"Well, that's all right, then." Milos cuffed me affectionately, as he would a horse, and strode off, whistling happily.

CHAPTER EIGHT

WIND IN THE DESERT

"PLEASE, ALINA, stay with the other women," Milos pleaded with me on the first morning when we set out for Jerusalem.

"Why? Are you embarrassed by your sister?" I glared at him. "You are so high and mighty since you've become a squire to Count Stephen. Of course having a sister trail in your wake hardly fits your new image of yourself."

Milos flushed. Suddenly I was sorry for him. This had to be good for Milos. Maybe Count Stephen would help him if Milos was able to prove himself. "What about Count Stephen, anyway? Why did he come all the way to the Holy Land to marry a princess he never met?"

"How should I know?" Milos scowled at me. "He owns a lot of land around Sancerre."

"I knew that." I shook my head in my frustration. I wanted to know so much more about the man, but I couldn't understand why.

"Why are you so interested all of a sudden? Anyway, I'll see you later." Milos kicked his horse and moved to join the knights at the front of the group.

My horse shook his head to dislodge a horsefly, yanking the reins out of my hands. I made a grab for them and readjusted my seat. Another horsefly landed on the horse's neck. Irritated, I swatted it with my bare hand, pretending it was Milos. It was his fault, after all. I hated feeling trapped, with no control over my future.

To distract myself, I kept my eyes on the wimples of Mistress Antonia and Mistress Lavinia, nodding as if to echo their expressions of disgust and disdain whenever I entered their line of sight.

I amused myself with coming up with new names for them—Mistress Loveless and Mistress Arrogantia, Mistress Nastyface and Mistress Sourpuss, Mistress Harridan and Mistress Sniffles. None seemed to be quite right, but it still helped my state of mind.

Their attitude toward me had, if anything, gotten worse since Acre. It made me miss Lana and her friends. Aissa, the young slave girl, was also no longer with us. Presumably she was on her way back to the west, at the mercy of her owner. In truth, there was nothing I could do for her, and I had other things to occupy my thoughts.

I looked around for someone I could ask about the court and about Sibylla, but didn't find anyone suitable. Also I was afraid of sounding uncouth and nosy. Of course I could ask Count Baltasar. He seemed to be well-liked by everybody, and I often saw him conversing with Count Raymond.

Meanwhile, the informality and the easy banter on the first leg of the journey didn't seem possible anymore. Especially since, with Count Raymond's sharp eyes roaming everywhere, I felt shy about approaching Count Baltasar.

Fortunately, Count Raymond ignored me completely...for the time being, at least. It was as if I didn't exist. He was usually surrounded by several older knights, as if he was holding court, and a dour-looking squire who followed him around like a dog trotting after his master.

Part of me hoped he would forget about us once we got to Jerusalem. And yet another part of me was intrigued by the thought of spending time with a princess, moreover one close to my age.

Our route took us south along the coast, past the towns of Caesarea and Jaffa, where we turned inland for the last leg of the journey. Aside from the horseflies, travel along the coast was pleasant. It was a green and fertile land.

South of Caesarea, we traveled on an old Roman road until we reached Jaffa. Some of the milestones had fallen over, and one could just barely make out the Roman numerals and the names of emperors. These roads were part of the system that used to connect the vast empire, but apparently nobody bothered to take care of them anymore.

After Jaffa we headed inland. The road turned into a narrow trail that passed through a harsh, dry region—nothing but rocky stretches with sand dunes and intermittent shrubs and stunted trees for shade. Occasionally my horse slipped and stumbled, so I had to concentrate to keep my seat.

"What happened here?" I asked one of the older knights when I noticed one of the dunes along the side. It looked as if parts of an old house peeked out from beneath the sand.

"That probably was a farming village. Shifting dunes have buried some of them."

How sad. It felt as if I was traveling through thousands of years in the blink of an eye.

On the second morning, when I was rolling up my blanket, Milos came up to me. To my surprise, he took it out of my hand and began tying it behind the saddle. He had never helped before. "Count Baltasar told me some things about Count Stephen." He looked at me expectantly. "Well, aren't you curious, after all your questions before?"

"Sure, if you won't take all day telling me." I was in no mood for playing games with Milos.

"He's a pretty important person. His uncle was the king of England, and he's bringing a lot of money from King Louis to assist King Amalric." Milos ran his hand over the leather fitting that held the left stirrup in place. "Tonight, when we stop, I could fix this for you. The thread is becoming loose."

I gaped at this unexpected offer. "Since when do you care about this sort of thing?"

"Count Stephen said that, as his squire, I have to be meticulous about my equipment and grooming."

I almost burst out laughing to hear this from my brother, who had never given a moment's thought to his clothes, which were most often ripped or stained or ill-fitting. I cleared my throat. "So what else did you learn?"

"Guess what, Froggie? He married a woman who was betrothed to someone else. Apparently, he abducted her on the very day of her planned wedding and rode away with her. He had to give up some of his lands to his new brother-in-law to compensate him for the lost alliance."

"Don't call me Froggie," I said reflexively as I stared at him. "Count Stephen must love his wife very much."

"She's dead. Besides, he can't be all that brokenhearted about it, coming all the way to the Holy Land for a new bride." Milos smirked. "Anyway, who gets to marry for love? Marriage is about money and politics. But the count sounds crazy to me. I heard him talking to one of the knights. He went on and on about a pond he wants to build."

"He wants to do what?"

"Build a pond. A fishpond. He sounded almost dreamy when he talked about drainage and fishing rights for the villagers. But he knows his horses." He took the pack from me and secured it behind my saddle. "And he speaks Arabic."

I was still thinking about the fishpond. "Count Stephen sounds like a farmer. Anyway, how do you know he speaks Arabic?"

"He asked about our music and then told me that Arabic poetry has influenced some of the lyrics written by troubadours." Milos sounded smug, evidently pleased that he could tell me something I didn't know. "He claims it's a beautiful language."

"I guess he studied Arabic in preparation for coming here." I was intrigued. Most of the knights I had met so far didn't speak Arabic.

"He also asked me about you."

"He did?" I was so startled, I dropped my headscarf. I picked it up, glad of the distraction. "What did you tell him?"

"Well, he wanted to know why we were traveling to Jerusalem, so I told him. He wondered what you would do once we get there."

"Oh." This might be a good time to explain. "I didn't get a chance to tell you—Count Raymond suggested that I spend some time with Princess Sibylla. Isn't that fortunate? It buys us some time."

"Why?" Milos frowned. "What are you supposed to do there?"

"Why shouldn't he ask me?" I was annoyed by his dismissive response. And it didn't help that I didn't want to explain what precipitated the count's request. "It seems perfectly reasonable. Apparently she doesn't have anybody close to her own age in Jerusalem."

The temptation to start yelling at Milos was almost overwhelming. After all, it was *his* fault. It was because he lost our money and his irresponsibility in Acre that I had to agree to Count Raymond's plan.

"Well, that's good." Milos had already lost interest. "At least it gives you something to do while I'm with Count Stephen. See, I told you it would all work out," he said grandly, and strode off after patting my horse.

So much for him worrying about what would happen to me.

That morning I kept glancing at Count Stephen as I rode along. Compact and straight-backed, and with broad shoulders, he rode calmly, with few movements. It looked like his horse responded to the slightest cues.

His simple tunic, the serviceable surcoat—a long vest-like garment with slits along the sides to ensure ease of movement—bare of any markings, and the plain leggings didn't reflect his rank. Others tried to engage him in conversation, but it appeared he wasn't interested. He responded courteously to questions from a knight riding next to him, but his replies were short.

I was tired of having to give in to Milos's wishes. It couldn't do any harm if I changed places occasionally. Gently nudging my horse forward, I began to work my way closer to Count Stephen when I sensed a pair of eyes glaring at me. I turned and saw Count Raymond frown at me with disapproval.

"You shouldn't be up here," Milos hissed.

I made a face. But this was hardly the place for arguing about it. Regretfully, I dropped back. Of course, my little excursion did nothing to improve my standing with the two merchants' wives. They glared at me and then quickly shifted their eyes, as if I carried a dreadful disease.

"Do not put yourself forward," reprimanded my aunt's voice in my head. "Girls should be silent, invisible unless called for, and always meek and humble." I supposed the merchant women would have agreed with my aunt.

But I was so intrigued by Count Stephen that I found their attitude merely sad and no longer hurtful, and I smiled at them as I fell in line behind them. They had no right to tell me how to behave.

The next day Milos stayed near the merchants' wagon, while our group had spread out along a narrow stretch of the road lined with olive groves on both sides. I happened to be riding behind the wagon, but I kept my distance because of the dust. Loaded up with trade goods, it lumbered along, leaving deep ruts in the road.

"So, why aren't you doing your squire duty?" I teased him.

Milos looked uncomfortable. "Count Stephen told me he wanted to discuss some things with Count Raymond." He hunched his shoulders and kicked his horse to move ahead of me on the trail, clearly not happy to have been relegated to the back of the group and too embarrassed to talk to me.

I didn't mind. I was tired, and there was something peaceful about jogging along in silence.

A clump of dirt hit my face. Startled, I straightened up. I must have dozed off.

Then my horse bucked, and I almost fell off as several small horses rushed past me at a gallop, their riders yelling as they barreled into Milos. One of them jumped onto the wagon's front seat, grappling with the driver.

Milos was on the ground, motionless. His horse lay on its side and groaned, desperately trying to raise its head.

I screamed, and without thinking pushed my horse forward and slipped off next to Milos, where I turned around to face the attackers. They stared at me, evidently surprised.

Afterward I realized how foolish I had been, reacting as I always had when Milos got cornered by the boys in the village. My sister and I had often rushed to his aid, yelling and hitting the bigger boys with our fists and any sticks we could find. "You should stick up for each other," our father told us when we were children. Somehow it always ended up being Milos who got in trouble while Maria and I were stuck trying to rescue him.

The man who had jumped the wagon driver fell back and rolled off the cart, hitting the ground with a thud and lying still. The wagon driver was shouting at the two others, who looked stunned by the turn of events, staring at their fallen companion.

The attempted raid took place when the merchant wagon was separated from the riders in the back, while the senior knights were far ahead of us. But in response to the commotion, the knights in the front had turned around, and the sound of their horses cantering toward us across the hard-packed ground grew louder.

One of the attackers pulled himself up on his horse, wheeled around, and took off into the grove in a cloud of dust.

The third one hesitated. His horse stood on the other side of the wagon, dragging its reins. He glanced toward the approaching knights and then moved toward me. Before I could back up, he grabbed my gown and wrapped an arm firmly around me.

"Let go of me," I yelled. Of course, I forgot—wrong language. When a cold blade pressed against my neck, I immediately stopped struggling. Relieved, I saw that Milos was moving and trying to stand up, although he looked dazed.

By now the knights who rode at the back of the group had caught up, trotting around the bend, while the returning knights pulled up their horses and formed a circle around us.

I could smell the sweat of the man holding me and hear his rapid breathing. Only the knife at my throat kept me from trying to kick him and free myself. I had fought often enough with Milos when we children, but of course this was different.

For a moment, no one moved. Count Raymond leaned on his pommel and said nothing, his eyes watchful and cool.

Milos was still on his knees, staring up at us in shock.

"Milos, are you hurt?" Count Stephen's voice was calm.

"No sir."

Count Stephen turned to the driver. "And you?"

The driver, an older man with a weather-beaten face, spat on the ground and shrugged. "No, but he is." He pointed at the man lying next to him in the dust, his arms flung wide, blood on his chest, and his eyes staring. He was dead.

For an instant I thought of Maria and my mother. Their faces had been calm and peaceful even though ravaged by sickness. This sudden, violent death was wrenching. The man's sandals were falling apart, and his tunic, which barely covered his skinny legs, was torn. He had a braided leather bracelet on his wrist that looked as if it had been made by a child.

"They came out of that grove," the driver added. "Maybe they thought the wagon didn't have any protection."

Count Raymond's squire dismounted, pulled out his sword, and moved toward us.

"Stop," Count Stephen shouted. "Can't you see he's just a boy?"

Startled, the squire looked back at him. With a sullen expression, he lowered his sword.

I could just see Count Raymond's raised eyebrows without moving my head. He refrained from saying anything. Apparently, he was willing to defer to Count Stephen in this.

Count Stephen slowly unbuckled his sword belt and allowed it to slip to the ground, then dismounted. Holding his hands shoulder-high, palms facing us, he focused on the man holding me and spoke to him in Arabic.

The young man glanced toward the dead man on the ground, where blood had pooled in the dust. He still pressed the flat of the knife blade against my throat, but I could feel him trembling.

Count Stephen said something else to the man. Then he turned to the knights. "Let him go. It does more harm than good to kill him now."

Reluctantly a few of the knights moved back, opening a passage. The man lifted his knife and shoved me away so hard I fell down. With a last desperate glance at the dead man on the ground, he snatched up the reins of his horse, mounted, and rode off.

Count Raymond's squire muttered angrily, "We should go after them and teach them a lesson."

"No," Count Stephen said sharply. "They just lost a friend, and none of us were seriously injured. They must have been desperate to try this. It's enough that we took one life today." He leaned down, offering me a hand. "Are you hurt, Mistress Alina?"

"No, thank you." I was embarrassed to find my legs trembling when I stood. To distract myself, I brushed the sand off my overcoat.

Count Stephen walked over to Milos, who crouched on the ground, looking helplessly at his horse. It groaned again, flailing around as if trying to get up.

"I think the mare broke her leg."

"Let me see." Count Stephen approached the distraught horse and ran his hands over the front leg. "Yes, it's broken. You'll have to end it for her."

"I can't." Milos looked as if he was about to throw up.

"Pull yourself together," Count Stephen said harshly. "You can't leave the horse to suffer out here in the sand."

Milos didn't move.

Count Stephen frowned and shook his head. He pulled a knife out of his boot and knelt on the ground next to Milos, blocking my view. He muttered something to Milos and handed him the knife.

After a moment of hesitation, Milos lifted his arm. I closed my eyes.

When I opened them, the horse had stopped moving, I could see Milos's bent head. Count Stephen stood up, gripped Milos by the shoulder briefly, and walked back to his horse. When he passed me, I peered at his face, which was closed and hard. I remembered how gently he had handled the horse in Acre.

Count Baltasar now took charge with his usual calm efficiency. He called out to two of the knights who had come to Acre with us. "Filipot and Jean, help me cover this poor soul decently. We will place him in the shade of the trees. If his relatives come back looking for him, they can see to his burial. Meanwhile, why were you so far behind the wagon?"

Jean hung his head. Filipot muttered something I couldn't hear, and Count Baltasar responded in an undertone. Both knights looked flustered.

"Milos, you'll have to ride one of the packhorses for now."

Milos glanced around uncertainly. He was pale.

"Get your saddle." Count Baltasar pointed at one of the packhorses. "Filipot, help Milos shift some of that roan mare's load to the other horses."

Later that day we started moving inland, heading farther and farther east. By the afternoon the land became hillier. Milos rode alongside Count Stephen, apparently over his shock. He always looked more self-assured and confident on a horse in any event.

He and Count Stephen were talking. It was as if Count Stephen was trying to distract Milos from what had happened earlier. I moved closer so I could hear them.

"Really, haven't you learned anything from your tutor back home?" Count Stephen glanced at Milos with a friendly grin. Our tutor, Brother Gervais, would have been sharp and impatient.

"Well," Milos hesitated. "He never talked much about the east."

I almost laughed out loud. Brother Gervais had talked at great length about Jerusalem and the first crusade, but Milos used to twitch in his seat, fiddle with something in his purse, or look out the window.

Evidently, now Milos was curious enough to ask questions. "But tell me, why did you say that King Amalric is in a vulnerable position?"

"Think about it," Count Stephen answered. "His kingdom is young—less than 100 years—and by no means secure. Its fate depends in part on the emerging power players in the east, and on the support it receives from the west. And it doesn't help that there is competition among the various crusader states."

Milos nodded as if he knew all about it.

Fascinated, I encouraged my horse closer and chimed in, "Yes, I remember—the County of Tripoli, the Principality of Antioch, and the County of Edessa."

"Ah, Mistress Alina." Count Stephen turned his head toward me. "You are interested in history."

I blushed and hung my head. Once again I had put myself forward, hardly behaving like a proper lady.

Count Stephen did not appear to mind. "You have to realize that the conquest of Jerusalem was almost what you might call an accident," he said thoughtfully. "The Byzantine emperor appealed to Pope Urban and the west in 1096 to help fight the invading Seljuk Turks in Anatolia, and that's when all eyes began to turn to Jerusalem. Anyway, conquest is not a good foundation for a young kingdom. Many of the city's inhabitants—Muslims, Jews, and even Christians—were killed during the crusade. You have to remember this—we are riding through a land of conquered people."

"But the crusade freed many Christians, right?"

"Certainly. Still, there is a price to pay. And another factor, of course, is that King Amalric needs a strong heir. His son suffers from leprosy, and his daughters are very young."

I wondered whether Count Stephen had sons. He certainly seemed to know how to handle Milos. He rode with elegant ease—his hands quiet on the reins—and his horse, an angular, sturdy bay stallion, twitched his ears, attentive but relaxed, comfortably picking his way along the trail.

An hour later we reached a small village of mud and stone houses clustered around a central well. An olive grove spread behind the village, and a few terraces on the hill were dotted with fruit trees. I heard shouting, and some of the riders in the front of the group had stopped. Count Stephen spurred his horse forward.

"What's going on? Why are we stopping?" I asked Milos.

Distractedly, Milos shook his head. "I don't know."

Craning my head past his shoulders, I saw a woman standing in the middle of the roadway, wrapped in a black shawl with a bundle in her arms. She was screaming.

"I think she is trying to sell us her child." Count Baltasar sounded bored, as if this sort of thing happened every day.

"Maybe it's got some dreadful disease," said another.

Some knights began to back away gently in an attempt to ride around the woman, putting as much distance between them as possible.

Count Stephen dismounted and approached the woman slowly, speaking to her in a quiet voice. She stopped screaming and held out her bundle. Count Stephen courteously bent to look. He reached into his tunic and handed whatever he found there to the woman. She tried to take his hand, attempting to place her forehead on it, but he pulled away and returned to his horse, which patiently waited for him with the reins trailing on the ground.

The other knights stared at him.

"What are you doing? Do you want to bring the bloody flux down on us all?" one of them asked angrily.

"No, of course not." Count Stephen frowned. "That's the widow of the man we killed back there on the road this morning." He remounted and without another word kicked his horse forward.

Count Raymond muttered something to the knight next to him. The knight, a bluff, rotund fellow with a red face, chuckled. The others were silent.

The last evening before reaching Jerusalem, we rested on the outskirts of a village. After days of traveling through blowing sand and rocky plains, I was surprised to find gentle green hills and groves full of fruit trees and olives. We ate roasted meat on sticks and flat pieces of bread, and Milos brought me a little beaker of red wine and a bowl with dried dates. As usual, I sat apart from the other women. But I didn't mind too much. Truly, I had nothing in common with them. On the other hand, it was unthinkable that I sit with the men.

Sand had gotten into everything I owned. I gave up trying to shake it out and resigned myself to being covered with a layer of dust until we arrived in Jerusalem. My hair was even more disheveled than usual, and I could taste the salty sweat on my cracked lips. My eyes burned from the hot glare of the day. I was tired.

And I was happy.

It was as if I was drunk on the colors of the desert, the silence, the vastness, and the impersonal harshness, drunk on traveling and on being far away from home. With one ear I tried to catch the sounds of the men talking. Occasionally I could make out Count Stephen's voice.

"Let's play some music."

Startled out of my reverie, I glanced around. Milos had walked over and crouched on the sand next to me. He helped himself to a date. "How about it?"

I hesitated. During the journey from France, it had seemed a natural thing to do in the evenings, but now with Count Raymond, Count Stephen, and other older knights, I felt uncomfortable. I hardly needed to draw more attention to myself.

"Come on, Alina. This might be the last chance we'll have for a while."

Reluctantly I took my lute out of its wrappings. "What would you like to sing?"

"How about *Can vei la lauzeta?*" Milos asked. "Bernart de Ventadorn is so young, people here might not yet have heard his music."

Bernart was a troubadour from Corrèze in Limousin, and a few months before we left for Jerusalem an itinerant troubadour had played this song and others by Bernart, and both Milos and I took a liking to them.

For a moment I yearned for home. Right now the hills would be covered with wild thyme.

I began to play a few chords, and then Milos began to sing, softly at first. Heads turned, and a few of the knights wandered over to listen to us.

Behold the lark
Dancing
In the sun's rays and
Swooping into the depths, borne down by the delight in its heart.
It makes me yearn to be one with all who have tasted happiness.

After the first few lines, I forgot my discomfort. Milos and I had done together this so often that we didn't even need to look at each other for cues about when to increase or lower the volume or when to slow down or to pause. For Milos, it was just one of many facets of his being. He liked to perform, but he had never hounded our father to teach him new songs.

For me, it was so much more—not just a joy, but something vital in a way I couldn't explain. Maybe in part it was because I could control it when I couldn't control anything else. Perhaps it had been like that for our father as well. Of course he was a man, and nobody could force him into a marriage or tell him how to act. So maybe it wasn't the same. Anyway, for me it was more than that.

When Milos finished, the last drawn-out note echoing through the still evening air, I made a sign to him and whispered, "Now it's my turn. I'll sing *Ar em al freg temps vengut.*"

Milos shook his head. "But that's about winter, and it's too long," he whispered.

"We'll do just a few verses," I said stubbornly. All afternoon I had watched the shifting light transform the desert into a glowing purple void, the silvery green leaves of the scrubby desert brush the only signposts reminding us of the ground beneath our feet. I had kept thinking of the right music to convey all this splendor. Finally, I remembered the song my father taught me by the trobairitz Azalais de Porcairagues. Gently I strummed the strings and began.

Winter is upon us, and time stands still,
Trapped in ice and snow and mud.
All birds have fallen silent
(for none wants to raise her voice in song).

Milos picked up his flute and followed my voice. The melody was sparse and severe, a song of immeasurable sorrow, glorying in desolation. It was as if one could hear the high-pitched whistling and groaning sounds from a frozen lake, echoing across the ice.

Now, with the heat of the day drifting away into the darkness, the flute's plaintive notes evoked the wind sweeping over the sands. I kept my eyes on Milos as I sang. A hint of sadness in his eyes reminded me of our father and his lost, hungry expression at the end.

When we drew to a close, Milos lowered his flute, but I didn't want to stop yet.

I concluded with one of my father's pieces. Eerily, he had composed it a year before my mother died. It was about a dreamer who walks through a misty valley, blind to the flowers at his feet, in search of his love. He walks and weeps and does not hear the birds all around him. Faster and faster he rushes through the woods. His steps lead him to the brink of a ravine. He never falters as he steps into the void. I didn't sing the lyrics, instead just picked out the chords of the simple melody.

A last dark note and I placed my fingers on the strings to still them. When I raised my head, I looked directly into the face of Count Stephen. He had moved quietly to join the others listening to us. The fire lit up his features—plain, with a jutting nose and a wide mouth slightly off-center, a broad forehead, and grey eyes under thick brows. Courteously he inclined his head toward me and smiled. It transformed his face.

I realized that I was staring at him, and felt myself go red, hoping he could not see this in the dark.

"Thank you, Mistress Alina. I hope we will hear you perform again." Then he turned and walked away.

The next day we arrived in Jerusalem.

CHAPTER NINE

SIBYLLA

I DON'T know why I thought Jerusalem would be in a desert.

We had been climbing steadily along rocky terrain over the past few days, and I had imagined small, sad, stone buildings spread out across a merciless plain with the sun beating down.

Instead we were greeted by a vista of green hills with Jerusalem nestled among them, a densely constructed town with glowing white sandstone walls and imposing gates. I squinted up at the sky, marveling at the tall tower above the walls of the city.

"Thy neck is like the Tower of David builded for an armoury, whereon there hang a thousand bucklers, all shields of mighty men."

Startled, I turned around and saw Stephen had ridden up behind me.

"That's beautiful," I murmured, unsure where to look as my face flushed, but when I sneaked a glance at him, he smiled at me. It was a quote. I knew that much.

"The Song of Songs has some very apt descriptions," he said before nudging his horse on.

My eyes on his straight back and my cheeks burning, I remembered how my father used to tease me like that with quotes from various works, delighted when I recognized them.

Soon we reached the gate and entered the town. After the days of quiet riding through the plains, it was strange to hear the clip-clop of the horses' hooves echoing from the stone walls amidst the sounds of a busy town.

The streets were crowded, and we had to maneuver carefully around people leading donkeys with carts carrying carpets, fruits, vegetables, and large clay jars, and many others going about their business. Children ran alongside our group, shouting and calling out in their excitement. We rode on a central street up a hill and emerged on a plaza with another gate flanked by tall brick walls leading into a courtyard.

Laughter reached us as we came to a stop.

A girl clad in a flowing silver-grey robe, her long, dark hair loose down her back, stood in front of two young men smiling at her. The men looked relaxed, their surcoats tossed onto a bench, and the padded doublets knights wore under their armor open at the neck. She had her hands on her hips in a provocative pose. "You think I can't do that?" she challenged. Her voice was surprisingly deep and husky.

The men chuckled.

Count Raymond, meanwhile, had dismounted and walked over to the group. The men looked askance, bowed hastily, grabbed their surcoats, and moved away.

"Sibylla," he said, with a stern note in his voice.

The girl flicked her shawl as she turned to him, managing to look irritated and provocative at the same time. "Oh, Cousin Raymond, you have returned from Acre."

Count Raymond frowned. "Sibylla, I want you to welcome these knights, who have traveled a long way to serve the Kingdom of Jerusalem." Quickly he named them, beginning with Stephen.

Stephen inclined his head, his eyes grave and kind. Count Baltasar smiled, bowing in practiced courtier's fashion.

"Kind sirs, you are most welcome." The girl went into a deep curtsy. When she rose, I could see her eyes flick across the other knights, as well as Milos. Her mouth curved into a slow smile. "Now if you will excuse me, I will call servants to show you to your quarters."

She picked up the hem of her gown, but before she could move off, Count Raymond blocked her way.

"Just a moment, Sibylla. I also want to introduce a young lady who will join your personal retinue, Mistress Alina de Florac." He turned to me and stretched out a hand, helping me off the horse, as if I were a lady of rank. "She is an accomplished singer and lute player, and she and her brother Milos have come to Jerusalem to pray for their father's soul. While she graces us with her presence, I hope she will help to divert you on days when the hours grow long."

As I curtsied, I winced at the count's "while she graces us with her presence" which, of course, meant "as long as I allow her to stay." I was stiff from the long ride and uncomfortably aware of my grimy blue gown, while this girl wore a robe so fine it was almost diaphanous, with gold embroidery along the seams and the hem. Count Raymond did not say anything about my teaching Sibylla. Perhaps it was just as well. I suspected that she would not respond kindly to the idea of another tutor. "It is a privilege to be here, and an honor to serve you, my lady."

Sibylla frowned at me. For a moment I thought she was about to stamp her foot, but then her scowl changed into a beatific smile. "How delightful." Her slightly exaggerated tone made a mockery of her polite words. "My sister and I will be happy to have you stay with us. Come, let me show you around."

I lifted my lute and picked up the trailing end of my gown to follow her, barely having time to glance back at Milos, who sat on his horse with a dazed expression on his face. His eyes followed the shimmer of Sibylla's robe already disappearing into the dark hallway.

I groaned inwardly. Milos had to know there would be absolutely no point in swooning over someone so far above his station. But I didn't have time to worry about it now.

As I hurried along, I inwardly cursed Count Raymond and Milos. They got me into this—Milos through his stupidity, and Count Raymond through his deviousness. I was now ensconced as Count Raymond's spy. It was ridiculous.

The next few hours passed in a blur. Sibylla took me to the housekeeper and bade her assign me a room. It turned out to be a little garret with barely enough space for a pallet and a table with a chair. A harried-looking servant brought my bag. I never let anyone handle my lute, so now I placed it on the table myself. The servant also brought a bowl and pitcher with water. I had just brushed my hair and cleaned my face when Sibylla reappeared. To my amusement, she had changed into a slightly less provocative, long green gown, and had pinned back her hair and covered it with a cap. She had also draped a pale green shawl around her shoulders.

"Do you need more time to change your robe?"

I shook my head. "Everything I have is dusty from travel. This is the best of a bad lot." I didn't want to admit that my choices were limited.

Sibylla frowned and then waved her hands dismissively. "It's not really important. Besides, it's not as if you're a lady of the court."

Her remark annoyed me, though I couldn't really argue the point. My mother raised me to be proud of who I was, though, and I was not about to let this little princess get to me with her arrogance. She couldn't be older than I was.

"Then we should go," Sibylla said. "It's getting late. Let me introduce you to the queen, Maria Comnena, and my sister Isabella."

"Isn't your mother called the queen?"

"No, silly. Don't you know anything? My father's and mother's marriage was annulled. Maria Comnena is his second wife— a good thing, too, because she brought with her a huge dowry from her granduncle, Emperor Manuel— just in the nick of time, because funds were running low." Sibylla grinned at me like a schoolboy who just tricked his teacher.

"And your mother?" I was bewildered by this confusing information.

"My mother is now married to Reginald of Sidon. She's not at court right now."

I shook out the wrap I meant to wear around my shoulders. My aunt had given it to me, saying, "Here, you can have this. I wore this at court a few years back and have no use for it anymore." At the time I had thanked her politely, although it seemed hardly a generous present. Made of dark green wool, it had a few holes where moths had nested over the winter months, and it smelled musty. Confronted with Sibylla's effortless elegance, I was mortified. At the same time, I resented feeling this way. Clothes had never mattered before.

"Let's go," Sibylla said impatiently. "The queen is waiting. Don't worry, she won't eat you." Then she pointed at my lute. "Bring that along," she added in a peremptory tone.

I bit my lip. I hated being ordered about like a servant, but this was not the time to show it.

We went to the great hall, where Sibylla introduced me to the queen. Maria Comnena was a young woman still, maybe ten years older than I, but with hard features and heavy-lidded eyes that missed nothing. Her dark eyebrows, arched like crescent moons, stood out on her sallow skin, she was heavy with child, and it looked as if her time was near. She put down the embroidery she was working on and studied me with a calculating expression. "Welcome, Mistress Alina. I trust that you will enjoy your stay."

A pudgy little girl with a mop of curly hair approached me. "Are you going to play that?" She pointed at my lute.

"Mistress Alina, this is my daughter Isabella. Pardon her manners. She is but a little girl."

I smiled at Isabella. Another princess and perhaps future queen, I thought, wondering whether I should address her as my lady. She could not be older than two or three. "I will play if you would like...and if your mother permits."

"Play, play, play." The little girl bounced up and down in excitement. I noticed an irritated look on Sibylla's face.

I sat on a stool and plucked a few notes to warm up. I kept it short, and stuck to simple tunes my father taught me—evoking images of sheep grazing on sun-drenched hills, the neighing of wild horses, the incessant gabble of flammant-rose flamingos in their nesting grounds in the Camargue, and the mistral wind, so fierce in the winter, yet gentle and loving in the spring and summer.

I was overwhelmed with longing for home, and, with a lump in my throat, I stilled the strings on the last note.

Isabella crouched in front of me, her thumb in her mouth, and her eyes following my every move.

"Delightful. Thank you, Mistress Alina." The queen sniffed. "I understand that you will be with us for a while. We look forward to hearing more of your music."

Clearly I was being dismissed. I stood and curtsied.

Sibylla adjusted her shawl. "I will show Mistress Alina around."

Much as I disliked being grateful to the princess, I was glad not to have to brave the long passageways to find my room. Sibylla introduced me to the housekeeper and showed me where I could eat my meals. She walked me back to my room, taking a path through the inner courtyard, fragrant with lemon and orange trees.

I thought she would leave me at my door, but, to my surprise, she pushed open the door and stepped inside.

"So, why are you here?"

I stared at Sibylla, taking in her plucked eyebrows and lightly tinted cheeks and eyelids. "My father died, and my brother and I decided to go on a pilgrimage to pray for his soul." That seemed innocuous enough. It also had the advantage of being true.

Sibylla frowned. "That doesn't answer my question."

"Count Raymond thought you might enjoy being with someone close to your own age," I said carefully.

"Did he?" Sibylla laughed. "Well, you are definitely an improvement over the sourpusses who have been inflicted on me over the years. Most of them didn't last long. You'd think Count Raymond would have better things to do since he got out of prison than trying to find a suitable companion for me. You certainly are a hit with my sister." She took off her wrap and tossed it on the bed. "Here, you take this. I'm tired of it, and it looks like you could use it." Without giving me a chance to respond, she swept out of the room, leaving behind the scent of roses.

I looked at the shawl. It made me think of a rippling brook in the spring, reflecting the fresh green from the willows along its banks. It was a strange kind of slap-in-your-face generosity. My only point of comparison for receiving gifts had been Aunt Marci's mean-spirited manner of passing on her daughters' worn, stained gowns.

That was my introduction to Sibylla.

I was torn between feelings of pure dislike and admiration. She was different from any girl I had ever known—groomed, polished, and self-assured, with the demeanor of a grown woman. If she wanted something, she could probably simply crook her finger, and everybody would rush to do her bidding.

I couldn't imagine what it would be like to grow up with the knowledge that one would be queen one day. My mother had little patience with Maria and me if we put on airs or were rude to servants. "You are noblewomen. I expect you to act accordingly," she would say sharply. If she found us preening ourselves or fighting over clothes, she quickly gave us a task. "You have too much time on your hands."

It would be strange to have to spy on this young woman. She probably had a good idea of what my role was supposed to be. If she complained to Count Raymond, he would be angry at me and would have no reason to keep me here, and I would have no way to protect Milos. I could easily imagine what would happen if Count Raymond told Stephen his new squire was a thief.

Oh, how I resented being in this position. I was trapped in a tangle of lies and would have to pretend to everybody. When we were children, our father reprimanded us sharply when one of us told tales about the others. I certainly did not like Sibylla, but to tell on her was impossible. I was revolted by the very idea. Maybe I could just come up with innocent tidbits or make them up if need be to keep Count Raymond satisfied.

CHAPTER TEN

CITY OF QUEENS

THE FIRST morning in the citadel, I got up early.

I needed time to think and to clear my head. Rather than go directly to the great hall, I decided to sit in the courtyard for a few moments. It was quiet. Eyes closed, and feet stretched out so my toes were warmed by the sun, I breathed in the scent of the lemon trees.

"Nice wrap. One of Sibylla's hand-me-downs, no doubt."

Surprised and at a loss for words, I opened my eyes and looked up at a young woman in the simple robe of a servant. Her shiny, dark hair was brushed back and secured under her cap. She was pretty, with a small, up-turned nose, full lips, and rosy cheeks, complimented by a solid build and ample curves.

But her eyes, sharp and observant, lent her face a curiously shrewish expression.

Gazing down at me, she wrinkled her nose. "I heard that you play the lute."

"Yes." I wasn't sure what to make of this young woman. "My name is Alina. What's yours?"

"I know your name. I already met your brother Milos. I am Beryl. I help out with Princess Isabella."

It bothered me that she seemed to know a lot about me already. I tried not to show my discomfort and smiled at her. She probably had a better sense of her place here than I did—I wasn't exactly a servant, but I certainly wasn't a lady of the court.

"I have to go inside," I said awkwardly, unsure of how to take my leave without offending her. I stood up and tried to nod graciously, inwardly wishing I had paid more attention to Aunt Marci's lectures on proper comportment with servants and equals. I felt Beryl's eyes following me as I walked away.

On my way to the great hall, I ran into Count Raymond. He greeted me courteously. "Mistress Alina, I trust you have settled in well."

"Yes, thank you, my lord."

"That's good." He acted like a gracious host seeing to one of his guests. "I heard that the ladies enjoyed your music. Have you made friends with young Sibylla?"

"It has been pleasant here," I responded blandly. I really could not think of anything else to say. "Everybody has been trying to make me feel welcome."

"And your brother? Not too many distractions to keep him from his duty with Count Stephen, I hope."

I looked down, at a loss for words.

"Very well. I have no time now and must go. Hopefully we will chat again in a few days." He walked away.

I felt vaguely soiled and uncomfortable.

Over the next several days I got used to life in the citadel. At home I always had chores, because my parents insisted on putting me to work if I was idle.

Life at court seemed luxurious. I had no worries about food and shelter, and my duties were restricted to being companionable and playing the lute on demand. But at times it was stifling, and all I could think about was to get away.

My father once brought my mother a pair of linnets from one of his journeys. Their cage was made of wicker and had a wooden base. A tiny bell hung from the top, and we heard it tinkle whenever the birds moved around.

"Oh, Guy, what will I do with you?" my mother said, upset and yet smiling. "Such an expensive gift." She cherished the birds, and was sad when one died and the other sat quietly and refused to eat. "It's grieving, Guy."

Together they went out for a walk the next day and returned without the bird.

In Jerusalem I was like a linnet in a cage—luxurious, silk-lined, and lemon-scented, bathed by sunlight and dry breezes from the hills, but still a cage. There was no one to take me outside and set me free.

The ladies of the court all rose early. To be honest, I previously had a very different idea of what ladies at the court of a king did all day. I had expected that they would sit around and chat while servants brought them mulled wine and spiced cookies. I had pictured them playing on a harp or a lute, or listening to the latest court poet in fashion recite his work.

Certainly, there was a harp and a *lyra*, as well as a beautiful lute that I eyed enviously whenever I spent time in the great hall. There also were several tables with games of dice and checkers and a chessboard. Plenty of servants ran around carrying trays with food and drink, but everything else was far removed from my original image.

These ladies worked all day long.

Both my mother and my aunt had always worked. They never sat idle, and their hands were never empty. I remembered how my mother deftly organized the household for my father, and yet he was hardly ever aware of all she did. I had not expected that it would be the same at court.

The queen, together with other court ladies, spent time going over accounts. They ran the household and decided what needed to be purchased. They reviewed the menus with the cooks and suggested alternatives when provisions ran low. They checked the cost of building repair and upkeep and interviewed tradesmen to do the work.

They talked to Hospitallers about organizing better care for the sick people in the city, reminding the knights of the Order of St. John of their original calling. They talked to the steward about making provisions for the poor. They read manuscripts and wrote letters. They worked with the younger children. They regularly looked at their prayer books and read out loud from the Bible.

And they played games, but only occasionally. When their hands weren't occupied with paper or a quill, the fingers would move busily over a piece of cloth or a tapestry, pulling colored threads in and out, without even looking at their fingers half the time. I watched entire landscapes emerge in front of my eyes.

They worked and they talked. They talked incessantly, gracefully slipping from French to Latin with occasional Arabic words spicing up their conversations.

Once again I had reason to be thankful that my father had let me sit in on Milos's tutoring sessions in French and Latin as well as Provençal. I listened, fascinated by what I learned about daily life in the citadel, the world of politics, and the unending stream of gossip.

Most of the ladies were gracious in an absentminded way, uninterested in what I was doing. Undoubtedly they thought I would be returning home soon enough and was hardly worth their trouble.

At first, especially at mealtimes, I was nervous, not sure about the customs at court. I found myself grateful for Aunt Marci's harshly administered lessons on the proper behavior of a young lady. My parents had emphasized the importance of kindness and consideration, but our life at home had been mostly informal and relaxed. Aunt Marci's rigid rules became a useful crutch for negotiating life at court.

"So, Mistress Alina, tell me a little about yourself. Who taught you to play the lute?" Dame Alice looked at me while accepting the platter of flat oatcakes being passed around. She was a cheerful, kindly woman, short and stocky, with her hair discreetly hidden under a cap, dimpled, plump cheeks, and a ready smile. And she was in charge of Princess Isabella.

Sibylla grinned at me from across the table. "Dame Alice knows just about everything there is to know about the court, because she's been here since I was born."

"Indeed I have," Dame Alice responded with a good-natured laugh. "And Princess Sibylla stopped listening to me almost immediately. For now at least, I have better luck with her little sister."

She helped me sort out what seemed to be a bewildering array of queens at court—far too many past, present, and future queens for my taste—not only Sibylla and her sister, both of whom might be queen one day, but also Sibylla's stepmother, Maria Comnena.

Sibylla's mother, Agnes of Courtenay, was sort of an ex-queen. To my amazement, she had been married repeatedly—at least four times, as far as I could make out. It was impossibly far removed in every way from my memories of the stable and loving marriage of my parents, or the staid and respectable life embraced by my uncle and aunt. Sibylla's mother seemed to be related to just about everyone by marriage or birth, and even though she wasn't at court, the court ladies gossiped about her with abandon.

"Of course, I knew Sibylla's grandmother, Queen Melisende. She ruled Jerusalem on behalf of her son for thirty years," Dame Alice said proudly while she offered me a bowl filled with honey. "This is one of the few luxuries we have here these days. Food supplies have been a little bit tight."

Surprised, I accepted the bowl and spooned a bit of honey on my oatcake. "Why are food supplies tight? I thought the king could have whatever he wanted."

"Did you see the villages when you came here from Acre? They grow barely enough for their own needs—in poor soil, with lots of rocks and little rain. The king imports much of the food, and recently it hasn't been easy."

I thought about this as I chewed. I remembered Stephen helping the widow of the man who was killed when we were attacked. She would have a hard time feeding her children.

Later, in the great hall, Dame Alice showed me Queen Melisende's psalter. It occupied pride of place on a table, opened to one of her favorite beautifully illustrated pages, as if she were still present.

"Would you tell me a more about the people at court?" I asked her. "I find it all confusing."

"Of course, it's confusing." She smiled at me. "You've arrived at a difficult time. The king is not well nor is his son. That means that all the noblemen are trying to establish their positions for what is to come. And all eyes are on Sibylla. After all, her future husband will be their king one day."

"What about Count Raymond?" I asked. "What is his role?"

"He is a cousin of the king and has a lot of power even though he spent years in prison." Dame Alice settled in as if happy to find someone to instruct about the court. "The king listens to him. Only lately he has also been listening to Miles of Plancy, another distant cousin to the king. Count Raymond is not happy about that." Dame Alice frowned. "I wouldn't like to cross Count Raymond to be honest. I have heard such stories about what he does to those who interfere with his plans."

I shivered and pulled my wrap tighter around my shoulders. I didn't want to appear too interested. "Who are the Ibelins?" I asked to change the subject.

"They are powerful knights and allies of Count Raymond. There are several factions at court, and they all have their own ideas about the future of the kingdom."

"And that means about whom Sibylla should wed," I added slowly. So that's why Count Raymond used every tool at his disposal to control the outcome, and I was such a tool.

It was strange to think Sibylla would marry one of those men, all so much older than she was. I tried to imagine her in a few years, when she would be a queen. For an instant I was sorry for her—so vibrant and fun-loving, yet with such heavy burden to carry. I just had Aunt Marci trying to arrange a marriage for me. Sibylla had to deal with an entire court.

I spent most of my time with Sibylla and her various tutors and court ladies. I enjoyed playing music in the great hall, and I became fond of Isabella, plump, small, and determined, plucking at my lute with stubby fingers.

"Play the song of the river, Alina," she would say, sitting at my feet. "Show me how you do it."

Or, "Play another one. Play the song of the sad knight." She began to sing along with me, whispering the words in her childish voice.

"Sing the song of the lost maiden," she pleaded another time. But when I got to the part when the maiden was despondent, alone, and afraid, Isabella frowned. "I don't like that story. Why don't you change it?"

I smiled at her. She was so young, really a baby still, and she already wanted to change the story.

Occasionally Sibylla watched us, but quickly lost interest, more intent on what happened in the courtyard below.

I found that I was happier when she focused on something else or was not around. Every gesture she made was graceful. My sense of being unpolished and uncouth increased whenever I looked at her, when I heard her laughter and the surprisingly deep, husky tone of her voice, and when her scent reached me, light and spicy, with a hint of peppermint and roses.

But I loved sitting in the covered walkway and looking at the arches that opened onto the courtyard. I could hear the tinkle of the fountain and horses trotting on the paving stones.

Sibylla showed me how to pick the seeds out of pomegranates, daintily sucking the juice off her fingers and managing to not get any stains on her silken robes. As much as I tried to copy her, I never could avoid splattering my arms and face, as well as my gown, with bright red droplets, ending up feeling sticky and clumsy into the bargain.

Sibylla made me laugh when we played chess. She would make comments about the other ladies and the knights at court in an undertone, irreverent, perceptive, and unimpressed by rank.

"That's Baldwin of Ibelin." She pointed discreetly at a heavyset, dark-haired man who was probably in his fifties. "Count Raymond thinks I should marry him." She smirked at the thought. "His older brother Hugh wanted to marry my mother, but then he was taken prisoner and she married my father. Of course my father later divorced her, and so she's now the Countess of Sidon."

My head spun with all this information, but Sibylla seemed to think of it as nothing more than a game of chess. "Of course, my father doesn't think my marrying Baldwin is a good idea. He needs someone from the west so he can get more support for another crusade."

"What about Count Baltasar?" I asked, fascinated by her matter-of-fact attitude. He appeared to be well-known among the court ladies, and he always had a polite word for me when he saw me in the great hall.

"He is friendly, rather sweet. He certainly tries hard."

Something in this cool statement made me suspect she wasn't impressed with him.

"Who is that?" I asked, nodding toward an older man with a pugnacious expression. He and Count Raymond hardly spoke when they were in the great hall together, and the tension between them was so obvious that I was intrigued. "Oh, that's Miles of Plancy. Actually, he also comes from Champagne, like Count Stephen. I think my father considered him as a match for me."

"And why does he seem so hostile toward Count Raymond?"

"They are constantly competing for more power at the court. Besides, Count Raymond hasn't forgiven Count Miles for persuading King Amalric to agree to a deal struck with Egypt instead of forcing Egypt to submit." Sibylla calmly arranged the chess figures on the board.

A court lady who overheard us put down her embroidery. "I think it's much more unforgivable that Count Miles didn't permit the unarmed inhabitants of the city of Gaza to take shelter in the fortress when Gaza was attacked in 1170." She scowled. "All those deaths are on his head."

To be king of Jerusalem hardly seemed to be an attractive prospect.

Occasionally I caught glimpses of Stephen when he entered the great hall to pay his respects. I wondered what he thought of Sibylla, who was quiet, subdued, and impeccably dressed in his presence, her sharp, malicious wit in check. While I was impressed by her ability to shift and adjust her behavior depending on the occasion, it made me distrust her.

Stephen was unfailingly kind and gracious, greeting all the ladies courteously. Sometimes he smiled at me.

Once I actually got to talk to him. I happened to be walking along the arcade on my way back from the great hall, glad of a few hours of freedom. Holding on to my lute, I sat down on a stone bench in the shade and closed my eyes.

I was tired and worried at the same time. There seemed to be no way out of this trap unless I could get Milos away from here. And yet, oddly, I was happy. Never had I had so large an audience for my playing, nor had I dreamed that I would get to see or live in foreign lands, much less spend time at a royal court and meet people like Stephen, Sibylla, and even Count Raymond.

"Mistress Alina, I look forward to hearing you sing again."

Startled, I opened my eyes. The sunlight had traveled around the column, and I had to squint. Stephen stood there, looking down at me with a quizzical expression on his face. I couldn't think of a response.

"May I join you?"

Mutely I nodded, and he sat. He was more elaborately dressed than I had seen before, in a dark blue tunic with gold embroidery along the cuffs and the collar. Perhaps he had just come from a meeting with the king.

"How have you settled in? How do you like Jerusalem?"

"I haven't seen much of it yet. My duties keep me in the castle for the most part," I responded, surprised that Stephen should care.

"I suppose we are both strangers in a strange land, and it takes some time to adjust."

"But you already speak Arabic."

"I had a bit of time to prepare, as well as to set my affairs in order, after the invitation from King Amalric reached me."

"That's more than what most appear to do before coming here." I hadn't forgotten the uncouth knights from the journey.

"People come here for a multitude of reasons. Preparation is not always possible."

"That hardly excuses their behavior," I burst out, irritated all over again with what I had seen, and with Stephen for being so even-tempered. He reminded me of my father. I had never been able to argue with him. Sometimes it is so much more satisfying when someone responds in kind. Like Stephen, my father had always been able to consider both sides of an argument and impossible to rile.

"A journey to the Holy Land is a harsh school." Stephen smiled at me. "Nobody who comes here will be quite the same, if and when they return."

I gazed at the frayed leather of my sandals, thinking of Milos.

"Your brother is learning things every day." Stephen seemed to have read my mind. "This might well be the making of him."

I pushed a pebble back and forth with my sandal. "I hope so."

"Don't worry too much," he said, standing up. "Milos is very young yet."

"And I am an old crone and know better," I snapped. How old did he think I was? Then I flushed with embarrassment. I had spoken to him as if we were equals.

He grinned, and the years dropped away from his face for an instant. "A wise old crone with the voice of a young lady." He walked off.

I flushed even more and hoped desperately nobody else would walk by and see me there.

But once I recovered from my embarrassment, I was comforted. It was as if Milos and I had a friend in Stephen.

Come to think of it, I hadn't seen Milos at all for days. He was usually off somewhere with Stephen.

I envied him and felt lonely and bereft, cooped up in this cocoon of once and future queens, trapped in silken webs of deceit, and sticky with pomegranate juice. I would never have guessed how segregated the world of women would be in the Kingdom of Jerusalem. Here, the worlds of men and women generally intersected only during public events and formal meals in the great hall. Once a week, the king and his courtiers joined the ladies in the great hall, but on that day as well the men for the most part talked among each other even though music and games helped to create a more relaxed atmosphere.

During the first weeks, I sometimes saw Count Raymond go by in the halls for a meeting with the king, and he didn't even glance at me. I breathed a sigh of relief every time it happened. Maybe he had forgotten about me.

But I was wrong.

One morning I was walking along the arcade on my way to the great hall, absorbed in my thoughts, when I heard a voice behind me. "Mistress Alina, my lord Raymond would like you to join him for a few moments." It was Ralph, the count's dour-looking squire.

Reluctantly I followed the man to the room Count Raymond used to conduct his business.

Ralph held the door for me as I entered and found myself in a room crammed with piles of scrolls and manuscripts. Several pewter goblets and a jug on a small side table did not distract from the impression of a place where someone worked hard. A desk was covered with paper next to quills, an inkwell, wax tablets, and styluses. The window was open, and one could hear faint sounds of men and horses in the courtyard below.

Count Raymond, immaculately dressed and groomed, sat at the desk reading a scroll. He looked up when I entered. "Ah, Mistress Alina, I have meant to speak with you, but affairs of state have kept me busy." He studied me intently. "Well, now you've had some time to observe how things stand here and spent time with the princess, what can you tell me about her?"

"I have not had that much time yet," I said apologetically. I had tried to think of things to tell him, but it was hard. "I am just getting to know the princess. She speaks several languages."

"If you plan to tell me that she is fluent in Latin, Arabic, and Greek, you are wasting my time." Count Raymond sniffed. "I know that just as I know perfectly well that she is smart and well-read."

"She likes chess." Flustered, I couldn't think of anything better. I definitely didn't want to tell him the princess was spoiled and willful. He might think I was speaking out of turn. Besides, I suspected he already knew that, too.

The door hinge squeaked, and a servant entered, her head lowered, struggling with a large wooden pail and some rags. Evidently she had come to clean.

"You're not supposed to come in here without knocking," Count Raymond barked. "What's your name?"

"Gilla," the girl whispered. Some water had slopped onto the floorboards. She put down the pail and frantically swept up the puddle.

"Leave immediately. I don't want to see you here again. I will complain to the steward."

Stunned I watched the girl scurry out of the room.

The count glared at me. "Well?"

"Count Raymond, I will do my best, but what is it you are looking for?"

"I thought you were smarter than that. Do I need to spell it out? How does Sibylla spend her time when she is not in the great hall? I want to know whom she befriends. I want to know what she thinks of Count Stephen. Is there someone else whom she favors? I suggest you take your position here a bit more seriously. Next time we talk, I hope you will have spent your time productively." He stood up, taking the scroll from his desk. "I need to attend to important matters. You may go now."

I could see his stained teeth and smell his breath as he loomed over me.

"Remember, you and your brother are here at my mercy," he hissed.

CHAPTER ELEVEN

DANCING THE CAROLA

MY EARS were ringing as I walked away from his room.

Count Raymond could kick Milos and me out of Jerusalem without a coin to support us, and he probably wouldn't even blink. Thoroughly shaken, I made my way back to the great hall.

"Alina, are you well?" Sibylla asked when I came in. "You look frazzled."

"Thank you, I'm fine." I tried to think of something innocuous. "I was just thinking about my father."

"Oh," she said, apparently already having lost interest in my state of mind. Then she grinned at me. "Today we are doing something sure to distract you. I got some of the others to agree to dance the Carola with us."

"The Carola?" I asked. "I don't know how to dance."

"Really? You've never danced?" Sibylla looked at me with amazement. "Don't worry, I'll show you. You'll like it. Ah, the musicians have arrived, so we're just about to start." Proudly she gestured toward four strangers arranged along the side of the great hall.

Their loose-fitting gowns were decorated with bells, tassels, and beads, and they had pointy hoods, one red, one blue, one purple, and one black. One held a bow and a string instrument with a rounded, pear-shaped body and three strings. There was a flutist. And another man held a stringed instrument that looked like a harp.

Most interesting, there was a man with a pipe in one hand and a drum in the other, and he played both instruments at the same time. The pipe looked like a recorder, but I could see only three melody holes, so he would need just three fingers to play it. A strap around the arm with the pipe held the drum to his body, leaving his other hand free. He could literally play his own accompaniment.

"Do you like them?" Sibylla asked me. "Count Baltasar found them for me. They're street musicians."

How interesting. Count Baltasar knew street musicians. He also apparently had taken the time to arrange this for Sibylla. "That was nice of him."

"Yes, wasn't it?" Sibylla said dismissively. She had to be used to people doing things for her all the time.

"Come." She took my hand and led me into the center of the hall. To my surprise, most of the court ladies joined us, as well as several men who happened to be in the great hall.

I saw Count Baltasar, looking smug. He wore a long flowing robe over a richly embroidered doublet, and he had cut his hair. I had to suppress a smile. The cut emphasized his round face. He acknowledged my presence with a brief bow.

Balian was there, as well as Count William Longsword, a cheerful, unpretentious, and unfailingly courteous man in his thirties who had the added advantage of being tall and handsome.

Only Queen Maria Comnena, heavily pregnant, stayed in her chair. She had a relaxed and contented smile on her face as she watched Isabella, who hopped up and down in her excitement, pulling on Dame Alice's hand.

Sibylla clapped her hands and directed us to form a large circle. At a sign from her, the musicians started to play.

First we went round and round to the beat, holding hands. Then we formed pairs, holding up our hands to create a gate for the others to pass under. Next we traveled through the great hall in figures of eight, then returned to the circle and moved toward the center with a clapping of hands and back again. The men outdid themselves in including Isabella, making a point of crouching down low when it was her turn to create a gate with her partner, Dame Alice.

Finally we stopped. I was out of breath, my hair had worked itself loose from under my cap, and my feet hurt, but none of it mattered. "Thank you, that was wonderful," I said to Sibylla.

She beamed at me, for once entirely without artifice. "It was. I am glad it worked out."

Both of us turned at a screeching sound behind us. Isabella, flushed and overheated, was sitting on the floor, screaming and waving her arms.

"Hush, child." Dame Alice bent over her. "You cannot do that here."

"I won't." Isabella screamed louder. "I won't."

"Let me take her, my lady." Beryl had been waiting at the edge of the great hall and now came forward. She crouched in front of the little girl. Taking a little white linen cloth out of her sleeve, she wiped the girl's face with a gentleness that surprised me, and Isabella quieted down, her thumb in her mouth, and her large, dark eyes on Beryl's face, which had lost all its sharpness. "Come, my dear, I have a warm bath waiting for you. Your lady mother gave me some rose oil to make it smell nice."

The girl stretched up her arms, and Beryl lifted her and carried her out of the hall.

"She's good with her," I said.

Dame Alice, still flustered, her wimple having slipped sideways, pursed her lips. "That she is." She shook her head as if annoyed.

"You don't like her?" I was surprised, because Dame Alice seemed to like everyone.

"Oh, I don't know," she said vaguely. "I am sure my lady the queen has her reasons for keeping her on. She is certainly good with Princess Isabella."

Sibylla had a pinched expression on her face. "Why do we need to discuss a servant maid?"

That was odd. I wondered why she had turned snappish all of a sudden.

Then in a complete turnabout, she beamed at me. "Come, Alina. I want to show you the musicians' instruments. You'll like them."

I forgot about Beryl. "I'd love to see them." Eagerly I followed her to where the four musicians stood, chatting and getting ready to pack up their instruments. They allowed me to hold them and try out a few sounds when they learned that I play the lute. I especially loved the harp and its sweet sound, but when I tried to hold the pipe together with the drum, I almost lost my balance. "This is hard," I exclaimed.

They laughed, but not unkindly. "It takes practice, my lady."

When I returned to my room, all the weight of my predicament returned. It would be increasingly difficult to deal with Count Raymond's questions, but I had to keep him satisfied somehow, because the notion of tattling was revolting. Unfortunately, I liked Sibylla more than I had expected. It would have been so much easier if I despised her.

The next morning I encountered Sibylla as she was coming from a hallway in the back of the citadel. She looked flushed, the hem of her usually immaculate robe was dirty, and she carried a bundle under her arm. She practically ran into me as she came around the corner.

"Oh, Alina, are you already on your way to the hall?" Sibylla looked flustered, and spoke in an unusually friendly tone, almost cajoling.

"Yes," I said slowly, unsure what to make of this.

"Good. I will see you there. I just was in the courtyard. It's beautiful outside." She spoke quickly. "I have to brush my hair. Don't wait for me." She ran off, heading toward the wing she shared with Isabella and her stepmother. For a moment the bundle spilled out from under her arm. A dark hood and the top of a remarkably plain cloak poked out before she snatched everything up again.

Puzzled, I watched her until she disappeared around a corner. She hadn't come from the courtyard, yet she had clearly been outside. I began to walk in the direction she came from, down the long passageway, until I heard steps behind me.

"Mistress Alina," a familiar voice boomed in my ear.

Startled, I turned around. "Oh, good morning, Count Baltasar." I had a hard time not showing my frustration. I would have to postpone my exploration.

"Where are you headed?" he asked, a curious look on his friendly, round face.

"Oh, I am on my way to the great hall, but I thought I saw a cat. I love cats." It was lame, but I couldn't think of a better way to explain my venturing down this particular passage.

"Cats?" He smiled at me. "At home in Aurignac, there are feral cats, and we sometimes have to reduce their numbers. Otherwise, they would take over completely."

"I'd better get back." I walked off, feeling his eyes follow me.

I got up early the next morning so I could explore the passageway where I encountered Sibylla, hoping no one else was around that early.

I had become just like Aunt Marci, who watched my every move. I shook my head in disgust at myself. But I really wanted to know.

I walked in the direction she had come from and found a narrow passage that didn't seem to lead anywhere other than to the door at the end of it. I opened it and looked around in disappointment. There was no other door leading out of this space.

It was a dimly lit little chapel. A simple silver cross hung above a modest stone altar. In the flickering light of the oil lamp I could make out a bowl filled with rose petals, a prayer stool, and a tapestry showing a lady next to a fountain. The torches on the wall were unlit.

It seemed unlikely that Sibylla had come here to pray. She would go to the chapel reserved for the king and his family. Besides, she hadn't looked like someone just returning from prayer.

Maybe there was a secret door behind the wall hanging. I moved my hand over the rough threads. Something hard bulged out from the wall. Perhaps it was a latch. Reaching behind the heavy cloth, I touched a cold piece of metal. It shifted when I pushed on it.

Sounds of doors banging in the distance jarred me out of my absorption. I had to come back another time. Right now I needed to get out of this room without anyone seeing me. I pulled open the door to the hallway and poked my head out. Nobody was in sight, so I stepped out into the passage and quickly walked back to the main hallway. I had to find another time when I might explore the chapel.

A low chuckle made me slow down. Sibylla. I was still surprised by how deep her voice was. She was standing close to a man I recognized as William Longsword. He looked down at her with a smile. Then she noticed me.

"Ah, Alina, I was just talking to Count William about your music," she said airily.

"You are very kind," I responded, trying to keep my face bland. They had not been talking about music, much less mine, when I came upon them. Then I was ashamed. Here I was speculating about what Sibylla had done while I'd just been sneaking around myself.

Count William bowed courteously and walked off.

Sibylla looked at me with an expression that was a curious mixture of pleading and defiance.

I pretended I hadn't noticed anything. "My lady Sibylla, I was wondering whether you need me this morning. If not, I'd like to go for a walk in town."

"Silly, of course you can go for a walk. You don't need to ask." Sibylla laughed at me, her face relaxed and self-assured again. "This isn't a prison—at least not for you!" She spoke lightly, but there was a funny twist to her smile.

"Thank you. I think I'll go today, then."

Sibylla turned away, having lost interest in my plans. Then she glanced back at me. "You know, I never asked. Do you need money?"

I gaped at her. So much had happened since Acre, and so quickly, that I hadn't had time to worry about money. So far the need had not arisen since I didn't need to spend anything on food or shelter.

But the travel funds from Uncle Garsanc were gone, and I would be penniless if it weren't for the money we received from Count Baltasar during the journey. Unfortunately, what I had left wasn't enough to get us home when the time came. I definitely would not be able to afford anything to improve my wardrobe. The blue cloth I bought in Acre made a serviceable gown, but did little to inspire me with self-confidence when I had to sit in the great hall.

To make matters worse, Sibylla continued to casually toss shawls and gowns on my bed while dismissively eying my clothes. Ever since my first encounter with Beryl, I had resented it. In any event, I didn't know how to wear any of Sibylla's things without feeling foolish. So, I stuck stubbornly to the blue gown, though I ended up using the shawls for variety's sake. Now this girl, younger than I was, had figured it out that money might be a problem. I flushed with embarrassment.

Sibylla eyed me speculatively. "I thought it might be the case." She sounded like a frustrated middle-aged lady when she continued. "Sometimes I wonder what men are thinking about when they make arbitrary decisions for people. Look, I will arrange for a weekly amount to be given to you out of the royal coffers, starting today. Would that do?"

"Yes, thank you. That would be very helpful." My face still burned.

"Well, I'll take care of it right now. Just check with the treasurer before you go. And tell me later about your walk. I don't get to go out by myself."

Again, I was at a loss for words. I hadn't realized how confined the princess was by her rank. I almost was sorry for her. Then I remembered her secret escape route. She had been outside at least once. In any event, her next question quickly made me forget any feelings of sympathy.

"How is your delicious brother? What's he doing these days? I haven't seen him at court."

I blinked at her. I hadn't seen Milos either. He had told me he was going on an excursion to survey the region with Stephen, but Sibylla didn't need to know that.

"I haven't talked to him for a while."

"Well, be sure to tell him I asked about him." She tossed her shawl over her shoulder and sauntered off.

I had no intention of telling Milos about Sibylla. He had enough troubles without being obsessed with a young woman who was so far above his status. And she certainly didn't need a new toy for her collection.

CHAPTER TWELVE

A WALK IN TOWN

WHEN I emerged into the sunny courtyard and walked through the gate into the town, I wanted to sing and shout. This was the first time since our arrival that I left the citadel. For a while I was free to take everything in without worrying about my peculiar position or the possibility of an uncomfortable interview with Count Raymond.

I marveled at the tight-knit town with its impressive gates and many churches. My first goal was the Temple Mount. I wanted to pray for my father, my mother, and Maria. I asked for directions from a man who was rushing along with a rolled-up carpet under his arm.

With a gap-toothed smile, he pointed toward the other side of town and said in heavily accented Latin, "Just follow this road."

I had heard that the Templars used part of a building that was a mosque. The street leading to it went slightly uphill, and I could see it at the end of a plaza—a large structure, glowing in the sunlight, with stone arches along the facade. I entered through the central arch into an enormous hall dominated by white columns throughout the central aisles, and was transported.

Powerful, dark beams stretched between the arches, as if holding them up, and the dome was covered with mosaic tiles, but I could not see an altar. Perhaps the Templars had set one up in the area where they assembled. There was chanting in one of the halls to the side of the mosque. I had never heard anything quite like this, though the words were familiar, a prayer to Mary, mother of mercy, *Salve, Regina, Mater Misericordiae.* Deep, strong voices travelled throughout the building.

It was as if the white columns trembled from the sound.

Awash with emotion, I felt naked and exposed in this vast, luminous space. I bent my head and murmured the words of the rosary, trying to keep my thoughts centered on my family, and especially my father. I had a hard time thinking of him as a sinner for having ended his life. He had just been lost, overwhelmed by grief. I spoke a brief prayer of gratitude for Uncle Garsanc's intervention, without which we would not have been able to bury my father next to my mother and sister, and with the proper rites of the church. It was odd to feel grateful for anything my uncle had done.

Footfalls behind me startled me out of my absorption. I turned around.

Stephen, together with one of the young knights who came with us from Acre, entered the mosque and gazed at the columns and arches.

Another man walked in behind them wearing a plain white robe and carrying a rolled-up carpet under his arm. He took off his shoes at the entrance and headed down the central aisle where he spread out the carpet. Standing with his hands folded over his chest, he began to recite something in Arabic.

The young knight with Stephen became agitated. He walked up to the praying man, grabbed his arm, and tried to turn him eastward. "That's how you should pray," he snapped.

The man backed up, saying something in Arabic.

At this Stephen shook his head and rushed over. "Let him say his prayers." He bowed to the older man, who appeared a bit shaken, and spoke to him in Arabic. Then he pulled the knight away. "Muslims have been granted the right to pray here as they always have," Stephen explained, speaking in an undertone. "You can't know that they turn toward Mecca in the east when they pray. Come, let us join the Templars."

Confused, I watched the two men make their way toward the hall where the Templars were chanting. I had never thought about why we faced east in prayer—something to do with the rising sun, I assumed. More importantly, it would never have occurred to me that Muslims would come to pray in a space where the Templars held their assemblies. Stephen had not been in Jerusalem any longer than the other man, but he made an effort to learn as much about the people living here as he could.

I walked outside and down a steep road. Following the crowd, I turned a corner and looked around in amazement. The street, while open to the outside along the sides, had a vaulted roof, shielding the merchants and shoppers from the sun. Stalls offered all sorts of boiled meats and roasts. I turned the corner and ended up walking along another covered street.

I was awed by the colors of the fruits and vegetables brought in by farmers, by the different garb people wore, and by the babble of languages— French, Latin, Greek, Arabic, and others. I stopped at the tables laden with spices, many of which I could not identify.

"That's ginger," the merchant said when I pointed at a pile of odd, tree-root-like things. He sliced a tiny sliver off the top of one of them. "Here, smell it." The sharp, sweet and sour scent made me want to sneeze.

Next I touched the pile of brown, nail-shaped flower buds. In the fall my mother used to have the cook boil pears with cloves stuck into their skin like tiny crowns of thorns so the pears absorbed the rich, warm, sweet aroma. She would have loved this market.

Piles of small brown balls puzzled me for a moment. Then I remembered. They were called nutmeg. My mother had kept one of them in a jar, and used it sparingly by grinding it back and forth against a rasp and sprinkling the pungent brown powder into stews and puddings.

One merchant sold sugar from a barrel in front of him, carefully measuring out amounts and pouring them into linen bags. I had tasted sugar once when a man traveled through our village after returning from the Holy Land. He had called it "sweet salt." I stared at it longingly.

"Young mistress, this is the finest sugar you can buy—straight from the sugar factories in Tyre. Try it. It's much better than honey." The merchant lifted one of the linen bags. "Come, let me fill this for you."

"No, thank you. Another time, perhaps." I backed away.

At the end of the street, several shop signs showed a fat purse and coins, with lettering beneath, some in Latin, others in what I assumed was Assyrian—they had to be money changers.

I walked on and turned into another street, also covered, and found it was much cooler in the shade. Sounds of people talking and carts clattering through the streets echoed off the stone walls. I stopped to admire a display of glass vessels and beakers in colors ranging from the deepest blue to a rich purple. I reached out to pick up a small, pear-shaped, blue flask. The light shone through it.

The merchant pounced on me immediately. "Finest glass from Antioch, Mistress. Perfect for scents."

Hastily I put it down and shook my head. "Sorry."

Knights wearing their distinctive tunics wandered around looking grave, but I decided they were enjoying the market just as much as I was.

One I recognized from a distance. It was Count Baltasar, walking in the direction of the castle and carrying something wrapped in a bundle. He looked pleased, as if he had come upon an unexpected treasure. I remembered his intent expression when studying the icons in the church near the Rilski River. Then I forgot about him as my attention was drawn back to the wares on display all around me.

A few sellers displayed trinkets on their tables, and I stopped at one covered with an array of flasks and caskets made of ivory or silver, some elaborately inlaid with enamel. I picked up a silver and gilt box, about the length of my hand, which showed a lute player surrounded by several other figures. One played a recorder.

"Mistress, this comes from Constantinople. Do you like it?" The merchant gazed at me appraisingly.

"It's lovely. But I know it's not something I can afford."

"I believe I've seen a larger version of this on an ivory casket," someone said in a deep voice, and I turned to discover Stephen. He courteously inclined his head in my direction.

The merchant, scenting a sale, directed his attention to Stephen. "Yes, my lord, you are right. It is a copy of a large casket in Constantinople, more than a hundred years old. I can offer you a fair price."

Stephen glanced at me.

I shook my head. "No thank you."

"See, you could keep your earrings in it." The merchant showed us how the lid opened. "I'd give it to you for practically nothing."

"You heard the lady." Stephen took my arm and steered me away.

"Thank you," I said, flustered. "I have a hard time saying no."

"I realize that. These merchants can be persistent. Anyway, I am sure he would have charged you an outrageous amount. Are you going on?"

"Yes, I want to spend some more time in the market."

"I will leave you then, Mistress Alina." He bowed and walked off.

I watched him until he disappeared into the crowd.

"Young mistress, look at these wraps," I heard a voice to my left. I turned and saw a table covered with wraps, headscarves, and piles of uncut linen and woolen cloth. The colors were amazing.

The moment of hesitation doomed me. The seller, a grizzled old man with a twinkle in his eyes, came from behind his table and draped a light blue wrap around my shoulders. "This silk would be lovely on you."

I had never even seen anything like this. Soft and smooth to the touch, the blue wrap shimmered like flowing water. "Thank you, but I can't afford this." Of course, now the seller knew I was interested.

He named an amount.

I ran my fingers over the silk, amazed how light it was.

"For you, so young and beautiful."

This made me laugh. No one had ever called me beautiful.

"It would be very little, practically a gift from me to you!" He smiled at me, and I could not resist smiling back. He named a lower amount.

I hesitated. It seemed frivolous to spend money on something so fine, but then I opened my purse and pulled out a silver denier and several smaller coins, all marked with the eight-pointed Templar cross.

The seller took them and bowed. "Come back. I am always here on Wednesdays."

Elated, I walked off with my new shawl floating off my shoulders, deciding to explore further before returning to the citadel. I hurried as fast as I could through the open-air poultry and livestock market, overwhelmed by the smell, while the chattering and screeching from the cages clashed with the bellowing of cattle in small stalls.

In another area merchants displayed various types of treated leather goods, but I went on until I arrived at a gate, not the same one we used to enter Jerusalem. Curious to see what lay beyond it, I walked through and down the hill, finding myself in an area less tightly built up, with small stone and mud houses, huts, and gardens, a whole little community at the foot of the town.

I thought I should turn back when I realized that I had lost my way, and I was looking around to see which of the little roads led back to the gate when I became aware of a commotion ahead of me.

Several boys ran out from another road and rushed toward a man walking along with a basket swinging off his arm. The boys yelled at the man, and when one stuck out his leg and tripped him, the man fell down, upending his basket. A small pile of barley spilled out, and oranges rolled away in the dust. The boys jeered at the man and began to pelt him with oranges.

"Hey, stop that," I shouted as I ran over, nearly tripping over several stones in my haste.

These boys were just like the village louts who liked to attack Milos. Distracted, the boys looked at me. One of them started to grin unpleasantly, and it occurred to me that once again I had acted without thinking. *Don't show any fear,* I thought to myself. Holding on to my new shawl, I raised my chin and tried to assume the expression Aunt Marci had when reprimanding one of the servants.

Meanwhile, the man had made good use of the distraction and was back on his feet, looking remarkably calm and unperturbed. He leaned down and retrieved his walking stick, holding it loosely in front of him without any evident intent of using it as a weapon.

At this point, the boys apparently decided the tide had turned. One of them spat on the ground, barely missing my gown, and said something in a language I couldn't understand, but the intent was clear. It was something rude. Then they ran off.

"I am so sorry about your oranges and the barley." I bent down to pick up some of the oranges. "These aren't damaged."

"Thank you," said the man, in oddly accented French, smiling at me. "I guess the barley is a lost cause."

He was unlike anyone I had ever seen. Tall and slender, he wore a dark tunic, with a dark cap on his head, and long, soft, dark curls reaching down to his shoulders. His dark grey eyes were huge, and his features finely drawn—a face that had burned off all unnecessary elements, leaving only the essence of a human being. He probably was in his twenties, but he had an air of someone a lot older. I realized that I was staring at him and looked down.

"I'd better go back." I shifted my weight and winced. I must have twisted my ankle when I stumbled.

"You hurt yourself?"

"I'm sure it's nothing." It was my reward for being foolish.

"Let me help you. Come with me. We live close to here, and my wife will take a look. She knows what to do."

"Oh, I'm sure it'll be fine." I was embarrassed. "Just show me how to get back. I need to return to the citadel."

"No, I insist," the man responded. "Come along, and I will go with you back up the hill in a little while."

Gravely he held out his arm. I hesitated, but then took it.

Together we went around the corner to a little house with a kitchen garden in front.

I noticed a small, oblong, metal case affixed at a slight angle to the doorframe on the right. I couldn't read the symbols on it, and it puzzled me that it hung at an angle. But we were already inside. My host slipped off his sandals, and I followed his example.

"Sarah," he called out. He led me to a bench covered with pillows. "Here, sit down."

Steps echoed on the stone flags, and a young woman emerged trom the back of the house. She was tucking in the corners of a scarf that covered her hair as she came toward me, her heavy eyebrows raised in a question above large, dark eyes.

The man muttered something in another language and then switched back to French. "Sarah, this young lady came to my aid when I was beset by some youngsters just below the tanner's house, and she hurt her ankle while helping me. I am afraid we have to do without barley, but the oranges survived." He placed the basket on a table.

"How far do you have to go?" The young woman looked concerned.

I blushed, realizing I hadn't told them my name. "I have to go back to the castle. My name is Alina de Florac. I am—" I faltered, unsure of how to explain my peculiar position. "I am sort of a companion or lady-in-waiting to Princess Sibylla."

"Well, you have met Sarah, my wife. And my name is Meir ben Eleazar."

Sarah frowned. Her face, with its thick dark eyebrows and a hint of freckles on her snub nose, looked vaguely pugnacious. With an abrupt movement, she shoved a lock of her hair back under her scarf and stood up. "I will bring you something to drink so you can rest a bit."

Sarah didn't seem happy to have me in her house. "Please, don't trouble yourself," I said, but she had already walked out of the room. I wished I had just limped home. This was awkward.

I glanced at my host, trying to think of something to say. "Your name... is that a Jewish name? I thought there weren't any Jews in Jerusalem..." I faltered, realizing that this sounded rude at best.

Meir didn't appear to be bothered. "No, there haven't been many of us since the first crusade. But perhaps this is not the time to relate that sad history. There have always been Jews in this city, and always will be. Right now there are about two hundred of us. Now excuse me for a moment. I'll be right back." Softly he closed the door, leaving me alone.

Uncomfortable, I looked around the room. It looked like a scholar's study, with a table covered with scrolls and writing implements, and other scrolls on shelves. The oil lamp on the table wasn't lit, but the light from the lattice window made it bright enough.

Benches with pillows lined the whitewashed wall, and there was a clay urn filled with olive branches. Near the front door I noticed a small, rectangular area where the stone was exposed. It looked neat, with clean edges, as if it was planned that way. But it didn't make sense for the wall to be left unfinished.

Suddenly I remembered something my father told me a long time ago. Actually, he hadn't done it intentionally. He had been talking to Mother, unaware that I was listening. It was something about Jews being expelled from the Rhineland and even some areas in northern France. Apparently, some were killed as well.

"Why?" my mother had exclaimed in dismay. My father had shrugged in his customary detached manner. "I don't know. Perhaps because they're different. Often people do terrible things for no good reason at all." It was odd and sad, but I soon forgot all about it. Later, when I was older, I heard Father Otho talk about Jews in his sermons. He claimed that they poisoned wells and took the blood of little children for their bread. I was tempted to giggle, because it was ridiculous. Nobody could possibly believe any of it.

I heard muted voices in the other room. My cheeks burned. I wished I hadn't remembered that bit about the poisoned wells.

Sarah returned carrying a tray. She handed a mug to me, a closed expression on her face.

"Thank you, you are very kind." I sipped carefully. It tasted of mint sweetened with honey, and the fragrant steam was comforting.

"Let me take a look at your ankle," she said after studying me silently for a few moments. She crouched down in front of me and gently lifted the skirt.

Embarrassed I looked around.

"Don't be concerned. Meir is in the back." She ran her hands over my ankle. "I think you just pulled it a bit. It should be fine if you rest it and don't jump around too much tomorrow." Sarah held out a small flat loaf. "Have some of this with your tea."

"Thank you." I nibbled on it. I hadn't eaten anything all day, and my stomach growled. It tasted slightly sweet, with something pungent mixed in. "It's very good. What do you put in it?"

"Oh, it's simple...wheat, herbs, and a bit of honey."

Meir walked back into the room carrying a tiny bundle in his arms. He sat down on the bench across from me and began to rock the bundle gently back and forth.

"Oh, you have a baby," I exclaimed wistfully.

"Yes, this is Alon Benjamin." Proudly Meir lifted the cloth away from the scrunched-up little face so I could see his son. "Alon means oak tree in Hebrew. Our very own little tree." Meir tugged on the tiny foot sticking out of the blanket and grinned at me. "I guess he has a bit of growing to do before his parents can rest in his shade."

"And Benjamin?" I asked curiously.

"We named him Benjamin after my master. Benjamin means son of the right hand."

"Who is your master?"

"Benjamin of Tudela. He's one of the foremost historians of our times. He has traveled all over Palestine and Egypt, as well as other lands. He wanted to describe all the Jewish communities in the region and spent over ten years recording everything he encountered. I am very fortunate to have been able to assist him in his work."

"More than ten years," I said. "That's a long time for one project."

Meir smiled but did not respond.

"Do all names in Hebrew mean something?"

"Most of them do."

"What about Meir?"

"'The illuminating one.'" Meir grew pink above his beard. "At least, that was my parents' hope."

"And Sarah?"

"A princess, of course."

"Of course." I smiled at Sarah. "How old is Alon?"

"He was born just a few weeks ago." Sarah had relaxed slightly. "When he's a bit stronger, we can leave."

"Oh, where are you going?"

"Bohemia."

On our journey to the Holy Land, we hadn't traveled through Bohemia because it was too far north of our route. I wondered why they wanted to go there but didn't want to appear rude again.

"And what about you, Mistress Alina? What brought you to Jerusalem?" Meir asked, bridging the silence.

Sarah picked up some sewing from her basket. The silvery threads in her dark hair, peeking out from under her headscarf, gave her a surprisingly matronly air. This sparely furnished, clean, and tidy house seemed a universe away from the court. I cradled the mug in my hands.

The last time I felt like this was just before my mother fell ill. I had been sitting next to her on the ground, looking at the flames in the hearth, while she mended one of my gowns, humming softly and occasionally running her hand over my head. It was one of my last good memories of her, and for once she hadn't been scolding me or trying to get me to be more ladylike. My eyes stung.

"You don't need to tell us."

I looked at Meir, once again struck by his chiseled features and his gentle, grey eyes. "I came here with my brother Milos." I hesitated. Then I told them about my father's death and our journey, and about being asked to be a companion to Sibylla for a while. I didn't mention my predicament about the strange bargain with Count Raymond.

Meir kept rocking the baby. Sarah stitched with her head bent, listening attentively.

It was tempting to tell them everything. I fell silent. Just then the baby began to fuss, making little mewling sounds.

Sarah looked up and put down her work. "He needs to be fed."

I realized how much time had passed. "You and your husband have been very kind to me, but I should go." I moved my foot and was relieved to find that the pain had already lessened.

"I will take you back to the gate," Meir said.

Sarah looked up. "Must you?"

"Oh, please, there really is no need to come with me. I'm sure it'll be fine."

"No, I insist." Meir handed the baby to his wife and went into the next room. In a moment he returned with a long walking stick. He waved it around with a pleased smile, making me think of a little boy with his first toy sword. "No louts will bother us now. Come on."

"Thank you, Sarah." I got up, moving carefully as I put weight on my ankle. It was tender, but I'd be able to walk.

"You're welcome," she said distractedly. She looked at her husband, her heavy brows drawn together, then brushed a speck of dust off his tunic. "Be careful, Meir."

"Don't fuss, dear."

With a frown, she watched while we went outside, her dark eyes troubled, before she gently closed the door.

"Things were bad for our people during the first crusade. Sarah worries whenever I go into the town," Meir explained as we walked.

I didn't know what to say. Unbidden, an image of one of the Templars came to mind. He was strolling through the market this morning, and I saw him help himself to some fruit from a vendor. The vendor watched him but stayed silent. It made me feel ashamed to be associated with them, however indirectly. Now, again, I was ashamed.

"Don't trouble yourself about it." It was as if Meir had read my mind. "Anyway, Sarah and I will leave Jerusalem in another month or so."

"And what about your master?"

"Master Benjamin? He wasn't well, and he wanted to return to his family in Spain. I still have to finish sorting and copying his notes."

"May I ask you something?"

Meir raised his eyebrows.

"Why is part of the wall in your house unfinished?"

"Oh, you noticed. Well, how to explain? It's a form of prayer, reminding us of the destruction of the temple when the Romans attacked Jerusalem. I also like to think it reminds us that things in this life are impermanent."

"It's sort of sad, but I like it." I thought of my father's pensive expression when he played sad songs.

We walked through David's Gate. I looked around. "This isn't the gate I used when I left the citadel."

"You probably used Tanners' Gate, and our little community is right below it. Anyway, there is the citadel." Meir lifted his walking stick and pointed.

"Oh, right. Thank you so much." I looked at him. Hesitantly I added, "Could I visit you and Sarah again?"

"You'd be most welcome." Meir smiled at me and turned to go. After a few steps, he glanced back. "By the way, before I forget, your name means 'light' in Greek." With his dark coat flapping, he strode toward David's Gate.

CHAPTER THIRTEEN

SALADIN

STANDING AT the entrance to the citadel, I watched Meir for a moment as he made his way down the hill. I was already wondering when I could see them again.

"So, who was your escort?"

Startled, I looked around and saw Beryl leaning against the side of the gate. She carried a bundle in her arms, and her sandals and gown were dusty.

"Do you always creep up on people?" I asked, disgruntled at being dragged away from my musings.

"Oh, creeping can be quite useful," she said calmly. "You'd be amazed how much you can find out about people."

Something about her sharp-nosed curiosity bothered me. "Where were you coming from just now?" I asked, deciding to attack to distract her. I didn't want to be queried about Meir. That afternoon with Meir and Sarah was a precious gift I wanted to keep to myself.

"I went to visit my little girl. She's with my parents in a village not far from here."

"Really, you have a little girl? Why aren't you with her, then?" I was surprised and then a little ashamed. In my irritation with her nosiness, it had not occurred to me to wonder about her own life.

"I have to earn a living." Beryl turned down the corners of her mouth, for a moment looking like a much older woman. "Besides, the villagers don't look kindly on me since I don't have a husband."

"Oh." I was flustered. That had to be hard. "I am sorry."

"Yes, well, who knows—I might find a husband here. What about your brother? I mean, when he isn't ogling Sibylla, that is."

My sympathy evaporated quickly. "Leave my brother alone. Anyway, why do you spend so much time watching what other people do? It's none of your business."

"Oh, you never know. Knowledge can come in handy. Sometimes it even pays. I've got my little girl to look out for."

"Well, you know what they say—curiosity killed the cat," I snapped. I was about to go inside when I heard two riders entering the courtyard.

I turned to see Milos and Stephen clattering in, their horses and gear covered with dust. They jumped off, and Stephen handed his reins to Milos. He clapped Milos on the shoulder and said a few words I didn't hear, and I couldn't help watching him as he walked off.

"Hey, Froggie!" Milos beamed at me. His lips were chapped, and sand had settled in all his pores and in his hair. "Do you have to be somewhere? I want to tell you about our ride. Just let me put the horses away."

This was new. Milos had never told me anything unless I pestered him endlessly. Come to think of it, we usually spent more time bickering rather than talking

"I can help you," I said, suddenly longing for my old life at home. Besides, I hadn't seen Milos for at least ten days. When I was younger I sometimes helped out in the stable. Right now, even sitting over a tub full of washing held a certain appeal—at least in those days I knew what I had accomplished at the end of the day.

"No, absolutely not." Milos grinned. "The others would laugh at me if I let a girl help me."

So I waited, sitting in the shade of the colonnade and imagining Stephen and Milos riding through the vast land between Jerusalem and the sea, envious of their freedom.

After a short while, Milos strolled up to me and sat on the bench, smelling of dust and sun and sweat. He looked happy.

"That was fast."

"Yes, a stable boy wanted to help, and I wasn't about to turn down the help. Anyway, you won't believe the time I had. I even met Saladin."

"Saladin? Who is that?"

"He's the new vizier—I guess you might say the ruler—in Egypt. He's been leading a lot of forays against the crusaders. Stephen thinks Saladin is going to be the biggest enemy of the Kingdom of Jerusalem in the years to come."

"And you met this archenemy?" I asked incredulously. "Perhaps he even fed you and spoke to you in French."

Milos took out his flask and pulled off the stopper, wiping the rim with his sleeve before he drank, allowing some of the water to run over his chin. He looked tanned and more muscular than I had ever seen him. "In fact, Saladin did feed us, and he even spoke a few words in French. We ate something called hummus, a paste made from ground up chickpeas, on an odd kind of flatbread—very tasty." Milos licked his lips.

Food in the citadel was not particularly inspiring, and I had heard the cook complain about the ongoing grain shortages. But the spices used to flavor the food as well as the pomegranates and oranges made up for a lot. "Enough about the food. What happened?" I asked impatiently.

"Well, there was this horse—the most beautiful gray I've ever seen."

I glared at him. "Milos, if you're just going to go on about a horse, I'll just go inside."

"It was quite a horse. I can't tell you how much I would have liked to keep it." Milos grinned, pleased with himself. "Sweet-tempered as well."

"Milos," I growled.

"All right, let me tell you. See, Stephen wanted to inspect the land south of us. We rode first to the castle of the Ibelins at the coast and then to Ascalon. After that, we kept going south toward Egypt. He even made me change my tunic so that we wouldn't be recognized immediately as crusaders. He called it scouting the territory, and we rode all over the region. And Stephen insisted that I write down a report of everything we had seen. He would dictate whatever he wanted me to record, but he wasn't particularly interested in Arab encampments, although I had to make a note of those as well—no, he made me write down what the farmers grew in their fields, the condition of the houses, even the condition of trails and roads, and he insisted I record every source of water we came across."

"So you were like a secretary." I laughed. "Brother Gervais would have loved that." The old tutor would have been stunned to see his reluctant pupil display such enthusiasm. It intrigued me that Stephen had apparently decided to spend some time and effort on training Milos. But I also couldn't help feeling jealous of my brother.

"Stop interrupting me," Milos said, but he looked pleased. "Anyway, that's how we found the horse. That is, we found bloody tracks which we followed into a little grove. There was the horse, standing quietly in the shade of a tree. Its rider was lying on the ground, motionless. At first, we thought he was dead, but he was only unconscious and bleeding from a wound in his side. His turban had fallen off, and he wore the robes of an Arab. The horse was exquisite, and his saddle was richly decorated, and a curved sword with a jeweled hilt was lying on the ground. I was all for taking the horse, but Stephen wouldn't let me."

"Of course he wouldn't," I said sternly.

"I'm just joking." Milos chuckled. "Anyway, Stephen tore up his spare linen shirt and wrapped it around the man's side, then decided to take him and his horse straight to the next encampment of Arabs. They had been making forays into the north, so it wasn't that hard to find them."

"Why? Weren't you taking a terrible risk?"

"That's what I thought. But Stephen said this was not only the right thing to do, but it was also a perfect way to get into the camp. He told me we might as well make use of it and learn something about the enemy. We put the young man's turban back on his head and cleaned his face with water. Then we wrapped him in my blanket, tied him to his horse, and rode straight into the next encampment. The first sentry we encountered immediately recognized the horse. He called out, and before we knew it, we were surrounded by a large group of men, shouting at us.

"There was a tense moment while we sat on our horses at the edge of the enemy camp, leading a horse with its wounded rider. But Stephen was right. He told me if they didn't kill us right away, we'd be safe, because then we would be treated as guests, however unwelcome. They made us leave our horses and led us to a large tent. Inside there was a man who looked about thirty, sitting on a pillow and playing a board game with a boy. It looked like checkers. The man was plainly dressed, and he had piercing, dark eyes, but I couldn't see his hair since a turban covered it. That was Saladin. Another man, fluent in French, acted as an interpreter. Saladin wanted to know what brought two French crusaders to his camp.

"Stephen muttered to me: 'Bow.'

"So I did. To my surprise, Stephen told Saladin who we were and explained how we found the young man and decided to bring him to the camp. Then Saladin invited us to have tea with him."

"Really?" I laughed.

"He clapped his hands, and in an instant a servant came in. I wish I could do that when I need something. Saladin barked an order, and the servant vanished again. Then we waited in silence. I was nervous, but Stephen seemed relaxed. Finally, the servant returned with a tray and several copper beakers filled with steaming tea, followed by another man who knelt on the floor next to Saladin, whispering in his ear. Then Saladin spoke again, and the interpreter translated."

Here Milos paused for effect.

"What did he say?"

"Well, it turned out the man we rescued was Saladin's cousin, and that he had brought an important message about a plan to assassinate Saladin. So Saladin was grateful to us. Of course it took a lot longer for him to say this, with lots of bowing back and forth.

"And then Saladin and Stephen talked and talked. I thought we'd never get out of that tent." Milos shook his head. "Stephen acted just like he was at home in his castle."

"What did they talk about?" I was amazed by this story and the cool courage it showed.

"You won't believe this. They talked about wine, and Stephen told Saladin about his vineyards in Sancerre. He even talked about what he wanted to do on his land to improve it. They talked about books and poetry until I lost track. In fact, I got sleepy, what with all the back and forth between the interpreter, Saladin, and Stephen. It seemed to go on forever.

"Finally, it was time for us to leave. In the end, to my surprise, Saladin switched to French. He had a thick accent, but he spoke clearly, looking Stephen full in the face. 'I hope you get to see your vineyards again. You love your land as I love mine. We share that. Something tells me that one day you and I will meet again, facing each other across battle lines. For both of us, I hope this is far in the distant future.' I remember every word, I was so amazed.

"Stephen just bowed, and we left. A few riders escorted us for about an hour. Then they raised their swords to us in greeting, wheeled around and raced back to where they came from." Milos fell silent.

"I wish I could have traded places with you. I would have loved to meet this Saladin." I also wished I had heard Stephen talk about his home and his vineyards, but I didn't want to confess it to my annoying brother.

Milos had a pensive expression on his face. "It's all so different from what I expected about the crusades and the Arabs."

"Oh, you mean Father Otho's ravings during his sermons?" I remembered the priest's flushed face when he recounted improbable stories about the infidels, but maybe I wasn't fair. I could never think of Otho without recalling his false sympathy after my father's death.

"Yes, in part. I'm sure some of the horrible things Father Otho talked about do happen, but still, it's all different and much more complicated."

Milos had changed, and so had I. Reluctantly I stood up. "Milos, I need to go. I'm supposed to play in the hall."

"Wait, I have something for you." Milos reached into his satchel and pulled out a piece of silk brocade with a floral pattern in dusty red, shot with gold threads, large enough for a wrap. "I got it from a merchant in Ascalon. I hope you like it."

I stiffened, remembering the little silver balls in Acre. Perhaps he had sold them to someone. I had not seen him practice juggling in a long time, but then I had not seen much of him lately. "But Milos, you didn't have money, did you? This silk looks very expensive."

"You know the usual thing is to say thank you. In fact, I did have money. Stephen has been paying me wages."

He looked so offended that I felt guilty. "Oh Milos, it's beautiful. Really, it is. Thank you very much."

"Well, there you are then." Milos stalked off.

I gazed after him. I had gotten so used to always worrying about him that it never occurred to me that it might hurt him to realize it. I sighed and turned to go inside. I had to get ready for an evening in the hall. Just then I heard hurried steps. It was Sibylla.

"Milos," she called.

Curious, I waited in the shadow of the pillar to watch. Milos had turned back from the doorway to the stable. Tall and slender, he loomed over Sibylla, looking down at her with a fond smile. He pulled another small parcel out of his satchel and handed it to the girl. "This is for you."

Sibylla beamed. For an instant, she sounded like a little girl. "A present?" She pulled the string and looked inside. "Oh, it's beautiful." She held up a purple glass ball, as large as an egg. I could see the light shine through it from where I stood.

My hand began to hurt, and I unclenched it. I had crumpled up the swath of silk brocade from Milos, and the stiff threads had been digging into my skin. At least he hadn't bought jewelry for her. That would definitely attract someone's attention. But if anybody saw this little scene, he might be in trouble anyway. Then I realized I was spying on them, turned to walk inside, and bumped into Beryl. She must have been standing right behind me. "Do you have to lurk in corners all the time?" I snapped.

"I wasn't the only one lurking, was I?" Beryl said carelessly, her gaze still directed over my shoulders.

I had no response to that, so I glared at her and walked away, my thoughts churning worriedly. Moving quickly, I collided with the bulky frame of Ralph, who grunted at the impact.

"Oh, I am sorry."

"Mistress Alina, I was just looking for you," he said, frowning at me.

"I'm in a rush." I squeezed past him and ran on.

"My lord Raymond wants to see you," Ralph shouted.

I really didn't want to talk to Count Raymond just now. "I've been called to the great hall," I called back over my shoulder, picking up my pace.

That night I decided to explore what was behind the secret door. I lay on my pallet as long as I could bear it, waiting for all the sounds in the citadel to die down, until the only ones out and about would be the guards, and most of them would be stationed around the king's and the queen's quarters and the royal treasury. There was no guard stationed at the little dead-end hallway.

I pulled on my soft slippers and wrapped a shawl around my shoulders. *This is stupid*, I scolded myself, but I was determined to find out where Sibylla had been before I encountered her in the hall.

Nobody had seen me by the time I reached the little hallway, and I quickly entered the chapel, illuminated only by the soft glow of the perpetual light on the altar. I lifted the tapestry to reach for the latch when I heard a boom somewhere in the distance. I dropped the heavy cloth and stood frozen in the dimly lit space. Someone was making the rounds, and a door had banged shut. They might come in here. No, I couldn't do this. I might get trapped inside even if I managed to open the secret door. Shivering with fear, I slipped out of the chapel and ran up the hallway to the arcade.

As I came around the corner, I saw someone make his way swiftly down the other end. It looked like a man, although all I could make out was a dark doublet. He was coming from the royal quarters.

I flattened myself against the wall so whoever it was wouldn't see me when I stumbled. My hand brushed against the wall to prevent myself from falling, and I couldn't stifle the small sound I made when I cut my palm on one of the sharp corners sticking out. The person turned and peered back at me. For an instant I saw eyes glimmering, the rest of the face obscured by a dark scarf. Then it was gone.

By the time I reached my room, I was drenched with sweat and trembling with fear and exertion, and wondering whether I should tell anyone about what I saw. But if I did, I would have to explain what I was doing prowling the hallways in the middle of the night.

I didn't fall asleep sleep for a long time.

CHAPTER FOURTEEN

A COURT HEARING

IN RECENT weeks I had run down to visit Meir and Sarah several times. Now familiar with the area, I could get there quickly. When I opened the door, there was Sarah, smiling at me. But she had shadows under her eyes.

"Alina, I am glad you came. I was just about to sit down for a bit. Meir will be back in a little while."

I held Alon on my lap while I watched Sarah prepare mint tea. She handed me a steaming mug, sat down at the table, and began to peel oranges. Alon grabbed my curls with one of his chubby fists and kicked with his chubby legs, giving me a charming, toothless smile. He just had a bath, and his silky curls were still damp. I glanced at Sarah. "You look tired."

"Last night he wouldn't let us sleep at all, crying and fussing and crying some more. Meir thinks he's already teething, but it is much too early."

"Sarah, when Meir brought me to your house the first time, you weren't happy to have me here. Why was that?" Sarah had relaxed with me, and the initial discomfort that I sensed had faded, so I felt I could ask without offending her.

Sarah looked up, an orange peel in her hand. Her strong brows were drawn together, and she looked sad. Then, with a shrug, she gave me a piece of fruit and said, "I was afraid. You are a Christian, and life has been hard for Jews in Jerusalem since the crusaders came. Things are quiet right now, but I didn't want to draw attention to us just when we are getting ready to leave."

I had never been in a position where someone feared me because of what I was. It was strange and uncomfortable. "And now?"

"Now you are a friend."

Despite all our differences of country and religion and background, they thought of me as a friend. With a lump in my throat, I bent my head, breathing in Alon's clean baby scent.

"Meir, you are back." Sarah beamed at her husband, who stood in the doorway with a sheaf of papers in his hands.

He kissed her gently and sat down. "Alina, I was hoping you would come for a visit. After you talked about the songs written by troubadours and trobairitz, I thought of something I want to show you." He pulled a different sheaf of papers out of a drawer and handed them to me. "Poems by Yehuda Halevi."

Curiously I glanced at them. The writing was Hebrew. "I can't read this," I said regretfully. "Who is Yehuda Halevi?" I stumbled over the unfamiliar name.

"A Spanish physician and a poet. He died about thirty years ago. Just listen. I translated them into French as an exercise." With his carefully modulated voice, Meir began to read aloud.

I listened spellbound as the words flowed over me. The poems were more vivid than many troubadour songs, so unlike the lofty phrases about courtly love that troubadours produced with the ease of kitchen maids shelling peas. One about Jerusalem evoked images of a once glorious city in ruins and yearning souls soaring like eagles above a wasteland. A few lines described aspects of day-to-day life in a way that was real—almost palpable. Some made me laugh outright such as a short one about Halevi mocking himself when finding a first gray hair on his head.

On the way back to the citadel, I kept thinking about what Halevi had written about the sea. The words sounded like music.

And what of the flood that left the world a desolate wilderness
With no hope of dry land, no sound of beast or bird, no hope of human voices?

I would have to write down as many phrases as I remembered. One was about a ship, nothing but a fragile little thing living on borrowed time on the swell of a wave. It was just how I felt—I was trapped by my brother's foolishness, degraded every time Count Raymond questioned me, and now also ashamed of my own burning curiosity about Sibylla. Yet, because of all that, I was still here in Jerusalem, happy because I might hear the sound of Stephen's voice, catch a glimpse of his square hands, callused but clean, or see his rare smile transform his blunt features.

When I reached the citadel, Count Raymond's squire cornered me on my way to the hall. "Mistress Alina, come with me. My lord Raymond is asking for you."

In anticipation of my meetings with Count Raymond, I had begun to making internal lists of things I could report to him that would not make me feel thoroughly contemptible. A few times I was tempted to tell Sibylla about the arrangement with Count Raymond, but quickly dismissed such thoughts. I was beginning to like her, and sometimes I even felt sorry for her, with everyone around her watching her every step and trying to manipulate her. But I had seen how she dealt with people who displeased her in any way. She would not be forgiving, especially since it had already gone on for some time. I had been lying to her for weeks.

I was running out of things to report. Again and again I wished I could hate Sibylla. I really did not want to tell Count Raymond about the tunnel or Count William or anything else, most of which was speculation anyway. But I had to pretend I was doing everything he wished so he would leave Milos alone. I pulled my shawl closer around my shoulders and followed the squire reluctantly as he led the way to Count Raymond's room.

"Thank you, Ralph." Count Raymond waited until the squire had backed out and closed the door. "Well, Mistress Alina, do you have anything to tell me?"

He appeared to have filled out since Acre, less gaunt and sallow.

"My lord, I have been playing the lute often for the queen and her ladies, so I don't get much chance to spend time with the princess."

"Well, still, anything that might be of interest?"

"She seems to have a tough time staying within her allowance. I heard that she was berated by one of the older ladies for having borrowed money and not returned it." That seemed innocuous.

"That is not news to me. I see the accounts. Hardly surprising. She is an expensive young lady." Count Raymond frowned. He looked distracted as if worried about something. Perhaps he was just getting bored with me and was trying to decide when to dismiss me. "Anything else?"

"No, my lord."

"What is her relationship with Count Stephen?"

"I don't know. I don't see them together often."

"And Balian?"

"Count Balian?"

"Yes."

"Well, she has known him longer, and they seem to be on friendly terms. I really can't say anything else. Oh, we had a dance the other day. Count Baltasar helped with the arrangements. Count Balian was there, as well as Count William, but not Count Stephen. Princess Sibylla enjoyed herself." He probably knew all about that already, but at least he might get the impression that I was trying.

"William? Interesting. We will talk in a few days." He turned to go and then glanced back at me. "Oh, before I forget, Count Stephen has spoken highly of your brother. That's fortunate." With that, he left, striding ahead of me toward the great hall.

I definitely did not need that reminder. Sighing, I followed him. Today there was a public hearing presided over by King Amalric, and I was supposed to play the lute in the background, near the ladies of the court.

As I entered, two older men stood in an alcove, so absorbed in their conversation that they didn't notice me. I recognized William of Tyre. Sibylla had told me that he was writing a history of the kingdom. Portly and satisfied-looking, he gesticulated while he talked, looking across to where the court ladies sat as he spoke in a low voice. "Her mother should never have been queen of so exalted a city as Jerusalem."

"Queen Agnes need hardly concern us any longer," said the other man impatiently.

"To be sure, but her daughter is not promising to be an improvement." Count William lowered his voice further.

"I wish the king would reconsider taxing the clergy. It's creating bad blood at court."

Count William chuckled. "Well, he has to replenish his coffers somehow. It's not as if Constantinople is forthcoming with funds or help, never mind how often the king asks."

"Did you hear that Count Stephen has suggested that the king institute a general tax levy?"

I shrank back against the wall, pretending to be struggling with the straps on my sandals.

"Well, that's sure to ruffle quite a few feathers."

"Hah! More feathers will be ruffled when he presides over this court hearing."

"And we have to listen to this court hearing because...?"

"Well, I suppose the king is using it as a setting to introduce Count Stephen as his successor."

I had to move on. Turning my head, I passed by as if not even aware that there were people inside the alcove. I wondered whether Stephen realized every move of his was under scrutiny.

"Sit here," Sibylla said as I approached. She pointed at a stool next to her, bent toward me, and whispered into my ear. "Today will be interesting. Count Stephen is supposed to decide in a dispute among three heirs who've been arguing for the better part of a year." She was more formally dressed than usual, her robes golden damask on a dark red background, her hair swept up and pinned underneath her wimple, making her look older than her years.

To my surprise I saw Isabella sitting stiffly on a stool next to Dame Alice, her governess. Wearing a heavy robe of blue velvet with golden trim, the little girl looked like a miniature woman. She tried to get off the stool when she saw me, but Dame Alice held on to her firmly.

Sibylla noticed my surprise. Her lips quivered as if about to burst out laughing. Out of the corner of her mouth, she muttered, "My father wanted us to attend today—I suppose he thinks it's never too early for us to learn about our future duties."

King Amalric sat on the dais flanked by several knights. Stephen stood next to him, calm and attentive. The king looked the part: tall, with a slightly crooked nose, and a full beard, although his blond hair had begun to recede from his forehead. His florid complexion made me think he must spend a great deal of time outdoors, but he was corpulent, his pudgy arms resting comfortably on a bulging paunch. Evidently, he hadn't been affected by the kingdom's food shortages in recent years.

I passed the king a few times in the hallway, and he smiled at me every time. Once he even chuckled and tried to pat my back, but my experience on the road had taught me how to sidestep this sort of thing—shifting away as I searched for something in my scrip, or stumbling, or suddenly remembering I forgotten something and rushing away. In this, he seemed no different from the young knights on their way to Jerusalem.

Stephen whispered something, and the king laughed so hard his shoulders and belly shook.

At that moment three women swept into the hall. I grinned—they seemed like characters out of a tale, one tall and gaunt, one medium-sized and handsome, one short and pudgy. All three had flaming red hair, and they all looked disgruntled. They stopped in front of the dais and each of them went into a deep curtsy.

One of the courtiers stepped up next to them. "My lord, the Ladies de Milly—Lady Stephanie, Lady Agnes, and Lady Sibille."

I had to suppress the urge to giggle, wondering whether this Sibille, dressed in a rich, stiff brocade that did nothing to distract from her short neck and her pug-nosed, pasty face, minded having a name that sounded just like that of the young princess.

"We welcome you to our court." King Amalric inclined his head in greeting and waved courteously, permitting the three to rise. "We have considered your dispute, and have decided to hand your case to Count Stephen as an impartial outside advisor. Count Stephen has my complete confidence, and he is fully competent to speak on this matter. I assure you that whatever Count Stephen decrees will be right and just." He spoke haltingly, as if struggling to get the words out. But his ponderous speech made him appear stately in a manner befitting a king.

Stephen stood next to the king. "King Amalric, members of the court, ladies de Milly, it is an honor to be asked to speak on this matter." His deep voice carried well. Without raising it, he carefully pitched it so it reached into the far corners of the hall.

"Mistress Alina." A small hand tugged on my sleeve. "When will you start playing?" Isabella's voice was loud enough to be heard by others in the hall.

"Hush." Distracted, I shook my arm. "Let me listen," I snapped at her without thinking.

The little girl started to wail, and I flushed with embarrassment. This was hardly the right way to speak to a princess.

The king glanced in our direction, looking irritated. Then, to my relief, Dame Alice picked up her charge, whispered in her ear, and sat down again, holding onto the plump body.

Sibylla smirked. Out of the corner of her mouth she muttered, "So, when are you going to play? Isn't that why you're here?"

Frustrated, I shook my head, trying to keep my eye on what was happening. It hardly made sense to have me play the lute in a proceeding like this. I craned my neck past Dame Alice's shoulders to watch Stephen.

He looked around calmly until quiet returned—like a performer, he knew when to wait and when to resume. "My Ladies de Milly, let me begin by expressing my condolences to you upon the death of your father in 1165, and your only brother, who sadly died just a few years after his father. Those are grievous losses to bear. It is understandable that you have struggled to come to terms with their deaths and to settle your father's affairs at the same time.

"I have reviewed your respective claims to the property left by your father, Lord Henry de Milly, also known to us as Henry the Buffalo. Now if your brother had lived, you would not be standing here in front of us today. But

alas, Baudouin died and left no male issue." Stephen looked at the three ladies kindly and with a trace of regret. "However, you have most properly concluded that, for the health of the kingdom if not your own peace of mind, this
matter cannot be left unresolved for too long, and have accordingly brought
it before us."

It seemed an elegant way to summarize what had apparently been years
of acrimonious bickering among the three sisters. I couldn't see their faces,
but their rigid postures showed that they were listening anxiously to Stephen's exposition.

"Now it appears to me that three considerations affect this matter." He
paused, his expression grave, impartial, and courteous.

I glanced around the court. The hall was quiet, no one was chatting. All
eyes were on this man who might well be the future king.

Stephen straightened imperceptibly and continued, speaking slowly so
no word would be missed. "Three considerations," he repeated. "Namely,
your duty to your father's legacy, your duty to your king and the kingdom
of Jerusalem," he bowed toward the king, "and the question of fairness and
balance of power."

The king inclined his head, his expression hard to read.

"Your duty to your father's legacy dictates that his estates be administered to the best of your capabilities. Your duty to your king and the kingdom
of Jerusalem dictates the proper obeisance and respect in the form of lending
support and aid to your liege as needed. Finally, there is the question of
fairness and a healthy balance of power, which is beneficial to all parties to
this dispute. Hence, having duly considered these various aspects and your
respective claims to your father's estates, we decree the following."

Again Stephen paused.

All eyes were on him. Only Sibylla appeared distracted, playing with the
end of her shawl.

"It is right and proper and fair, not to mention in the best interest of your
father's legacy, that the dispute be settled as soon as possible. In the interest
of a balance of power, it would not be beneficial for one party to have more
control of resources than the other parties. You all have equal claims to the

material property he left behind. Hence, I decree that this property shall be divided into equal parts among you. Meanwhile, to ensure the utmost of possible support to your king and lord, King Amalric, we decree that the two younger sisters submit to the eldest, Lady Stephanie, in all matters bearing on policy and the defense of Christendom." Stephen stopped speaking and bowed once again to the king.

"We approve and concur with this decree. This matter is now settled." The king inclined his head graciously toward the three sisters, who, after a moment of hesitation sank again into deep curtsies.

"Thank you, my lords. We will act on this as instructed." Lady Stephanie spoke quietly, rose, and began to make her way out of the hall, her two sisters following in her wake.

I almost wanted to laugh. The three sisters, all looking equally gloomy as they made their way out of the hall, made me think of my father settling one of our fights when we were small. No one was ever the winner. We were reprimanded in equal measure, and yet ultimately we were once again at peace with each other.

I felt a small nudge and turned around.

"Would you play something for the little one?" Dame Alice smiled at me, a pleading expression in her eyes. "She is getting restless, and I don't want to draw the king's attention to her again."

I nodded, although in truth I would much rather have continued watching Stephen, who stood next to the king and listened attentively while the king spoke. I picked up the lute. Out of the corner of my eye, I saw Stephen walk over to greet the ladies of the court. He graciously bowed, first to the queen, and then to Sibylla. He said something to her in a low voice which made her face pinken, and I had to admit she looked especially beautiful that day.

My hands slipped on the strings, making a brief grating sound. I played, but I could not concentrate.

Isabella began to fuss anyway. Dame Alice admonished her, but it didn't help. With an apologetic glance at me, Dame Alice whispered, "She's tired from all the excitement."

I was relieved when the queen dismissed me. Outside the great hall, I passed two courtiers talking to each other.

"Balance of power, fairness, duty to one's liege," said one in a mocking tone. "My word, he thinks he is the shining light of Christendom."

"He won't last long. Idealists never do."

"He would certainly have to wake up to the political realities if he wants to become king."

Thoughtfully I returned to my room. Clearly, Stephen had enemies here. In my mind I painted a scene where I told him about what I overheard. I imagined how he would look at me gratefully. He might even take my hand. Maybe he would say he didn't want to marry Sibylla.

CHAPTER FIFTEEN

THE TRUE CROSS

"AH, YOU are becoming another Countess de Dia." Sibylla threw her piece of tapestry work on the table and began fiddling with the pieces from a game of checkers.

Surprised, I stopped plucking the strings. I was making up harmonies together with stories for Isabella. The little girl had quieted down, gazing at me intently, her finger in her mouth.

It was the afternoon after the court hearing. Queen Comnena had withdrawn for a rest, and only a few court ladies sat in the back, heads bent over their work.

It didn't seem that there was anything I could, or should, say. Beatriz de Dia was a renowned trobairitz in the south of France. Her social status was higher than mine, and her family was wealthy. I admired her music greatly, even though much of it was written for a flute. I wished I could compose songs that were as memorable.

Of course it was a foolish dream that I might become a trobairitz in my own right. Besides, most likely Milos and I would soon be on our way back home, where we would once again be at the mercy of Uncle Garsanc and Aunt Marci.

Still, it was a remarkably snappish comment, just when I had thought Sibylla and I were on the way to becoming friends.

Sibylla's face had a greenish tinge, and she looked agitated. I put down my lute. "What is it, Sibylla?"

With tense motions, she began to stack checker pieces on top of each other. Isabella, meanwhile, had become bored and wandered off in search of Dame Alice.

"What is it?" I asked again.

Sibylla glanced around nervously.

"Look, there's no one around to hear you."

She shook her head and bit her lip. After a moment, she spoke in a low voice, "I did something I shouldn't have done, and now I don't know what to do."

"What?"

"The True Cross has disappeared."

"What's that?"

Sibylla raised her carefully tinted eyebrows. "You haven't heard about the True Cross?"

I shook my head.

"It's the most valuable thing in the king's treasury." She frowned at me. "I can't believe you don't know about it. It's a silver cross with slivers of wood from Christ's cross embedded in it."

"And?"

"Can't you see how important that is? It's gone. And it's my fault. I told someone about the secret entrance to the treasury, and I think that person told someone else, who took the True Cross."

"Whom did you tell? And why?"

Sibylla made a face, as if she had bitten into a rotten apple. "I can't tell you. But I wish I hadn't."

Actually I had an idea whom she had told. There couldn't be that many people around who knew secrets and bullied others into revealing theirs. "How do you know it's gone? Maybe it just fell behind some scrolls or something."

"Cousin Raymond told me. He found out yesterday, and he is livid. He somehow thinks that I had something to do with it. He knows my father introduced me to some of the royal secrets when I attained my majority." She knocked over the pile of checkers and started over.

So that's why Count Raymond had been so distracted yesterday. "But who would steal something like that?"

"How should I know?"

Perhaps Beryl herself had taken the True Cross. Then I froze. I remembered the mysterious person with the covered face in the citadel at night. My heart thumped in my chest. Milos. *Please, please, don't let me find out that he took it.* I needed to talk to him as soon as I could. Sibylla had to deal with her own problems. But I shouldn't rush off right away. It would look odd.

Fortunately, one of the court ladies came over and asked Sibylla to participate in a game with the others. She complied, politely and with complete composure. Once again, I was amazed at her ability to disguise her feelings so easily. But as she walked off, she glanced back at me over her shoulder with a pleading expression on her face. I shook my head, trying to convey with my eyes that I wouldn't tell anybody. Finally I could make my exit, and it was a struggle to keep from running.

Once outside the great hall, I rushed toward the courtyard. As I turned the corner, I ran into a man walking in the other direction. I stumbled. "Oh, I am sorry."

"Watch where you're going," the man growled. It was Ralph, Count Raymond's squire. He looked angry. "Oh, it's you, Mistress Alina." He gave me an exaggerated bow. "You think you're so high and mighty at court. Well, you better watch your brother. He's sticking his nose into things that are none of his business—not to mention making eyes at every girl in sight."

I stared at him, taken aback by his hostility. Fortunately, he didn't expect a response and stomped off. Still shaken by this encounter, I walked into the courtyard and headed toward the stable, hoping to find Milos there.

At the entrance to the stable, I stopped in my tracks, studying the curious scene in front of me. Milos sat on the ground with a saddle between his legs and moved a brush back and forth over its leather fittings. Next to him was

Beryl. She perched on a pile of hay and waved a long stalk at his head, trying to tickle him.

"Milos, do you have a moment to talk?" I asked uncertainly.

Beryl got up and shook the hay off her gown. "I'm leaving anyway. He's all yours." She left before I could say anything to her.

"What did she want?" I asked, my voice sharper than I intended. "You realize how dangerous she is, don't you? She peddles secrets to the highest bidder."

Milos shook his head. "Oh, Alina, let me be. You aren't my mother."

"Well, just be careful." I was exasperated. I wanted to say more, but his quip had stung, and perhaps this was not a good moment to bring up my worries about Sibylla. "So where were you the past few days?" I asked, trying to change tack.

"Do I ask you when you go to visit your new friends? You don't tell me anything about that, either."

I glared at him. "Well, you aren't my father."

Milos glared back. Then we both started to laugh.

"Do you remember pushing me into the pond?"

"Well, you deserved it—putting the poor rooster in my blanket chest." I sat down on the pile of hay.

Milos chuckled.

Then I remembered why I wanted to talk to him. But how does one ask something like that? *So Milos, did you creep around at night, wearing a mask, and steal the True Cross?* I couldn't bring myself to do this. "Milos, please be careful. There are so many eyes watching whatever you do around here. Count Raymond's squire just ran into me outside, and he sounded very nasty. He said you're sticking your nose into too many things."

"Oh, Ralph," Milos scoffed. "He hates everybody. You know what they call him? Count Raymond's camel! He sort of looks like one too, with his broad, flat nose and his habit of spitting."

I burst out laughing. "Milos!"

Milos smiled at me affectionately. "This is a strange place, isn't it? You are right. It feels like everyone is watching and fighting everyone else while all are waiting for something to happen."

"Oh, something will definitely happen. I just don't know what." I grinned at Milos.

At that same moment, feeling my lips stretched in amusement, I thought of my sister. She used to tease Milos mercilessly, and had grinned just like that. When I looked at my hands and the shape of my fingers, I saw Maria's hands, as clearly as if she was sitting next to me.

In his final days, my father had occasionally called me Maria—we had become blurred in his mind. Sometimes the memory of her warmed me. Mostly, though, it was as if I was condemned to keep walking around and around a gaping hole that couldn't be filled. I would never be able to touch her or to hear her laughter or to see her dance again.

Milos was silent. He appeared to have picked up the sense of a shadow. Then he raised his head, his expression grim. It occurred to me that he looked much older than even a few months ago.

"Stephen thinks Saladin is going to be the biggest threat to the kingdom ever. He's worried about all the infighting between Edessa, Tripoli, and Jerusalem, and he also has been trying to find out what happened to the funds he brought to King Amalric from King Henri. Did you know that Shawar, the former vizier of Egypt, had been an ally of King Amalric?"

I shook my head. I had never heard of this Shawar.

Milos didn't wait for my response. His face intense and focused, he went on. "Now King Amalric is short of funds, and Emperor Manuel keeps promising to send more help, but it's never enough. Stephen thinks the king should institute a general levy to raise the funds he needs to defend Jerusalem, but the nobles and people like Count Raymond are totally opposed to this idea."

I had no idea that Milos was interested in this sort of thing. I also was getting irritated by this constant "Stephen thinks." I got up. "It sounds all rather complicated. Listen, watch your back. You don't need people like Beryl spreading rumors about you."

"I know what I'm doing. You watch your own back," Milos snapped.

I stalked off, frustrated and angry all over again.

The next day, I went down to visit Sarah and Meir. When I arrived at the little house, Sarah was alone with the baby. She smiled at me. "Ah, Alina, we were wondering how you have been doing. Meir is out talking to someone about our journey, but he will be back soon."

"I brought you a wrap for the baby."

Sarah spread out the white blanket-like shawl, her fingers running gently over the soft threads. "This is lovely. It will be wonderful for Alon when he gets chilly on the journey. Thank you."

"You're leaving soon?" I asked, trying not to sound too upset about it.

"Perhaps in a few weeks, once Meir has been able to make all the arrangements. Watch the baby for a moment. I will make tea for us."

I held Alon on my lap, hugging his firm, round body, and breathing in his sweet, milky smell. He grabbed the top of my gown and gave me a gummy smile. I wished I could go with them.

"Why are you going to Bohemia rather than back to Spain?" I asked when Sarah returned.

"Meir received an invitation from the local rabbi to help build a school in Prague. There has been a Jewish community there for some time, but they have had their troubles. Now things look more promising since Duke Soběslav has granted Jewish residents more rights and privileges. Meir wants to go to support the community there."

"You are brave." I tried to imagine the uncertainty they had to live with at all times.

"Well, you aren't exactly timid yourself." Sarah grinned at me. "You didn't hesitate to go on a long journey to a foreign land."

I shook my head. "I just couldn't face the idea of staying with my aunt, not to mention having her marry me off to some old man."

"Maybe you have to be more patient with your aunt. She might eventually suggest a good husband for you," she said before disappearing into their kitchen.

I bit my lips, tempted to retort sharply. But I was unfair. Sarah and Meir were introduced by a marriage broker, and it had worked out. Then again, she hadn't met any of the prospective bridegrooms Aunt Marci picked out for me.

"Sarah, I am back." Meir walked through the door just as Sarah brought in a tray with beakers of tea.

"I just told Alina about our plans." Smiling at him in her discreet fashion, she handed him a beaker and turned her attention back to me. "What is troubling you, Alina?"

"I'm worried about Milos. He is being stupid about something, and there's nothing I can do to protect him."

"I don't suppose there's all that much you can do to protect him in any event. He's not a baby," Sarah said. "But what is he doing that worries you so?"

"I have seen him with Sibylla. He brings her presents. He's just a squire, and he could get in trouble for that. And there's a servant girl, Beryl, who keeps following him around. I think she's dangerous. She as much as told me that people pay her for information. What if she tells someone about his friendship with Sibylla?"

"Ah, the old problem of being one's brother's keeper," Meir said thoughtfully. "As I see it, you're doing the best you can. Can you protect him always? I doubt it. Certainly you can't protect him from the consequences of his own actions. He must be responsible for himself. Don't be too hard on yourself."

"I'm not even sure he's done anything wrong yet." I couldn't bring myself to tell them about my fear that Milos might have something to do with the disappearance of the True Cross. I shook my head. "I'm just afraid."

"Well, then you have to watch and wait. And maybe you could try trusting him."

All the way back to the citadel, I thought about what Meir said. It was true. I hadn't trusted Milos since our father died.

Glad to be free for the rest of the evening, I strolled through the arcade toward the stables, yawning. I could hear the horses in their stalls munch their feed, a comforting sound that reminded me of home.

Then the muffled sound of voices made me slow down. I saw a couple standing close together at the entrance to the stables. It was Ralph, holding on to the arm of the woman next to him. I couldn't see her because she stood in the dark entrance to the stables. He was talking to her in a low, intense murmur.

She struggled and pulled herself free of his grasp. "Take your hands off me." The woman laughed, but there was a brittle quality to it, part satisfaction and part fear.

I recognized that voice. It was Beryl's. I coughed. I didn't want them to feel I was sneaking up on them.

"You'll regret this." Ralph turned away and stalked off. His eyes swept over me as he passed, his scowling features making me uncomfortable.

"Ah, Mistress Alina, I thought that was you lurking in the shadows. I hope you enjoyed yourself." Beryl moved away from the stable door, brushing off her gown and tucking stray locks back under her headscarf. She looked outwardly composed, but she watched me with the intensity of a bird of prey.

I wanted to strike back, she had put me on edge and made me feel unsure so often. Now it was my turn. "Well, it wasn't all that interesting—of course I wonder what Count Raymond would say if he knew you were meeting his squire in the stables." I had no intention of going around telling tales about anyone, but I couldn't resist pretending I would. "It might be tough on your little girl if you were sent away."

Beryl's face tightened. "What if I told you something that nobody else knows? Would you then keep this to yourself?"

I stared at her, amazed that she really took my threat seriously. I almost burst out laughing, but then curiosity got the better of me. "What would that be?"

"Promise you won't tell anyone about tonight."

I was tempted to prolong her misery. "It would depend on what you tell me, wouldn't it?"

"What if I told you that the princess has a way to get in and out of the citadel unseen?"

"Sure, I promise. I won't say anything. But how do you know this?"

"I followed her."

"You must be worn out with all your following other people around," I said snidely. "And exactly how does she get out?"

"I had been watching her. You never know when you might pick up something useful." Beryl almost preened herself. "One morning I happened to see her make her way down a passage that leads just to a small chapel at the very end. You can reach it from that hallway above the arcade." Beryl pointed toward the northwestern part of the citadel. "She didn't come back for a long time, and I had to go back to work. But then I saw her come back from that same direction on another morning, her gown and her sandals dusty. That got me thinking. So the next time there was no one around to see me, I went exploring. It took a while, but I found it."

"Well, what did you find?" I asked impatiently, feeling a little sickened that Beryl would assume I traded in the same coin as she did. And yet, I was hardly blameless. I had done just as much sneaking around as she had, and I was curious how far she had gotten with her exploration.

"In that chapel there's a secret door behind the tapestry. It leads to a tunnel that comes out on the other side of the western wall. I tried it out, and it's a bit gloomy and damp in there, but it's not too long a walk. The other branch of the tunnel on the right of this chamber leads to a gate on the eastern side of the city."

I was fed up. "Oh, that. I know all about that," I snapped. "You're not the only one who has eyes around here. You better watch out your snooping doesn't get you into trouble."

"But you won't tell anyone about me, will you?" Beryl looked confused, and her voice had a pleading note.

"No," I snapped. "I don't do that sort of thing." I stomped off, disgusted with myself.

I had just been mean and petty. I had no right to act superior to Beryl. Maybe, if I had a little girl to take care of, I would be doing exactly what she did.

I put Beryl out of my mind. I had enough to worry about.

The next morning, I woke up early as had become my habit, wrapped a scarf around my shoulders, and went downstairs. I craved those moments alone, away from the prying eyes everywhere at court and from all the gossip. Pigeons swooped in and out of the arches, their shadows playing on the stone flags in the sunlight. Enjoying the mild day, I walked along the arcade, humming. I had begun to experiment with different combinations of chords, and a whole world opened up. When I played the lute and sang, I forgot about my worries.

A man's voice mixed with that of a woman chuckling in a low tone reached me. Distracted, I glanced around...it appeared to come from inside.

Then a scream bounced off the stone pillars, followed by a dull thump. Without thinking, I rushed toward the steps leading up to the second level of the arcade.

A girl lay on the flagstones, her arms flung wide in a helpless sprawl. Bright droplets shimmered on the floor like vermillion beads, splattered in all directions, and a red pool spread from underneath her head. Benumbed, I thought of pomegranate juice. My fingers twitched as if to rub off the stickiness.

It was Beryl. I tried to move, opening my mouth to shout for help, but I couldn't. My lips were frozen. Even my breath seemed locked inside my chest. She must have fallen from the arcade above.

I glanced up—and stared in disbelief at the white face of my brother.

CHAPTER SIXTEEN

KING SOLOMON'S QUARRY

"MILOS," I whispered.

His eyes bulged, and he gripped the balustrade, as if afraid of falling.

Racing up the staircase, I stumbled in my sandals and stubbed my toes on a stone step. I was almost grateful for the sharp pain as I limped toward him.

Out of the corner of my eye, I saw a shimmer of gray and rose sweep around the corner at the end of the hallway, and thought I heard footfalls behind the columns, but I had no time to think about that.

"What have you done?" I panted.

Milos shook his head. "Done? I didn't..." he stammered. He was still holding on to the balustrade, his hands clenched so hard that they were white. "She is dead, right?"

"Do you doubt that? Did you push her?"

"I pushed her...?" He stared at me. "You think I did this?"

"How would I know?" In my fright, I spoke harshly.

"I didn't." Milos began to tremble. "I heard voices when I came up the steps. I was looking for...for"—pointing downward helplessly, he swallowed convulsively. "Then there was this awful scream." He stretched out his hands, as if to grab Beryl at the last moment.

"I didn't do this," he repeated, sounding bewildered and lost. He glanced down into the courtyard and quickly turned his eyes away. "We have to tell someone." His voice was shaking.

"What would we say? Wouldn't they think you did this?" If Milos were found here, he would be accused and condemned, with no chance to defend himself. Nobody would believe me—just a girl, and his sister, with nobody to support me.

Milos shook his head. Then his eyes widened. "Oh no, I forgot!" All of a sudden his face was flushed. "People saw us argue yesterday. What am I going to do?"

I heard steps in the outer courtyard.

I had to get him away. It was all I could think of.

I had an idea. "Come with me." I grabbed his hand and pulled him along while he stumbled obediently in my wake.

We fled down the long hallway, then around the corner, along another passage, and into the little chamber.

"I never saw this chapel before," Milos muttered behind me.

The gently flickering oil lamp threw just enough light for us to make out the alcove with its stone altar and the prayer stool in front. I bowed my head, momentarily comforted by the cross, and was tempted to kneel on the stool and pray for Beryl's soul.

But someone might come at any moment.

I shoved aside the tapestry. The latch was heavy, but I managed to lift it and push the door open. A slight, damp draft of air breathed out from the dark space.

I pulled Milos along behind me, making sure the tapestry covered the opening. Then I stopped. "Wait." Quickly I turned back and grabbed a torch from its wall fastening and lit it on the flame of the oil lamp. Back inside, I held it high in front of me and set out with Milos following in my footsteps. Beryl had said that the tunnel led to the western wall, which meant it went across town to the Temple Mount, and from there to outside the city.

"Where does this go?" Milos's voice echoed off the walls.

"I think the tunnel is part of the quarries of King Solomon." I had heard the court historian William of Tyre talk about these quarries with another knight. The light flickered, and I tried to hold the torch more steadily as I walked ahead of Milos. "Ouch. Watch where you're going."

"Oh, sorry." He had stepped on my heel. "How do you know about this?"

"The quarries?"

"The tunnel," Milos snapped.

"So she didn't show you?" I was exasperated with him. "Sibylla uses this when she wants to leave the citadel without anyone knowing."

Milos was silent except for his breathing as we plodded along the rubble-strewn path. Water dripped from the walls, and the light of the torch made our shadows appear huge along the curved ceiling.

Partly to cover my own fear, and because I could never resist thinking of words to fit the occasion, I began to intone the lines of the 23 Psalm.

Yea, though I walk through the valley of the shadow of death, I will fear no evil: for thou art with me; thy rod and thy staff they comfort me.

"Stop that," Milos grumbled. "You're just like Father, always quoting something. I wish I had a real staff right now."

"Well, a little prayer can't hurt," I said lightly. In fact, I found comfort in the familiar words.

Finally we reached a large chamber. It was littered with piles of discarded rocks, and the torch's flickering light showed gaping hollows along the back, caverns leading deeper into the quarry. Water dripped from the ceiling, and had carved out a little basin, filling it to overflowing. Beryl told me another branch of the tunnel on the right of this chamber led to a gate just outside the eastern walls of the city. Hopefully I had picked the right one. My hand cramped, and I changed my grip on the torch. After a few paces, I saw an opening in the rock wall. "That must be the passage out."

This passage was much narrower than the other one, and I hit my elbow on a rock and stumbled. Milos ran into to me from the back, almost knocking me over. There were a few stairs, and after that the tunnel continued to lead downward.

It had just begun to level off when a gust of air blew out my torch.

"Alina?" His voice shook.

"Here, hold on to my gown." I reached for him in the dark. "I need my hands free." Feeling my way by running a hand along the wall, I continued until finally I saw a sliver of light ahead. A few more steps and my outstretched hand touched wood. I could see daylight through a crack. I put down the torch and fumbled on the surface until I found the latch. Again, it was well oiled and easy to lift. The door made hardly any noise when I pulled it open.

The fresh air and light streaming in were a relief.

"Wait," I whispered and stuck my head out. Boulders were artfully piled up to disguise the door, with just a narrow cleft on the side where we could slip through.

It seemed an age had gone by since I first saw Beryl lying dead on the stone flags, but it was still early morning, and there was nobody on the foot-path below the wall.

We had come out somewhere beyond the western wall of the city and had to make our way around to the settlement below Tanner's Gate where Meir lived. I took my shoulder wrap and draped it over my head since I had rushed out without a cap.

"Where are you taking me?"

"To Meir."

"Wait, who's that?" Milos tugged on my sleeve, forcing me to stop.

"He's a friend. Come on, we have to hurry."

"But what can he do?" Milos asked. "If I'm a suspect, they'll look for me. Anyone hiding me would be in trouble."

"Oh." I stared at him. "I hadn't thought of that."

Milos made a scoffing noise. "You don't think, do you?"

"You're a fine one to talk," I snapped. "At least I got you out."

We glared at each other. Milos's hair was standing up, frizzed by the hu-midity in the quarry. I touched my hair to find it, too, was tangled and damp. For some reason, this calmed me down. "We're squabbling the way we did as kids back at home. Look, there's no time for this. You have to get out of sight, and I need to get back."

"But where?" Milos asked, sounding scared again.

"I'm not sure." I chewed my lip. "Perhaps you could go to Mount Zion."

"I don't know," Milos said doubtfully. "Where could I hide there?"

I tried to picture Milos scrambling around on top of Mount Zion. No, it was too exposed and too close to the wall. I shook my head in frustration. "Then, how about the Spring of Gihon? You could pretend to be one of many going to drink water directly from the spring."

"And then?"

"You could hide in the tunnel at night. I think you'll be safe there for a while. I'll come as soon as I can and bring food. At least you'll have water."

Milos stood still, looking at me helplessly. "But what am I going to *do*?"

"How should I know?" I snapped, frustrated and frightened at the same time. "Look, we have to move before someone sees us here, and I need to get back."

Milos's face was ashen, covered with white streaks like salt tracks and making me think of an old marble head that had stood outside in the rain for too many centuries. He looked so lost and uncertain that it made me want to cry.

"I'll figure something out." I wrapped my arms around him. "Maybe they already found whoever did this. Maybe they're not even looking for you. Just wait for me. I'll come later today and bring you some food."

He nodded and began to make his way down the trail. In the sunlight, he seemed shrunken. It was as if all his newfound confidence, gained while working for Stephen, had leaked out of his lanky frame, making him appear disjointed, hunched, and frail. For a moment I watched him pick his way along the stony path.

Then I heard voices in the distance. The clip-clop of a donkey was coming closer. I needed to get back into the tunnel before anyone saw me, so I turned quickly and slipped into the hidden entrance.

It was dark inside, and I groped along the ground for the torch until I realized that I had no way to relight it.

The sound of dripping made me shiver in the dark, damp space, and I hesitated, running my hands along the wall.

This was impossible. I couldn't face going back up the tunnel without a light.

I turned around and ducked out of the opening again. The donkey cart had just passed by, Milos was gone, and I had no choice but to run around to Tanner's Gate, even if it meant walking all the way through the market streets back to the citadel.

Maybe that was just as well, I thought as I stumbled along the path, wincing when pebbles got stuck in my sandals. At least this way nobody could catch me coming out of the secret passage. I was out of breath and bathed in sweat by the time I reached the gate.

CHAPTER SEVENTEEN

IN HIDING

I BRUSHED the tunnel dust off my skirt and sleeves and tucked my hair back under my headscarf before I walked through the gate of the citadel.

It was quiet in the courtyard, and I slowed down when I entered the arcade. I felt as if I was dragging my feet through a swamp.

In my fear for Milos and my overriding wish to get him away, I had forgotten that a young woman had just died—someone I knew. Her body had been right there on the flagstones, but it was gone now. I averted my eyes, trying not to stare at the area where her blood had been splattered.

Hoping I could get to my room unnoticed, I went toward the hallway that led there, because I badly needed a few moments to think.

Two servants stood close together. They glanced at me briefly, dismissing me, and resumed their conversation in low tones.

"So who did this?"

"Nobody knows. Gustave thinks it was a retainer of Count Stephen."

I walked at a snail's pace, hoping I would hear more before they became aware of my interest. I didn't know this Gustave, but I hated him for suggesting something that could lead people to my brother.

"Of course, it could have been anybody."

"True. There were plenty of people who had it in for her," the young one said with a sneer.

I reached my room without anyone noticing me.

Once I closed the door, I sat down on my pallet, my head spinning.

I needed to get Milos some food and water. More importantly, I had to find a way to get him away from Jerusalem. Since Stephen's name was bandied about already, it would be a matter of moments before someone thought of Milos and the fact that he had spent time with Beryl.

Hopefully, no one had noticed how often he talked to Sibylla—he hardly needed to get in trouble for that on top of everything else.

Then I wondered why someone would connect Stephen to this deed. The idea that someone would smear Stephen by suggesting his name made me ill. Of course, then he wouldn't be able to marry Sibylla. That had to be the only good thing that might come out of this.

I needed to slow down my thoughts, so I took several deep breaths, as I did whenever I was getting ready to play music. To my surprise, it steadied me. Maybe I could figure out who did this.

How foolish of me. I hadn't really seen anything. I thought back to this morning—it was all a blur in my mind. I heard voices before the scream, and when I raced up the staircase, there was Milos. I also heard the scuff of feet behind the columns, but had forgotten them in my shock and worry for Milos.

But wait. There had been something else. Now I remembered. When I reached the top, out of the corner of my eye, I saw something dusty pink float down the hallway to the left, and I knew only one person who wore a robe with those colors. Sibylla.

That was it. Sibylla had pushed Beryl to her death. Beryl must have seen Sibylla doing something she shouldn't have and tried to threaten her, and Sibylla decided to act. It fit.

My head ached.

I would have to go downstairs soon, before anybody remarked on my absence, and I could hardly go to Count Raymond and accuse Sibylla. I would have to explain what I was doing there at the time, and it might end up giving Milos away. No, that was not an option. I would have to go to the hall and play the lute and pretend nothing was wrong while I worked out a plan to get Milos away.

Quickly I brushed my hair and washed my hands and my face. I picked up the lute and went to the great hall.

Sibylla saw me when I came in. She looked pale and tense, her hands clenched in her lap. "Where have you been this morning?"

"I wasn't feeling well and went for a walk." I thought it was better to admit that I had been outside just in case someone saw me.

"Something has happened." Sibylla's voice trembled. "You know Beryl?"

I nodded, keeping my eyes on the lute and fiddling with the strings.

"She's dead."

"What happened?"

"She fell off the balustrade above the inner courtyard."

I stared at her, at a loss for words, and surprised by her air of innocence. She looked shocked.

"You wouldn't believe the rumors going around. Count Raymond has sent people out to make inquiries."

"Is he looking for anybody in particular?" I asked, trying to appear relaxed and unconcerned.

"He made me come and talk to him. I despise that man. He asked me all sorts of questions, as if he thought I would stoop to doing something like that."

I was stunned by her tone of outrage. I looked down. She was so convincing that it made me angry.

Sibylla seemed to have regained some of her composure. "One of the rumors is that Count Stephen was seen in a compromising situation by Beryl and had one of his retainers kill her. Count Raymond told me that they're looking for anyone who might have been there at the time. He believes it's all linked to the disappearance of the True Cross." Sibylla studied me with a calculating expression. "He even wondered where you were."

"I told you, I went for a walk."

"Don't sound so defensive. Why should Count Raymond care about you? It's not as if you would have any reason to push Beryl over the balustrade. He also mentioned your brother and asked me whether I had seen him."

"And did you?" I tried not to react, struggling to keep my face blank and pretending not to care one way or another.

"That's silly. Why would I? I'm not in the habit of chatting up low-ranking retainers."

I almost laughed at that. Many people had to have seen her with Milos over the past weeks. I avoided meeting Sibylla's eyes.

"Anyway, it's ridiculous that Count Raymond is trying to pin this on Count Stephen—the last person likely to be caught in a compromising position. Besides, if that had happened, Count Stephen would have taken care of it himself; he wouldn't have involved anyone else. Of course he was away all day on one of his excursions into the countryside. You'd think the man was writing a book, he's so busy collecting information about the kingdom."

It was odd that she was so talkative, but I had to admit that her comments about Stephen had the ring of truth. She genuinely seemed to believe that Stephen would not have done something like this.

Fortunately Isabella came up to me just then and demanded that I play for her. I was so grateful to the chubby little girl for providing a distraction, I could have hugged her.

Sibylla watched us with a strange expression. If I hadn't known better, I would have sworn she was afraid. But that could not be. She was much too arrogant and secure in her position to believe that anyone would seriously accuse her of something like this.

After a while I claimed I was still feeling ill and asked for some time off. Sibylla nodded distractedly.

I went to the market and bought some fruit, bread, and dried dates, wrapping everything into a piece of cloth and stuffing it into my scrip. Milos would have to make do with this for a while. When I turned around, I almost flattened my nose against Count Baltasar's doublet. "Oh, I beg your pardon."

I was irritated that I had not heard him come up behind me.

"Mistress Alina, are you enjoying the market?" He smiled at me and waved at the baskets filled with fruits and dates.

"Yes, very much." I thought of how I could explain my purchase. "It's nice to have something in my room so I don't always have to go to the kitchen if I'm hungry."

He laughed. "I'm partial to a bottle of wine and nuts myself." He bowed and walked off.

How silly of me to overreact. A knight like Count Baltasar would hardly care if I bought some dates at the market. Still, I decided to linger there until I was sure he was gone. It would not do to have him notice where I went.

The spring was east of the temple in the Kidron Valley, so I decided to go out by using Tanner's Gate, which was closest to the market.

Fortunately I had been at the spring once before when several ladies of the court decided to visit it and asked me to accompany them.

Several tunnels and shafts led from the spring to the Pool of Siloam where water for the city was collected, and there was a remnant of a tower near the spring. Apparently the spring had been better protected at one point in time. Luckily the tower was abandoned now, so Milos wouldn't have much trouble staying out of sight.

By the time I reached the stone structure with the staircase leading down to the spring it was late afternoon, and there was nobody nearby when I approached. I waited for a while, glancing around to make sure that I was alone. Then I began to call out softly.

"Milos, it's me. Where are you?"

Silence.

I approached the stone steps and peered down. "Milos?"

There was a rustling sound, and then Milos emerged from behind a rock wall on the bottom of the steps. His face was turned toward me, pale and strained. He rubbed his arms as if he was cold. "I thought you'd never come." Stumbling a few times, he made his way up the stone steps and sat down on the ledge at the top.

I sat down next to him, shocked by how spent he appeared. "This is all I have for now." I handed him the bread, two oranges, and the dates. "Sorry, it's not a lot."

"Thank you."

I thought he would be ravenous, but he just held on to the little bundle. "What happened at the Citadel?"

Quickly I told him what I knew. "I definitely think you need to stay out of sight for now. The rumor about Stephen might be all Count Raymond needs to embarrass Stephen, but I am sure he would be thrilled if he could catch you—he could punish you as one of Stephen's retainers, which would shame Stephen, and there wouldn't be anything he could do to help."

"But I can't stay here forever."

"I thought I would go to Stephen and tell him what happened. He might have an idea for how to get you away safely. At the very least, I could warn him about all these rumors."

"No, please don't do that. I don't want him to think badly of me."

"Why should he? Milos, what did you do?" My stomach hurt. Maybe he had taken the True Cross, and Beryl had threatened to expose him.

"I didn't do anything. Please believe me."

"I don't know what to believe anymore."

"It's true that I was there, but only at the last moment. I had come up to talk to Beryl. I did flirt with her for a while, but yesterday we had a terrible argument when I told her I hadn't meant anything serious. She was furious. So this morning, I decided to talk to her again to see if I could make her understand. I've been such a fool."

I thought of what Meir had said. *"Maybe you could try trusting him."* I badly wanted to believe my brother. "Better a fool than dead or locked up in a cell." Then I was distracted by another thought. "Milos, did you see Sibylla up there?"

Milos stared at me. "Sibylla? You can't possibly think she had anything to do with this."

"I don't know what to think," I said slowly.

"I don't want you to tell Stephen about this."

"Now you really are being a fool. Stephen could help you."

"I don't want him to think badly of me. Please? Promise?"

"Fine. I won't say anything to him—for now. But Milos, something else happened. The True Cross has disappeared." I watched him carefully.

His face looked blank. "The True Cross? What's that?"

I explained, inwardly breathing a sigh of relief. If Milos really didn't know what it was, he couldn't be the one who took it. "Someone stole it. Sibylla told me."

"Someone stole it?" Milos asked, sounding puzzled. Then he sat up straight, glaring at me. "You didn't think I took it, did you?"

"What was I supposed to think?" I blurted. "I saw you take the silver balls. You've no idea how much trouble that caused."

"What do you think I am?" Milos looked furious. "I admit I thought about it. I was tempted. It was so easy—I even had them in my pocket. They would have been perfect for juggling. But I changed my mind and put them back. The merchant never knew any different, what with all that commotion about the complaining woman and her silly pearls." He ran his fingers through his hair, making it stand up. "And what do you mean? What kind of trouble?"

"Well, I saw you, and so did Count Raymond." I went on to tell him about the arrangement with Count Raymond and his threats.

"Oh."

"Oh, indeed." Actually, I was relieved to have everything out in the open. Maybe now we could figure out a way to get out of this predicament together.

"You know, Stephen warned me about Raymond. I just didn't understand." Milos shook his head. "What a horrible, manipulative man. Maybe this cross was just mislaid. There must be piles and piles of dusty, musty stuff in that treasury. Maybe Count Raymond knocked Ralph over the head with it and forgot to put it back. Maybe he took it himself to raise funds and is now coming down on others, all high and mighty, so he won't have to admit anything."

I almost started laughing. This was the irreverent Milos I remembered. Then I sobered up as I remembered the reality of the situation. "Milos, I need to get back. Let me think. We'll get through this."

"But what am I going to do? I can't stay here indefinitely."

"You don't need to keep reminding me." I got up, irritated with him for whining. "Just stay out of sight. I'll be back tomorrow."

"Great. I look forward to sleeping in the dark cavern."

"I'm doing the best I can," I snapped.

Some of this was his fault, after all. If Count Raymond hadn't seen him in the market in Acre we might not be sitting here right now. But then I looked at his bent head, and my frustration with him evaporated. "Just wait for me."

Milos looked up at me. "Thank you, Froggie." He grinned, for an instant reminding me of the carefree boy from years ago. "I will practice being a hermit of the caves."

As I walked back I decided to visit Meir and Sarah.

I found their usually calm and orderly house in disarray. Trunks were open. Piles of linens and clothes covered the table. Dishes, jars, and cooking pots stood on the floor, and Sarah was kneeling among them. "Do you think Jacob would like this back?" She held up a pan for her husband's inspection.

Meir peered at it with a look of distaste, as if he had never seen a pan before in his life. "I'm sure he could find a use for it, and if he can't use it, he'll know someone who can. Let's make a pile for him to pick up. We should take only what we really need for the journey, and I'm reasonably sure we can find a new pan in Bohemia."

Then he glanced in my direction, his harassed expression relaxed, and he smiled at me. "Ah, Alina, you catch us at our disadvantage. As you can see, we're preparing for our journey. It's surprising how much we have accumulated in the two years we've been here."

"When are you leaving?"

"We just got word that a group of merchants will be traveling from Acre, and if we want to join them, we need to be on the road in four days. That's why we have started the process of passing on most of our things. The most valuable part of our luggage will be the notes about our stay here and the travels before. Master Benjamin will need them for his work."

"So soon!" I was shocked. I had forgotten that this was their plan all along. Only now did I realize how much I had counted on their sympathy and their advice.

Meir looked at me with concern. "You looked exhausted."

I burst into tears.

"Come, sit down." Sarah pulled me onto a bench, pushing a few candle-sticks out of the way.

I hid my face in my hands, embarrassed. A moment later, Sarah pressed a beaker into my hands.

Gratefully I held it, breathing in the familiar, minty scent.

Meir sat down across from me. "What is wrong? Something happened. I can see it in your face."

"It's Milos. He is in trouble." I told them everything. They listened without interrupting, and their calm acceptance helped me regain my composure. "So now I have to figure out how to help him. He can't stay at the spring forever, and I can't even bring him food regularly. It's not that easy for me to get away."

Sarah frowned, a steep line down the middle of her forehead, and her brows drawn together. "I think I might have an idea about that. We could ask Jacob's son to bring him something."

"But you shouldn't take risks for us."

"Nobody pays attention to a young boy driving a donkey around."

"Oh, that would be a big help." I stood up. "I'd better get back. As soon as I think of something I'll let you know. Thank you. Thank you for listening to me. You don't know Milos, but he didn't do this." Mentally I crossed my fingers.

"I believe you," Meir said.

"And so do I," Sarah added firmly.

All the way back I thought about their words and their willingness to help, touched by their confidence. But my newfound sense of calm vanished when I entered the courtyard. One of Count Raymond's retainers approached me.

"Mistress Alina, Count Raymond wishes to see you."

For an instant, I considered pleading an illness or some other excuse so I could put this interview off for a while. But it wouldn't appear very credible. With a sigh, I squared my shoulders and followed the man into the citadel toward Count Raymond's apartment.

As we came around the corner, Count Baltasar stepped out of Count Raymond's apartment. He looked momentarily startled.

"How are you?" He smiled at me. "Where is your brother? Do you realize rumors are going around about him? If he is safe away somewhere, it might be a good idea to keep him there until things settle."

This warning made me even more scared than I had already been.

"Thank you. I am sure all is well." That sounded vague enough, yet it was polite.

"I am glad," he said emphatically. "Let me know if there's anything I can do." He walked off.

As he departed I glanced at his back, taking in the elegant doublet stretched over his well-padded shape. He was always so friendly and helpful. I wished I could confide in him. Then I shook my head. There was really nothing he could do.

When I knocked on the open door, I saw Count Raymond bent over his desk, papers spread out in front of him.

"Yes?" he grunted.

Uncomfortable, I stayed at the door. "My lord, you asked to see me."

For a moment it looked as if he couldn't remember who I was. His doublet was unbuttoned, his hair disheveled, and he looked tired. Then he beckoned me inside. "Of course, Mistress Alina. Has anything happened in the past few days that I need to know about? Anything unusual?"

I swallowed. "Nothing really." As an afterthought, I added, "Of course, everybody is upset because of what happened to Beryl."

"Indeed." Count Raymond raised his eyebrows. "And Princess Sibylla, was she upset?"

I almost smirked before I caught myself. It was hypocritical that he would ask me about Sibylla when he had talked to her himself. "Oh, yes. We all were."

"Yes, certainly, most unfortunate. We are still trying to get to the bottom of it. However, right now something more important has happened. A priceless reliquary cross has disappeared from the royal treasury. Needless to say, we are questioning everyone who might conceivably know anything about it."

"A reliquary cross?"

"Don't tell me you have not heard of it. It's a double-armed cross with a cavity in the larger cross arm containing fragments of the True Cross. Surely even an ignorant girl must appreciate the significance of such a thing."

I barely noticed his insulting and condescending tone, because I could feel my heart beating faster as I thought of Milos. But I could not allow this horrible man to have an inkling of my concern. I tried to compose myself. "No, I'm sorry. I haven't heard about it. I hope you find it soon." There. That sounded innocuous.

"Very well," Count Raymond said abruptly. "On to other things. How is your brother? In fact, we have been looking for him."

I kept my hands still by clutching my gown. "He didn't tell me, but I believe he may have ridden out to gather information about nearby towns. Count Stephen has used him for such excursions before." Too much. I was saying too much.

"Don't volunteer too much information," my father had once told me with a chuckle when he caught me in an elaborate lie.

"Indeed, how diligent of him. I have no doubt that he serves Count Stephen well."

I tried to keep my face blank, seething inside as he managed to throw doubt on both Milos and Stephen with one sentence.

That afternoon I sat in my room, reluctant to go to the great hall.

I was paralyzed.

I had no idea how to show that Milos was blameless in this. I had no proof, and besides, I was hardly in a position to get anybody to listen to me if I so much as dared to hint that Sibylla was involved.

Also, even if she was guilty and people at the court knew it, it would hardly change anything. She was the eldest princess and likely heir, given her brother's precarious state of health. A servant's death by whatever means would hardly change things.

Count Raymond wouldn't care very much about a servant girl's death. However, he would care about having the means to manipulate and control Sibylla and her choice of a husband while getting rid of Stephen at the same time.

I hated the idea of any shadow attaching to Stephen. I didn't want him to marry Sibylla, but not because of something like this. He should not be forced to withdraw from the marriage because of a cloud of suspicion hanging over his head.

Meanwhile, none of this would help Milos. I wondered whether I could contrive to approach King Amalric directly and plead for Milos.

This thought lasted for no longer than a few breaths as I tried to imagine what I would say to the king. But the king had no reason to believe me. He would simply call Count Raymond to deal with me.

Round and round my thoughts went until my head ached.

Finally I got up, cleaning my face and brushing my hair, making sure all stray locks were secured under my cap. Then I went to the great hall. When I walked inside, I noticed that Stephen was playing a game of chess with Sibylla.

Unhappy, I arranged my lute next to the stool where I usually sat. For a while I just plucked and strummed without singing, which gave me time to collect myself. It also allowed me to watch Sibylla and Stephen.

Sibylla had a look of grave concentration as she considered her moves. Stephen was equally grave, and occasionally he spoke in a low tone. She responded with a brief smile before returning her attention to the game.

They looked comfortable together. I struggled against a powerful urge to knock over the table and drag him away. I had to warn him about this young girl who had succeeded in getting me to like her, only to do this vile thing. He should not marry her. I had to let him know.

Finally the game was finished. Stephen bowed to Sibylla and walked over to where King Amalric sat with several courtiers, including Count Baltasar.

William of Tyre was reading something to the king from a thick sheaf of papers. Perhaps this was his draft for a history of the kingdom. The king interrupted frequently and asked questions. Sometimes William responded, making notes as a result of one of these exchanges. Several times Stephen interjected a comment.

At one point, the king's voice rose, and he waved his hands to make his point. "Gentlemen, let's be realistic. Do you know what someone said to me not long ago? He told me that he was sorry for me and that I would be king only as long as the Muslims wish it. He said that if a Muslim army entered our country, that army would have help and information from the peasants and even receive food and services. It makes one think, doesn't it?"

People in the hall stopped talking and looked toward the dais. At this, the king lowered his voice.

I decided it was a good moment to make music. I chose to play *Reis glorios*, one of Milos's favorite songs, filled with passion and sorrow, and perfect for his warm baritone. It was by Guiraut de Bornelh, a troubadour from Limousin. Both the lyrics and the melody worked just as well with a woman's voice.

Oh King, radiant in your glory,
Bringer of truth and light,
Almighty God, I plead with you
To be at the side of my companion.
My heart has yearned for him throughout the long night,
And soon the first gray light of the morning will be upon us.

As I sang, it felt like a prayer for Milos, alone at the spring. I was willing him to stay strong, to wait for me. But I was afraid. I had no idea what to do.

A pudgy hand pulled on my sleeve. "Alina, tell me a story."

Distractedly I glanced at the little girl while trying to keep my lute away from her fingers.

Isabella stamped her foot. "Tell me a story. You promised." She scowled.

"I am sorry, Mistress Alina." Dame Alice tried to pull her away. "This may not be the time for you to entertain a little girl."

"No, let her be." I gazed at the little girl. An idea had taken hold of me. "She's right. I did promise."

Expectantly, Isabella sat down next to me. I leaned forward, smiling at her, and began to play. Strumming the strings in a light, cheerful tune I remembered from my childhood, I made up the story of a shepherd boy who searched for one of his lambs and came across a sleeping maiden.

Isabella listened, her eyes wide and her thumb in her mouth as usual.

I kept spinning the story until the maiden was safely returned to her
home and the shepherd boy rewarded for his help. I even managed to let
him find the lost lamb.

I knew now what I was going to do.

I would tell a story with my words and my music to reveal what had
happened without pointing any fingers directly.

I knew I could do it because I had been composing new tunes for the
past several weeks. I just needed time alone. If I did it well, I might be able to
make Stephen think before he decided to marry Sibylla.

On the other hand, time was what I didn't have. If I wanted to do this,
it would have to be on the next day when the king and his courtiers joined
the ladies in the great hall. That would be my moment. That meant I had one
night to get ready.

I was appalled at myself. I'd been so involved in my thoughts about Stephen I had managed to forget Milos's predicament. They would still be looking for him, trying to pin the guilt on someone.

CHAPTER EIGHTEEN

A SONG FOR THE TELLING

I HARDLY slept that night; I was so busy writing out the lyrics and practicing them with the music until my fingers hurt and my voice cracked.

My father's face swam in front of my tired eyes. It was as if he watched and prodded me when I got tired. I remembered how he would take the lute and play for me.

"Listen," he would say, "you could do anything with this," his fingers running wild over the strings and then settling into a tune I had never heard before. "There are no limits. Don't be afraid to try something new."

I could hear his voice, dark as his face, though always with a hint of laughter before his sadness swept him away. "Froggie, you can use music to say what cannot be said. The words and the tunes are just tools to work with."

I woke up dazed and disoriented.

It was getting light outside, so I dressed quickly because I needed to run to the spring before I had to appear in the great hall.

I walked into the courtyard, hoping that, at this early hour, the only people who took note of my early morning walk would be servants.

But to my chagrin, I noticed Count Baltasar at the entrance to the stables. He really managed to appear wherever I went. I backed away, trying to hide behind one of the columns. But he had seen me already. "Mistress Alina, you are certainly up early." He smiled.

"Yes, I wanted to take a walk. It's pleasant to get out of the citadel sometimes."

"Well, enjoy your walk. Just be careful. You never know who might be out and about. I have to attend a meeting with Count Raymond. Will I see you in the great hall later?"

"Thank you, yes, I will be there." It was as if I could feel his eyes on my back as I walked off.

I gave myself a mental shake. Count Baltasar was just being friendly.

When I reached the spring, the sun had crested the horizon.

"Milos," I called softly into the tunnel.

Milos emerged slowly, blinking in the light. "I thought you forgot about me. Any news?"

"No." I handed him a loaf of bread. "Sorry, that's all for now. But Meir will send a boy to bring you something later today. His name is Daniel, and he'll have a donkey with him."

"Oh, Froggie, I don't know what to do." Milos shook his head despairingly. "I think I should just steal a horse and go to Acre."

"No, don't do that," I said, shocked. "You know you wouldn't survive all by yourself. Just wait. I'm working on an idea."

Which was a lie. I was worried sick. I hadn't been able to figure out how to get Milos away from Jerusalem safely.

Count Raymond's retainers patrolled the area around Jerusalem, and one of them would be sure to recognize Milos. Anyway, I didn't have enough money to buy him a horse. But I couldn't think about it right now.

I rushed back to the citadel and got ready. I could feel my heart beating when I picked up the lute and walked out of the little room.

The great hall was decorated with palm branches and bunches of sage and myrtle. Most members of the court were there, engaged in quiet talking. The mood was somber, but with an undertone of tension. King Amalric sat with some of his courtiers, looking tired and strained.

His son Baldwin sat on a dais in an alcove in the back of the hall.

I had never seen him before. Of course I had heard the stories about his leprosy and how he preferred to stay in seclusion.

Today all I could see of Baldwin were slender, long legs and wrists ending in hands that looked surprisingly strong. He wore a veil, the fine gauze in front of his face fluttering in and out with every breath.

Several knights stood to the side of the dais at a respectful distance, and I saw the Duke of Burgundy next to Count Raymond and one of the Ibelins. Count Baltasar gave me a gracious bow, which instantly made me wistful for the days of the journey, now seeming so carefree and innocent in retrospect.

Sibylla was next to one of the younger knights, smiling up at him. But something in her attitude made me think she was tense and distracted. I wondered whether the king had already found out about the disappearance of the True Cross and realized her part in it. I would give her more to think about. I had no doubt that she would understand exactly whose story I was about to tell.

One of Queen Maria's court ladies approached me as I walked in. "Mistress Alina, my lady the queen has asked whether you would sing for us."

I curtsied. "I would be honored."

"We were told that knights have been searching for your brother but could not find him. I hope nothing is amiss."

I didn't know what to say. I had wondered whether Milos staying away would make him appear guilty, but Count Baltasar's warning had convinced me that he was safer where he was. I shook my head politely as if I had no idea what she was talking about.

With a puzzled expression on her face, she said, "But come, everyone is looking forward to your singing."

"Thank you. I will start right away."

I sat down on a stool near the tapestry and arranged my skirt so it wouldn't distract me when I played. I picked up my lute and gently plucked the strings to make sure they were tuned. I already checked them earlier, but repeating the process always helped me calm myself before a performance.

Most people fell silent, their faces turning toward me expectantly; only a few continued talking in a soft murmur.

I played a few chords and then began with a song by Countess de Dia, *A chantar m'er de so qu'eu no volria.*

I must sing to tell my tale though I'd rather keep silent.

When I reached the final verse, I saw that Sibylla had sat down, her hands moving back and forth on her silken skirts.

Stephen stood in the back, his eyes—attentive, grave, and thoughtful—resting on me. After the last chord, I put the lute down on my lap for a moment.

My hands were clammy, so I pretended to recheck the lute strings to cover my nerves. Once I started this song, there would be no going back.

I cleared my throat and spoke, my voice sounding strange to me, loud and hard, "The following is a song by an anonymous composer, written in the style of a *tenso.* I hope it will please you."

A tenso, a form of musical dialogue or debate, was perfect for what I wanted to do. Drawing on everything I had learned from my father, I used three voices, the narrator or chorus, and a man's voice in a lower key alternating with a woman's voice. I wove a story of a man who came to a royal court to wed, only to find that the maiden he had chosen had been toying with him and had given her heart to another. But the maiden was overcome with jealousy of a rival, a court lady competing for the same man. In her anger and frustration, the maiden created a trap, sending the other lady into an abyss.

For the opening, I used two lines by Yehuda Halevi as I remembered them. Since I would never sing this song again, I thought it was acceptable to borrow the words.

Let me tell you a tale of a man,
a noble man, honest and brave,
without blame, learned, and filled with wisdom,
who traveled far to a distant land.

Riding a dappled grey, bearing gifts of silver and gold,
He came to a kingdom of glittering ice

where he beheld a wondrous maiden,
whose long, golden tresses shimmered,
her laughter like fragrant bells of spring.

I sing of love that cannot be spoken
Of betrayals and jealousies
And hearts that are broken.

Oh, wondrous maiden,
Let me behold thy beauty
For it is unlike any I have ever seen before.

My lord, behold it you may.
But I cannot linger here.
I want to be free.

And so I wove a story of a young princess shunning the prince while competing with her companion for another suitor. The princess took her companion for a ride in the forest, where the companion died by falling into a ravine. Suspicion was cast in all directions, but especially on the prince. The princess, who did not care for the prince, implied that he was behind the deed. In the end, I had the prince speak before returning to the refrain.

I am adrift, forlorn
in a sea of foul deeds.
Faces shift and truth is forsworn.
My heart yearns for the hills of my home.

I sing of love that cannot be spoken
Of betrayals and jealousies
And hearts that are broken.
I sing of love that cannot be spoken
As I watch and I listen and my heart aches.

I softened my voice and gentled the sounds of the lute as I drew to a close.

Some of the listeners looked puzzled, others bored. After a brief silence, people began to talk more loudly again. William of Tyre stood next to the young prince in his alcove, chatting with him.

I did not dare seek out Stephen, afraid of what I might see on his face. I caught a few speculative glances, and Count Baltasar had a peculiar expression on his face, as if he was puzzled about something.

Before I turned away, I stared straight into Sibylla's eyes, which were flat and cold and hard. Then she gave me an odd, twisted little smile.

Count Raymond, sitting next to Queen Maria, glanced at me, his expression unreadable.

I bowed to the queen and to King Amalric and left the hall.

I was shaking when I got outside. Oddly enough, it was not the realization that I probably was now in serious trouble with several people, all at the same time.

Right now I was elated. I had written my first full tenso with my own lyrics and music. To be sure, when I sang I realized where the weak spots were, but I didn't care.

It wasn't perfect, but it was mine.

I sat down on a stone bench in the shaded archway, dazed and giddy at the same time. Breathing in the clear, dry air of Jerusalem, with hints of citrus and myrrh from lemon trees and small thorny Commiphora shrubs grown in clay containers around the perimeter of the courtyard, I closed my eyes.

"May I join you?"

CHAPTER NINETEEN

BIRDS IN A CAGE

STEPHEN STOOD in front of me.

I blinked as I gazed up at his smiling face, the skin around his eyes crinkling into rays. It felt as if it had been just yesterday and yet also half a lifetime ago since we had sat together in this courtyard a few days after our arrival in Jerusalem.

Stephen sat down and stretched out his legs, as I had seen him do when he chatted with men. His tunic was plain, and it looked as if he had gone riding earlier. Fine grains of sand clung to the blond hair on his legs, and the skin on his hands had hairline cracks from the dryness and heat. I could feel the heat from his body and smell his scent, warmed by the sun, a bit spicy with a hint of sweat.

The silence was comfortable. I wished I could freeze this scene in my memory. For a moment I imagined sitting next to Stephen many years from now, on another bench at the edge of his vineyard, looking at the ripening fruit after a day of work and contentment. I blushed, hoping he couldn't read my mind.

"The first lines of your song reminded me of a poem by Yehuda Halevi."

Startled, I glanced at him.

His expression was sad, with a hint of amusement. "I do read, you know." He bent to the right and stretched out his arm to pick a lemon from the tree on his side. "Halevi's 'In Remembrance of Jerusalem,' would also have been fitting today."

"Yes," I said in a low voice, trying to recall the lines Meir had read to me.

Truly a feast for the eyes and the soul;

behold the City of Kings.

"I wanted to tell you that I am going back to Sancerre."

I looked down. This was what I had wanted. Yet sorrow welled up inside me. I would never see him again.

"Perhaps one day I will feel compelled to return and fight for our faith in this land, but not now, and not for some time to come. My responsibilities lie elsewhere, and I want to accomplish something yet in my life before I return here."

Stephen rolled the lemon back and forth in his hands. He seemed to have forgotten to whom he was speaking.

"I had an interesting conversation with the king the other day. He reminded me of the story of the Assyrian King Sennacherib who besieged Hezekiah, then King of Jerusalem. Sennacherib imprisoned Hezekiah in his own city, like a bird in a cage. It seems an apt description of Jerusalem, then and now. Ultimately, its fate will depend on the surrounding peoples. It's a fragile balance. As Christians, we are supposed to support and protect the people in our realm and defend the holy city. But when many of them are not of our faith, our values held most dear are in contradiction with our deeds.

"King Amalric invited me to come here as an outsider, bringing a fresh perspective to a fractured court. It turns out it is also exactly why I must leave. The outsider who was supposed to unite the kingdom would be the outsider whose very presence would split it at a time when it needs unity above all."

I listened to him, bewildered and confused, while I almost pitied Sibylla.

Stephen had never even thought of her as a person—all his thoughts were bent on the kingdom and its needs, on the world of politics and power, and not on the young woman whom he was supposed to wed. He hadn't even heard what I was trying to tell him.

He glanced at me, as if he only now recalled my presence. "You have made some things clear in my mind. Most of all, you have reminded me of my home. I have many ideas about what I want to do there."

"You want to build a fishpond," I blurted out.

Stephen raised his eyebrows. "Funny you should say that. I talked to your brother about fishponds. It's just one way of describing what I want to do. There is so much. I want to create a charter to protect merchants and assure justice and safety in the region, do something about the serfs, make it so people can marry without giving up their rights to property, make it so the king cannot act arbitrarily all over the land as if he were in his own rooms. Yes, I want to build a fishpond. I want to improve land use in my domain. I want to grow wine. None of which would be possible here."

Stephen stood up. With a courtesy generally reserved for great ladies of the court, he took my hand and bowed. His hand was warm and firm, and part of me wanted to clutch it and never let it go. Stephen straightened, looking down at me with a smile. "It is strange that the words that have swayed me came from the king who bade me come here, from Saladin, our enemy, and from a young girl from Provence who would be my daughter's age if I had had one, a singer whose music and words reminded me of what I love. For this, I owe you my gratitude. It occurs to me that you might want to leave as well. Please let me know whether I can be of assistance."

He turned and walked off.

He thought of me as a daughter. That stung.

As I watched Stephen stride out of the courtyard, my heart ached. Yet something warmed me as I thought of my music. It was like a promise I could wrap around my sadness.

I got up to return to my room.

Just then a servant approached me. "Mistress Alina, Count Raymond asked that you attend him."

Clearly, the long day had not yet come to an end. Obediently I followed him.

Count Raymond stood in his small apartment near the fireplace. He was lost in contemplation of a map while sipping from a goblet. When I entered, he turned around, frowning. "Ah, Mistress Alina, do sit down."

I sat on the chair he indicated. Again, I was grateful Milos was far away, safe in his cave. Still, I trembled.

"I must say I underestimated you. Your..." Count Raymond hesitated, sniffing in his customary way, "shall I say, musicianship...is remarkable—indeed, telling, if that's the right word to use when describing a piece of music."

I decided silence was my best option.

"Curious how someone so expressive in her music has so little to say to me in person. But enough of that. It may not have been quite what you intended, but it turns out that it was to our benefit. Your little exhibition helped to speed things up a bit, relieving me of the need to employ other means. Count Stephen informed the king of his decision to return to France."

I tried to keep my face devoid of any expression. Count Raymond was so pleased and smug that he had gotten rid of Stephen, it angered me on Stephen's behalf.

"You may not believe me, but in truth, I have only the well-being of the kingdom in mind. Bringing in an idealistic outsider is hardly helpful at this volatile point, when the kingdom faces challenges from emerging powers such as Saladin."

"So the well-being of the kingdom is a justification for spying on people and for manipulating things to your satisfaction?" I could not help myself—I could hardly get into any worse trouble. I almost added, "even having someone pushed over a balustrade when she gets in the way," but thought better of it.

"Ah, another idealist." Count Raymond sniffed. "How charming. I shall pretend I did not hear your impetuous comment. Meanwhile, when were you planning to start your journey home?"

"If my services are no longer required, I would like to leave soon." Of course he wanted me gone. Sending me away was just housecleaning.

"Well, it might be an opportune time now. Princess Sibylla will no longer be in need of a companion. I am sure she will express her gratitude herself."

Hardly, I thought, but I nodded politely. "Yes, my lord. I understand."

Count Raymond reached behind him and took a small purse from his desk. "Here, to assist you on the journey."

"Thank you," I said, taken aback. I had not expected any help from this man. Then I had an idea. It could hardly make anything worse for Milos or for me, and it might do some good. "My lord, could I ask you for a favor?"

He studied me with raised eyebrows. "And that would be what?"

"Beryl had a daughter. Her parents are raising her, and Beryl used to send things to her parents to help. Perhaps something could be done for the child."

"I didn't know." He looked surprised. "Yes, I'll see to it that something is done for the child."

I stood up, curtsied, and had turned toward the door when he spoke again, addressing my back.

"Oh, I almost forgot. I am certain you are troubled about the disappearance of the True Cross, and that the culprit who murdered the servant girl has not yet been apprehended. Let me assure you, we will not rest until we've found the culprit."

I stopped moving, frozen. I couldn't show him that I was afraid. Glancing back, I said, "I hope you will be successful."

"Of course, there are several possible contenders, because the young lady had an unfortunate habit of talking carelessly to too many people, and we would regret if any shadow attached to anyone associated with the court or with Count Stephen, even though he is leaving us. But don't let me detain you any further. I am sure you will want to begin to prepare for your journey."

My knees were wobbly when I went along the hallway, terrified and revolted. Count Raymond could not have been more explicit in his threat. In a way it was my fault. The very fact that Milos had gone into hiding would make him appear guilty if he were caught. And how two-faced of the count to pretend to care whether or not Stephen would leave under a cloud of suspicion.

At least I had money now, which would help with making arrangements. Milos definitely needed a horse to get away from Jerusalem quickly. Perhaps I could join a group of merchants traveling west. Yet, I couldn't bear the notion of returning to my uncle and aunt. Thinking feverishly, I walked toward my little room. Preoccupied, I pushed open the door.

"There she is, the famous trobairitz. What will you do when you've run out of people to besmirch?" Sibylla was sitting on my bed.

I felt as if I had stepped barefoot on shards of pottery.

Sibylla had my aquamarine silk shawl on her lap, running her fingers over it thoughtfully. "Nice. Did you pay for this out of money from Count Raymond for spying on me?"

I couldn't think of anything to say. Numbly, I shook my head.

"Don't act so surprised. Didn't you think I would have figured out by now why Count Raymond chose you, a mere girl with no connections or experience as a 'companion' for me?" Sibylla sneered at the word. Evidently she thought I was a ridiculous candidate for such a position. "The only reason I continued to put up with this was that you apparently never did tell Count Raymond anything of import."

"How do you know that?" I asked, surprised at her insight.

"You saw me with Count William, and you also saw that I had been outside one morning, but you didn't tell Count Raymond—and believe me, I would have heard about it." She tossed the shawl aside and stood up. "Well, Mistress Alina," she said, stressing the mistress, "it seems to me that it's high time that you conclude your stay here before you manage to alienate more suitors of mine with your fabulations."

I opened my mouth to speak, but she stopped me.

"Did you really think I pushed that girl off the balcony?"

"You didn't? But I saw you run off."

"I suppose you recognized my robe. But never mind. Come on, I was hardly the only one to rush away from the scene of the crime. It's true, I was there, but I did not give Beryl that little push."

"You saw it?"

"Not exactly. When I walked down the hall, I was hoping to see Milos. He had promised to teach me a trick with dice."

I scowled. "Go on."

For a moment, Sibylla looked embarrassed. "I just wanted to have some fun and not worry about the kingdom for a while."

"Never mind that now," I snapped. "What did you see?"

"I saw Beryl. That is, the column blocked my sight, but I recognized her voice. She sat on the balustrade, her skirts spread wide. Someone stood in front of her, but I could only see his back. I must admit, at first I thought it was Milos, which annoyed me. He had no business talking to Beryl. She was laughing when the man shoved her backward. I heard her scream and saw her skirts disappear over the balustrade. Before I could move, the man had disappeared. Then I heard someone come up the steps, and I ran down the hallway as fast as I could."

Aside from the fact that she had wanted to meet Milos, which made me angry all over again, it had the ring of truth. "But do you have any idea who did this?"

"How should I know? It all happened to fast. But something tells me Count Raymond was behind it."

"Count Raymond?"

"Well, you should have heard him. He could barely contain his delight at this opportunity to frame me. Actually, he said as much. It makes it easier for him to get me to do what he wants. He has been trying to get me married to one of the Ibelins. To throw suspicion on Count Stephen was just a bonus for him."

I stared at her. "But why would Count Raymond have Beryl followed?"

"I don't know, but I have no doubt that unfortunate girl had found out something about Count Raymond that he didn't want anybody to know about. Anyway, I have seen his grumpy-looking retainer sneak around in all sorts of places, and I suspect he's the one who pushed Beryl to her death."

"You mean Ralph?" It all fell into place. Count Raymond had managed to frame several people with one stroke—or at least make sure a shadow of suspicion hung over them. He had wanted to get rid of Stephen all along, and to continue having something he could use to control Sibylla. Milos, Beryl, and I were just pawns.

"Yes. He's been with Count Raymond for ages. He'd do anything for him. To be honest, I wasn't overly distressed that Beryl met her maker."

"Oh, are you talking about the True Cross?"

"Ah, you figured that out. Yes, Beryl had caught me with Count William." Sibylla blushed. "It was nothing really, but I definitely did not want Count Raymond to hear about it. She threatened me, so I fed her a little bone to distract her." She looked uncomfortable. "It was very wrong, but I could not think of anything else at that moment, so I told her about the entrance to the treasury. I thought it wasn't much of a risk since it is always well guarded. She must have passed that knowledge on to someone else, who then stole the True Cross. Whoever it was probably bribed or drugged the guard."

"But then you had a reason," I said hesitantly.

"A reason to toss her off the balustrade?" Sibylla interrupted with a pained smile. "Well, yes, it looks that way. Beryl definitely knew too much and talked to too many people. She was always sneaking around and claiming to know all sorts of secrets. I definitely did not like her, but that's not the point. I was afraid of my father finding out about my stupidity with the True Cross. On the other hand, even if she had told someone things about me, who would have believed her? Getting rid of her would not have helped me all that much—or helped me retrieve the True Cross."

It made sense. It was beginning to sink in how much I had misjudged Sibylla.

"Anyway, really, don't you think I would have come up with a more elegant way of doing this?" She laughed.

I was taken aback by her tone. Then I suddenly realized something else. Her callous attitude was in part a disguise. I remembered how shocked she was at first when Beryl was murdered, and then she became flippant, as if nothing bothered her.

There was no doubt that I had been wrong about Sibylla. Without knowing the truth, just judging from the flimsiest bit of evidence—literally a bit of greyish pink silk—I went ahead and did my best to blacken her name in front of the assembled court of the kingdom. Never mind that it was all innuendo, and no names were mentioned, and the details of what happened never made it into the song. Still, those familiar with events would have no difficulty guessing what I meant. I opened my mouth to speak, but no words would come out.

Sibylla looked at me quizzically.

"Sibylla, I am sorry," I said finally. "I was wrong." I owed her something more. "I was afraid for my brother."

"Silly, I know that. Although we aren't talking just about your brother, are we? Be honest. Isn't there someone else you like in all this?"

I flushed.

Sibylla laughed. "Admittedly, you've done me a favor. Bringing Count Stephen here was definitely not my idea. My father was the one who thought he would be perfect for Jerusalem. I happen to disagree. Perhaps it won't surprise you to know it's the first time Count Raymond and I have been in agreement on something.

"To be sure, Count Stephen is honorable and brave—even though he's a bit too godlike for my tastes. But I think his heart is in France. He would have made too many enemies here with his ideas about taxes and laws, not to mention his upright sense of morals and fairness. The kingdom would be split in half. Besides," Sibylla said and grinned at me, "I have my eye on someone else."

I smiled in response. Sibylla was manipulative and too clever for her own good, but I liked her. And in her own way she had always been honest with me. I had just failed to see it because I was blinded by my fear for Milos and my feelings for Stephen.

"But what about the True Cross?"

"I am afraid it's gone." Sibylla's expression grew serious. "Count Raymond and my father think it is a sign from God of bad times to come for the kingdom."

"I am sorry. Maybe it will still turn up." I hesitated, not wanting to appear presumptuous. "I hope you will marry someone you like."

"Thank you," Sibylla said. "The truth is that it won't be up to me—my marriage affects the future of the kingdom." Then her dimples returned. "If I were free, I might run off with your handsome brother."

I laughed to show that I understood she was just teasing. It occurred to me that she might become a good queen one day—with her intelligence, her knowledge, and her spirit.

"It might be in your best interest to get away from here. Count Raymond doesn't look kindly upon people who become too independent in their thinking."

"He already made that clear," I admitted.

"Have you thought of asking Count Stephen to take you along when he returns to France?"

I should have thought of that. Milos and I could go with him. In fact, Milos would love it. For an instant, I was bewitched by visions of months on the road with Stephen, making music while he listened, and walking through a vineyard in Sancerre danced in front of my eyes.

But no, it was all wrong. This was the stuff of troubadour songs, and I was done with that. I had a better plan now. "Thank you for that suggestion." I didn't want to elaborate.

"Well, then, come to me before you go, and I will give you some money to help defray the expense of your journey."

I was embarrassed and irked that I needed to be grateful again. "Count Raymond already saw to that, my lady. Thank you." I remembered something else. I cleared my throat. "Sibylla, take care. The tunnel," I hesitated, afraid of revealing too much. "It's not as much of a secret as you think."

Sibylla raised her eyebrows. "You do get around." She sounded cool again, but then she laughed. "Don't fret. I already realized that. In any event, it's time to let some of these things go. My brother is not well, and my father will need to rely on me more and more. But thank you."

She got up, gazing at me thoughtfully. Her serious expression made her appear old beyond her years. "You may not realize this, but sometimes I envy you. You have a gift, and you are going to find a way to make it work for you. You may even be able to leave something behind for the world to enjoy in the years to come. My life is defined by my position, and marriage is the only route open to me."

I stared at her, lost for words. I had seen that she was somewhat restricted in her movements, but it had never occurred to me how much she was a prisoner of circumstances.

She didn't have the option of running away, which is what I did when faced with my aunt's incessant demands that I get married. Moreover, I found something I love, something I can do well. My music became my anchor, and all other uncertainties seemed irrelevant as long as I could make music.

Sibylla squared her shoulders and flicked back her shawl in a practiced gesture. "Be well, and travel safely."

I curtsied, for once willingly. "My lady, I thank you."

CHAPTER TWENTY

AT THE SPRING OF GIHON

AS I walked away from my room, I began to run. I needed to see Meir and Sarah, but first I had to find Stephen.

After fruitless searching in the courtyard and in the great hall, earning me puzzled looks from some of the ladies sitting over their needlework, I had to ask one of his retainers to fetch him. After a short while, he came out into the courtyard. "Mistress Alina, you asked to talk to me."

"Yes," I said abruptly. Then I swallowed and added, "my lord." I had thought of him as Stephen so long that I stumbled over the proper address. I continued quickly before I lost my nerve. "You offered your help. Would you take Milos back with you to France?"

"Of course. In fact, it had already occurred to me to ask Milos to come with me. We will leave the day after tomorrow. Where is he? I have not seen him for the last week."

"I can't tell you that." Desperately I tried to think of what to say. "He didn't do anything wrong, but he needs your help."

"I see." Stephen studied me intently. "What about you? Can I offer you safe passage as well?"

I looked away to hide my thoughts. Weeks ago, I had dreamed of hearing something like this from him. "Thank you, but I have made my own arrangements already."

"I hope that these arrangements include music." He raised his eyebrows.

I nodded, grateful that he did not prod me with questions.

"Very well, then. Would you let Milos know? I suggest that he meet us at daybreak on the road to Acre."

"On the road to Acre?" I repeated doubtfully.

"Yes, he will know where from our various excursions." He placed his index finger on his lips, as if trying to think. "Incidentally, I wonder whether he had time to visit the horse trader who arrived a few days ago and has set up camp outside St. Stephen's Gate. You might want to mention it to him. With his love of horses, he would enjoy the selection of sturdy desert horses the trader brought with him. As it happens, I will be there just before sunset tomorrow. But I must take my leave now. I have a lot of things to attend to." He bowed and began to walk off.

Relieved and sad at the same time, I gazed at his straight back until he turned around once more. "You are wrong about Princess Sibylla, by the way."

He had heard me after all. I could not think of a response. I bent my head, ashamed of how wrong I had been.

"I understood what you were saying," Stephen said gently. "It was by no means all off the mark, but you should look elsewhere in this case. Still, I am grateful. Your words and your courage reminded me of all that I hold dear—my home and my family not least of those." He smiled at me, and then he was gone.

For a moment, I was unable to move. Stephen had seen so much more than I realized. It should not have come as a surprise. He was one of the most observant people I had ever met.

I wondered what he meant by looking elsewhere. Then I shook my head. I needed to get going.

Sarah and Meir immediately agreed to my request when I went to see them.

"We have already talked about this, and we were going to suggest that you come with us to Prague." Sarah beamed at me. "You could help us on the journey."

"Thank you. I am very grateful. You won't regret this."

"Of course not," Sarah said. "Come to us tomorrow morning. Everything is ready. The merchants traveling back to Acre agreed to let us join their group."

"I'll be here. Sarah, I am so glad you will take me with you. I can't go back to Uncle Garsanc and Aunt Marci. I never want to be at the mercy of someone's charity again. I don't know what I will do once we get there. But I will think of something."

Meir looked at me with a slight smile. "I have no doubt."

By the next morning, I was ready. I hadn't slept much, my eyes were sore, and I was still thinking back and forth until my head hurt.

This was the hardest decision I ever made, but it was for the best. Stephen would take Milos with him, which would give Milos a chance at a future. I would go off by myself with Meir and Sarah. I had to make my own way.

It was still dark when I gathered my things, wrapping the lute in one of Sibylla's hand-me-down shawls. Before leaving, I went to the kitchen to see if I could get some bread for Milos. I told the cook that I was preparing to travel west with some merchants. To my surprise, she quickly packed a satchel with bread, dates, dried meat, cheese, and a jar filled with olives wrapped in grape leaves.

I thanked her profusely, embarrassed by her generosity after all my subterfuges over the past days to cadge food from her.

"Take it, take it, Mistress Alina. You and your brother have been nothing but kind to me since you came. Your brother even brought me some nice beads when he came back from one of his excursions with Count Stephen."

At home, Milos never had a thought for any of the servants. I don't think he ever meant to be unkind. He had just been unaware of them as people. Perhaps I didn't know him as well as I thought.

This surprising discovery distracted me as I made my way out of the citadel and up the hill to the spring.

Milos sat outside on one of the stones near the opening. I forgot all my pleasant thoughts about him in an instant, irritated by his nonchalance. "What if somebody sees you? Count Raymond told me in so many words that his men are still hunting for you." I dumped the little satchel with food at his feet.

"Nobody comes up here this early. But to be honest, I truly don't care much anymore. It's got to be better than staying here indefinitely." He pulled open the satchel. "Oh, bread, thanks. I was getting tired of dates." He chewed hungrily. "And olives in grape leaves. This is a feast," he mumbled around another mouthful of food.

"Don't speak with your mouth full, you glutton." Huffily, I sat down next to him. "Are you listening, or are you too busy eating? I have a plan for you." I recounted what had happened.

"You think it was Ralph?" Milos sounded surprised.

"It would make sense. I think Count Raymond told him to get rid of Beryl."

"Ralph is a bully and a frustrated old man." Milos shook his head. "But I don't think he did this. I know he really liked Beryl."

"I doubt we'll ever know. But it doesn't matter. You would be accused of it anyway if Count Raymond's men found you." I told him where he was supposed to join Stephen the following morning.

Milos frowned at me. "What did you say to him?"

"Nothing. I just told Stephen you needed help, which is true enough. The rest is up to you." I was getting annoyed at him all over again.

"He was very discreet. I think he knows why you disappeared because he didn't ask any questions. Oh, I almost forgot—he suggested that you go to the horse trader's this evening just before sunset. He said he would be there. I guess he wants to make sure you have everything you need for the journey. Here, I got some money. It should be enough for a horse." I handed him half of the coins from Count Raymond. "Count Raymond is paying for it—not that he knows, but I think it's only fair." I stood up and brushed off my gown. "I'd better go."

Milos stared up at me, blinking in the sunlight. "But what about you?"

"I am going to Bohemia with Meir and Sarah."

"Why?" Milos sounded shocked. "Why aren't you coming with us?"

I could not tell him that the last thing I wanted to do was to spend more time in the company of Stephen. That was finished. "They offered, and I accepted."

"But what are you going to do there?"

I was surprised at how upset he sounded. I had thought he would be happy about it.

"Well, to begin with, I'll help Sarah, but eventually I want to compose and perform music." Trying to sound reassuring, I spoke as if I had been planning this for ages, and while I worked hard to convince him, I realized it was exactly what I wanted to do. I smiled at him. "Really, this is right for me. I might even teach. Of course I will return to Provence eventually, but not yet. Besides, you can hardly keep dragging me all over Europe when you are starting out as Count Stephen's squire."

"Perhaps you are right." Milos stood up as well. He had lost weight over the past few days. "Thank you, Alina." Then he smiled at me fondly. "I wasn't making up to Sibylla—I know that's what you thought, but I wasn't. Truly."

"Then what were you doing?"

"It's just that she is really a little girl."

I made a face. "Not that little."

"That's not what I meant. Of course, don't get me wrong. I'm not blind. Sibylla is beautiful. But mostly she just reminded me of Maria at that age. I was sorry for her. I think she was glad to have a friend who didn't want anything from her."

Dumbfounded, I stared at him. I remembered how Milos used to bring Maria little wood carvings. Maria would smile at him, her face dimpled and her curls dancing. Again I had been wrong. I had been wrong about almost everything—even about Count Raymond.

"Don't cry, Froggie." Milos touched my cheek and wiped off a tear.

"Oh, Milos," I said, my voice wobbly. "Don't be late for the rendezvous with Stephen. I think if you don't mess up, he'll help you to a knighthood." If I stayed any longer, I would lose my resolve. "I have to go. I'll send a message to Count Stephen when we're settled in Prague." I gave him a hug and pulled myself away.

"That's where you have been hiding all these days," a hoarse voice bellowed in my ear. It was Ralph. He stood on the path that led down the hill.

"I have been looking for you." Ralph moved toward Milos, raising his fists. "You killed her." His face was swollen, his eyes red-rimmed.

"I didn't kill her," Milos shouted.

"Ralph, stop," I screamed. "He didn't." I tried to grab his tunic.

Ralph's head swung toward me like that of a dazed bull. "Count Raymond told me it was Milos."

"He didn't hurt Beryl," I shouted.

"I wish you had never come." Ralph shook his head, as if trying to free himself from a bad dream. "You and your brother."

"Why do you blame us? Milos didn't do anything to you."

"Your brother made up to Beryl. It made her think she might do better than me. And you with your songs, thinking you're so fine when you were really no more than a servant."

"Will you listen to us? We didn't do anything to Beryl." I managed to get close to Ralph and grabbed hold of his tunic. "Count Raymond has been tricking you. He has been tricking all of us."

Milos lifted his hands to show he didn't want to fight. "Truly, Ralph, it wasn't me."

"She wouldn't have laughed at me if it hadn't been for you. I loved her, and she laughed at me." It was if Ralph couldn't hear us at all. Tears ran down his cheeks. "You are going to get what you deserved." He yanked his tunic out of my grasp and threw himself at Milos, pounding him with his fists.

Milos fought back while I was helpless. I thought of trying to trip Ralph, but I was afraid of either of them falling down the steps. Then, Milos struck Ralph on the jaw, and Ralph's head was knocked back.

"Why don't you listen?" I yelled. "Milos didn't do it. Help us figure out who did."

Ralph shook his head from side to side. He charged Milos again, enraged as a gored bull. With a resounding crash, they both landed on the ground next to the stone steps of the spring and lay still. They had knocked each other out.

"What a charming reunion." Count Baltasar stepped out from behind an olive bush. He wore a plain doublet with a dark surcoat with a big satchel hanging on a strap over his shoulder. He held his unsheathed sword in his hand. "Too bad they didn't kill each other. It would have saved time. As it is, let me assist them."

"Count Baltasar!"

"Mistress Alina." He sketched a courteous bow, as if we were in the great hall. "It's really most unfortunate that you are here. Much as I dislike hurting women, now I will have to dispense with you as well." He waved his sword delicately in my direction.

"How did you find us?"

"I followed you. In fact, I've been curious about your activities for a while now. But when I came up here, the conversation got so interesting that I decided to wait and listen."

"It was you!" I blurted out. I had remembered the masked figure. "I saw you in the hallway at night. You stole the True Cross."

"Ah, I thought I heard someone slinking around." He smiled at me. "Indeed, you are quite right. I did take it. Such a beautiful relic. I suppose you haven't seen it. What a pity."

"But why?" I clutched my gown to keep my hands from trembling. "It's not something you can sell on the market."

"It's always a good idea to have some insurance. I can think of several people in Europe who will pay a pretty penny for it."

"Then I'm sure you would love to get your hands on the icons from the monastery south of Sofia," I snapped. I thought of kindly and thoughtful Brother Gregorius. Although I suspected he had seen Count Baltasar for the kind of man he was.

"Indeed I would." Count Baltasar smiled. "Journeying back and forth has been quite lucrative. But as it happens, I have changed my mind. I will be the one to find the culprits," he waved the sword at Milos, Ralph, and me, "and will finally earn all the credit and respect at court that I deserve."

How odd that he was so willing to talk. Either he was terribly vain or convinced that he would be able to get rid of us easily. Out of the corner of my eye, I saw that Milos was still stunned from the collision, but Ralph was beginning to stir. I had to buy more time. "You made sure Milos would be suspected of killing Beryl. You must have whispered into Count Raymond's ears about this and told him Milos probably stole the True Cross as well."

"Yes, wasn't it convenient? Count Raymond actually entrusted me with the job of finding the culprit."

"But why did you have to kill Beryl?"

"You are not the only ones who felt threatened by Beryl." Count Baltasar scowled. "That foolish woman was going to expose me and destroy all my careful work, just when I was about to make headway with Sibylla. That was a pretty song, by the way. I wager you didn't make any friends with it. Incidentally, how did you manage to get Milos away so quickly? I searched for you, but you had both vanished."

"What were you doing? Hiding behind a column to watch what would happen after you murdered Beryl?"

"Yes. It was fascinating to watch the traffic up there, not to mention quite convenient to have an appropriate suspect appear." He looked pleased with himself. "Anyway, it's time to resolve all this." He shifted his stance, firming his grip on the sword. "You really did me a favor. I will dispense with all of you and will be revered as the savior of the True Cross." He smiled again.

All the way from Lyon, I had thought he was kind and gentle. I shifted my eyes for an instant. Milos had raised his head, and Ralph was on his knees. I had to distract Count Baltasar.

Then I remembered something he had just said. I started to laugh. "If you think Sibylla will marry you, you are sadly mistaken."

Count Baltasar frowned. "I am just as suitable as Stephen. Just because his uncle was King of England makes him no more suitable than any other nobleman."

"We laughed about you," I jeered. "Sibylla thought you were ridiculous, so sweet and smiling and friendly with everybody." That was true as far as it went, even though I was certain Sibylla had not spent even one minute thinking about him beyond that dismissive comment. "She said you were porky," I taunted.

He narrowed his eyes. "I think it's time to finish this," he said and moved toward me.

At that moment, Ralph lunged, pushing Count Baltasar as hard as he could until the count stumbled and lost his balance. Arms flailing, he tumbled down the stone steps. A thud was followed by silence.

I stared at the platform at the bottom of the steps. Count Baltasar lay in an awkward sprawl.

"He hit his head." Ralph was breathing heavily. "I think he's dead."

"That's justice for you." Milos had gotten up and was trembling as he leaned on the stone ledge, his face green. "He killed Beryl by making her fall, and now he died the same way."

"I killed him." Ralph sat down on the ledge. He rubbed his hands over his face.

"It's not your fault," I said. "It was an accident. And besides, Count Baltasar really would have killed us."

"Nobody is going to believe us," Ralph muttered.

"What do we do now?" Milos asked.

I almost laughed at the two faces turned toward me, one old, dour, and tired, the other young, pale and excited, with nearly identical expressions of shock and bewilderment. They both looked at me expectantly, as if they were sure I would have a solution. Then I glanced down into the well, and the urge to laugh was gone. "Let's pull him out of there. We don't want him polluting the spring."

"Porky?" Milos's eyebrows were raised in a familiar mocking expression I hadn't seen for a long time. "I can't believe you called him 'porky.'"

"Oh, you heard that." I could not help but smile at him in response. "It was the best I could come up with."

With much groaning, Ralph and Milos managed to drag him up the steps. Ralph also brought up the satchel that Count Baltasar had carried with him. When he put it down, it made a clunking noise.

"I wonder what's in there," Milos said, a puzzled expression on his face.

Gingerly I tugged on the strap. There were a few garments and other items for travel, and something hard and heavy, wrapped in soft cloth, about the length of my arm. I sat back on my heels. "I know what this is. You didn't hear Count Baltasar go on about this, bragging about how clever he had been." I was right. It was the True Cross, its silver and gilt surface glinting in the sunlight.

Ralph began to curse. He stomped around and tossed rocks into the distance. "For this Beryl had to die, and I have lost my position." After a few moments, he calmed down. "Begging your pardon, Mistress Alina. Count Raymond dismissed me. He said he couldn't trust me anymore, and I know he thought I might have been behind the theft of the True Cross. And now I find that this smooth-talking devil killed my Beryl and took this holy thing. I would probably throw him down the well all over again if given the opportunity."

The sun on the back of my neck reminded me of the time. "We need to move. We can't be found with him, or we would be suspected of killing him and having stolen the True Cross. We have to buy some time so that we can get away before he's found."

"But where would we hide him?" Ralph asked.

"Well, we don't have much choice. Let's take him over there." I pointed at the cluster of silvery shrubs about fifty yards away from the well. Together, we dragged the body toward the olive grove. Fortunately it appeared to be abandoned. Many of the trees were dead, and weeds had taken over. Using our hands and Ralph's sword we scraped out a hollow just deep enough for the body. We covered it up with dirt and rocks, finally pulling branches and leaves over the little mound, and then returned to the spring's entrance. Hopefully he wouldn't be found before I managed to get Milos away from Jerusalem.

I picked up my satchel and stuck the True Cross inside.

"What are you doing?" Milos asked worriedly. "We can't be found with that."

Ralph laughed. "Caught in the act! It would be what Count Baltasar had envisioned. Of course, he hadn't planned on being dead in an olive grove."

"Well, we definitely can't go to Count Raymond with this story. Nobody would believe us," I said. "I'll deal with it. I have a plan. Take the sword and his satchel and hide it in the bushes with his body."

Frowning at me, Milos did as I asked.

Ralph sat down on one of the stone walls, his face buried in arms. He looked so sad and broken, he was not even remotely like the threatening figure I had feared all these weeks.

"What will you do—you and your brother?" Ralph's voice sounded muffled.

"Milos will join Count Stephen tomorrow, and I'll travel with some friends and a small group of merchants. And you?"

"I don't know—and I don't care." Ralph shrugged. "The only man I ever served dismissed me. I guess I should be grateful that he paid me, but it hurts. I waited for him all the years he was in prison, working at his castle in Tripoli. Now with Beryl gone, there is nothing for me."

"I am sorry," I said helplessly. Then I had an idea. "Wait. Ralph, there is something."

"Nothing. You don't understand."

"Listen to me. You forgot Beryl's little girl. She will need someone now her mother is gone."

"I am not her father." He rubbed his hands over his face, leaving track marks of dirt.

"But she doesn't have anyone else. Beryl told me the people in the village are mean to her, and her parents are getting old. I told Count Raymond about her, but I doubt he'll actually do anything to help."

He shook his head again, but I could see he was thinking about it. He frowned.

Milos came back from the olive grove. "What about the True Cross?"

"Don't worry about that. Both of you have to get away from here."

"Where will I hide? Stephen won't be on the road until tomorrow. And I can't stay here. What if Count Raymond still has people searching for me?"

Ralph got up, brushing the dirt off his tunic. "I know a merchant who has stables just outside the wall. We could both hide there and leave early in the morning."

"Oh, Ralph, that would be a big help."

"We should get away from here," Milos said. "People will start coming up to the spring."

"Ralph, I hope..." Then I stopped. It was presumptuous to say anything about hope to this man who had lost so much. "Look, I am truly sorry."

Ralph stood straight and solid. "Go on, Mistress Alina. I will make sure your brother gets on the road safely tomorrow."

I smiled at him. "Thank you, Ralph." I hugged Milos. "Take care," I whispered.

He hugged me back. "You too."

CHAPTER TWENTY-ONE

THE SOUL OF THE LUTE

I DIDN'T have much time.

Meir and Sarah would be wondering where I was. My satchel, now loaded down with the True Cross, was heavy. I wished I had never found it.

I hadn't lied when I told Milos I had a plan, but I was afraid of what might happen to me as a result. I couldn't hand it over to Sibylla, because it would be difficult for her to return it without drawing attention to her own involvement in its disappearance. Besides I wanted to solve this for her. Somehow I had to get in to see the king.

When I entered the courtyard, I looked around for someone I could ask to help me. A few knights stood outside the entrance to the royal stables. One of them was Count William Longsword whom Sibylla liked to meet when no one was watching. He had been nothing but kind to me.

"My lord, may I speak with you?" I was out of breath.

"Mistress Alina," he said with a courteous smile. "I thought you had already left us. My lady Sibylla told me of your plans."

"Yes, I am leaving soon." I stepped away from the others, beckoning him with my eyes. Speaking softly, I said, "I need to do something first. Could you help me have a private interview with the king?"

He looked at me in surprise.

"Please," I said. "I can't tell you why. But it's important, and it would help my lady Sibylla."

Count William studied my face, his warm brown eyes full of curiosity. Then he nodded. "Come. I know the king is in his office."

"Can we hurry?" I was terrified of running into Count Raymond.

Count William lengthened his stride, and together we hurried along a hallway toward the royal apartments. In front of a door, he said, "Wait here, please," and disappeared inside.

Sweat trickled down my back while I waited. At least Milos was safe now.

After a moment, Count William returned. "The king will see you now."

"Thank you, Count William."

"I will wait for you." With a gracious bow, he held the door for me.

When I entered the apartment, I was amazed at its plainness. Bare of decorations aside from a silver cross on the wall and wall sconces, it contained just a desk and a few chairs. The king sat in an armchair, listlessly turning the pages of a manuscript. He looked tired, and his skin had a yellowish cast.

"Mistress Alina," he said, "I have heard from my daughter how sorry she is to lose your companionship. What may I do for you?"

I squared my shoulders. Stepping up to the desk, I pulled the True Cross out of my satchel. "I have come to bring this to you."

Slack-jawed, the king said nothing. His hand trembled slightly as he reached out to touch it. "I thought it was lost for good. How is it that you return it to us?"

"My lord, I beg for your indulgence. The culprit is dead and will trouble you no longer. I came upon it by accident, and I cannot tell you the story without harming innocent bystanders."

"I see."

I hid my trembling hands behind my back. This was when the king would probably ask for Count Raymond, and Count Raymond would force me to tell him what happened. I had thought about what story I could come up with in that case, but none seemed credible. I definitely did not want to admit that with Ralph's help my brother and I had killed a knight of the cross.

The king slowly ran his hands over the precious silver cross that housed the holy relic. Then he looked up and met my eyes. "Mistress Alina, we are in your debt for returning the True Cross to us. We cannot begin to express our gratitude. This will help us in the years ahead as we defend the kingdom."

"Thank you, my lord," I said, stumbling over the words. He was not going to ask any questions. "May I take my leave now?"

The king inclined his head. "We wish you a safe journey."

I curtsied and backed out of the royal apartment, dizzy with relief, and spotted Count William leaning against the wall. Holding my arm, he shepherded me past curious glances out into the courtyard.

"Thank you." I studied his face. I liked him. I knew Sibylla liked him. "Please tell my lady that the matter she was concerned about has been resolved. She might also find that another of her suitors has departed and will not return. I doubt she will be grieved by that."

Count William looked as if he was burning to ask questions, but then he merely bowed. "Godspeed, Mistress Alina."

It was getting late. Gripping my satchel, I walked as quickly as I could across the courtyard. As soon as I cleared the gate, I started running.

When I arrived at Meir's house, neighbors were in the process of helping get the cart ready.

"Alina, I am glad you've come." Sarah looked distracted, clutching the baby with one arm and trying to pick up a large sack with the other. "I have to run down to Jacob's house to drop off some things we aren't taking with us."

"Why don't you let me hold Alon?"

The baby was heavy. He had grown a lot in the past few weeks. He blinked at me sleepily and closed his eyes again.

"Is that all you have?" Meir asked, pointing to my bundle and the lute wrapped in Sibylla's shawl, which I had put on the floor.

"Yes. Be careful. The lute is in there."

Soon we were ready. Meir took up the reins of the cart mules, and Sarah and I perched in the back as we rolled along the road below the wall toward David's Gate, where the group of merchants was about to set out toward Acre. They had hired several men to ride along for protection.

The next few hours passed in a blur. Fortunately, Sarah didn't make any attempt to talk to me. Occasionally, when the baby began to cry, I heard her sing to him in her soft, low voice. We stopped for a short break, but I couldn't bring myself to eat anything. I just drank some water. We got back on the cart.

Exhausted, I began to doze and didn't wake up until the cart stopped. We had reached the village where we would spend the night. The guards sat in the shade of a tree. Sarah and Meir began pulling things out that they would need. I hopped on the ground. "Would you like me to take Alon for a bit?"

"Please do." She handed the baby to me.

I was grateful to hold him in my arms. His weight and his warmth steadied me as I walked back and forth, listening to his comfortable snuffling sounds and watching his parents make preparations for the night, but my thoughts were in Jerusalem. My eyes burned.

Hoofbeats in the distance startled me out of my reverie. The guards leaped to their feet, alert, their hands on their swords.

A rider approached, his face covered by a dark blue cloth to keep out the dust. He brought his horse to a stop in front of me and pulled the scarf down.

"Hey, Froggie, you didn't get very far, did you?"

Milos. Speechless, I stared up at him.

"You didn't really think I would let you go off by yourself?" He grinned, his face free of the haunted look that he had for so long.

"But what about Stephen?" I sputtered.

"We met at the horse trader's, and we talked for a while."

"You didn't tell him about Count Baltasar, did you?"

"No. At least not in so many words. I think Stephen understands. He even gave me some advice about how to deal with Uncle Garsanc."

"He did?" I looked at him in amazement.

"Yes. It was good advice, too. He told me that he had some experience with brothers and fathers and that I needed to think like Uncle Garsanc for a while. I would have to earn Uncle Garsanc's respect, and I would have to work my way up from the bottom. Stephen thought that once Uncle Garsanc respected me more, he would welcome me if only to preserve the estate for the family. Incidentally, Stephen sends you his regards. He said all sorts of complimentary things about you."

Flustered, I glanced at his horse, a raw-boned gelding with yellow teeth and ears laid back as if ready to bite. "Is that all you could find?"

Milos laughed, stroking the gelding's neck. "You didn't give me that much money. Besides, it was rather short notice." He dismounted. "And who is this?"

"Alon, Meir's son." The baby had begun to fret until I realized I was holding him too tightly.

"Stephen wrote a letter for me to give to Duke Sob slav." Proudly Milos patted his satchel. "Oh, I almost forgot. He gave me something else." He opened his satchel, rooted around in it, and pulled out a little parcel wrapped in hemp. "Here."

"Hold him for me, would you?" I handed the baby to Milos.

I laughed at Milos's bewildered expression and his awkwardly extended arms. "It's a baby, not a sack of barley."

"Don't fret. At least I'm not holding him upside down." Milos grinned. "Now open your parcel."

With fingers suddenly clumsy, I tugged on the rough brown wrapping until it fell away. Stunned, I stared at the silver-and-gilt box I had admired in the market. The lute player seemed to be smiling, one foot lifted as if about to dance. I opened the lid. Inside there was a scrap of paper, folded tightly. Turning away so Milos could not see my face, I flattened it out. Everything was blurry. Finally I blinked often enough that I could read the minute, neat script.

Something to remind you of Jerusalem as you embark on another journey. May the Lord shelter you, be the waves ever so wild or the road rough and full of stones, and trust in your music. S.

Stephen. He had remembered and troubled to get that box for me.

I didn't understand him. He lived in a world of complex politics I could barely grasp. He thought of me as a father might think of his daughter, which no longer stung. Blind to our differences in rank and status as well as age, I had turned him into a character in one of my songs, which had nothing to do with the reality of who he was.

But he would always be important to me because he had shown me what mattered. Thanks to Stephen, I now knew what I wanted. In truth, I had known for a long time, but doubt and fear had held me back. One day, after I had become an acclaimed trobairitz, I would travel to Sancerre. I would perform in his great hall. He would show me his new fishponds, and I would meet his family. I might even send him my oldest son to serve as a page.

"This little fellow weighs a ton," Milos said behind me.

I turned to take Alon from him. Tears ran down my nose.

"Hey, don't cry, Froggie." He slung an affectionate arm around me.

"I am so very glad to see you."

"Yes, well, that's why we shouldn't let you make all the plans. We need to stick together. Who knows? The lords of Bohemia might have a use for an extra sword."

The next morning we set out on our journey toward the west. Swaying in the cart and listening to the clip-clop of the horses, with my eyes on my brother, lanky and long-limbed, with a new air of self-assurance astride his tall horse, I thought of everything that had happened.

Again, I heard Meir's reply when I asked him about the unfinished wall in his house, calling it a form of prayer in remembrance of the temple's destruction. "*I also like to think it reminds us that things in this life are impermanent,*" he had added. Impermanence meant change, and change meant an opening to something new. I thought of Halevi's poems, humbled and awed by their purity. I could never match that, but that was as it should be. I had to find my own words. I thought of my father's voice as he carved an exquisite rose, the sound hole in the center of a lute. "*The rose is like a window into the soul of the lute. You have to make it your own through your music.*"

I was going to claim my rose. Drumming a beat with my fingers, I began to hum.

The taste of tangy lemons on my lips,
Jerusalem silk slipping through my fingers,
I face the dusty road ahead, curling toward the open sea,
And shape my tears into a new song.

HISTORICAL NOTES

Often in the course of working on this book, I wished someone wise had urged me to leave this one alone.

To put it simply, it's complicated. History is never linear or straightforward, and any attempt to grapple with the realities of a historical sequence of events is bound to be messy.

Upon closer examination, much of the history of the crusades reads like the present times—with its web of intrigues, its political machinations, the peculiar mix of ideology, faith, lust for power, and greed, and the all-too-human characters involved with their multitude of contradictory motivations.

Yet, just as in our times, there emerge individuals who stand out—unforgettable, fallible, human, and with streaks of greatness.

The central historical character of this book is Stephen, Count of Sancerre, a French nobleman of rank and distinction. We know little about him, but what we do know is tantalizing.

He was the third son of Count Theobald II of Champagne, and he inherited Sancerre on his father's death. His elder brothers Henry and Theobald received Champagne and Blois respectively. Stephen, Count of Sancerre, was the nephew of Stephen, King of England (c. 1092/6 – 25 October 1154), who was often referred to as Stephen of Blois and a grandson of William the Conqueror.

Stephen, Count of Sancerre was one of the richest men in the region, with few to match him, and his powers equaled those of the king. The family history (*Histoire de Sancerre*) provides a nuanced portrait of a man with royal aspirations and the heart of a farmer, a man deeply religious and yet also quick to engage in conflicts which often resulted in little profit to him. He negotiated complex power struggles between the powerful church and parties representing economic and political interests, in a shifting landscape, in particular in the context of the waning power of baronial seigneurs vis-a-vis the king.

Stephen was the first to claim the right to print money, and this currency was in circulation throughout his domains. Local disputes involved, among others, his construction of a pond and mills as well as a farm. In cooperation with the local bishop, these disputes were settled by a decree that the profits be divided equally among the contesting parties. Stephen amended a system of fines by setting limits on the amounts payable by the parties involved. In 1155, he granted the Customs of Lorris to the merchants of the town. This merchant charter was considered one of the most progressive of such charters of rights and privileges in the Capetian kingdom. He abolished a local custom which involved the liberation of a prisoner at Easter, which always led to bloody battles and frequent deaths. He also abolished certain laws regarding marriage, in particular, one known as *formariage*, which involved loss of property if individuals from his domains got married in another county.

Stephen eloped with his future wife Alice-Matilda de Donzy on the day of her wedding to another. Regrettably, there is some uncertainty about both her given name and the date of her death. In any event, he was a widower and about forty years old when he traveled to Jerusalem in the early 1170s. In 1169, King Amalric I invited Stephen to Jerusalem as a possible husband for the young princess Sibylla. Such a marriage would have made him the future king of the kingdom. For reasons unknown, Stephen decided against it after a brief stay in Jerusalem, and returned home to Sancerre.

His first act upon his return was to make a gift of twelve acres to the church. He also allowed the local monks to name their own abbots and granted them other concessions. He embarked upon a rebellion against the king of France in which he sided with his sister Alix de Champagne, wife of Louis VII; eventually, this dispute was settled by Stephen's bowing to the king's authority and pleading for mercy. In early 1190, he emancipated all the serfs in his domains and then returned to the Holy Land. He died in the third crusade at the Siege of Acre in the fall of 1190.

For my convenience I made adjustments regarding the year in which this story is set and the respective ages of the individuals involved. Some sources claim that Stephen went to Jerusalem in 1170 or in 1171; others claim that he went there in 1174. I find the latter date unlikely, since King Amalric died on July 11, 1174. I had Stephen travel there in 1173. Sibylla was born in 1160. In 1173, she was thirteen. Her sister Isabella was born in 1172. Regarding the cast of characters, the year 1173 allowed me to insert Raymond of Tripoli into the story, who had been imprisoned in Aleppo after a battle at Harim against Nur ad-Din Zengi in 1164 in which the crusader army was defeated. According to historical reports, in 1173, King Amalric freed Count Raymond by paying a ransom of 80,000 pieces of gold.

GLOSSARY

Cyrillic – a writing script that was developed in the First Bulgarian Empire during the 9th century A.D. and became the basis of alphabets used in various Slavic languages.

Doublet – a padded, sleeveless vest worn by medieval knights under their armor.

Harp – a stringed musical instrument with individual strings running at an angle to its soundboard and strummed with the fingers.

Hospitallers – Knights of the Order of St. John, a Catholic military order, founded to provide care for sick, poor, or injured pilgrims coming to the Holy Land.

Joglar – a medieval European person, generally not of the noble class, also known as a minstrel who performed songs whose lyrics told stories of distant places or of existing or imaginary historical events.

Joglaressas – female minstrels.

Lute – an instrument with strings running in a plane parallel to the sound table, with a neck (either fretted or unfretted) and a rounded back, sharing a common ancestor with the *oud*.

Lyra – a bowed, stringed instrument, after the 13th century referred to as a *rebec*. In its most common form it has a narrow, boat-shaped body and 1 to

5 strings. Played, supported by an arm or positioned under the chin, this instrument may have influenced the development of the violin.

Oud – a stringed musical instrument prominent in medieval and modern Islamic music, similar to the lute.

Provençal – a dialect of Occitan, also known as *langue d'oc*, a Romance language.

Scrip – a small leather pouch carried on the waist by pilgrims and monks.

Surcoat – a long, flowing garment, either sleeved or sleeveless, worn by medieval knights over other clothes, frequently emblazoned with their personal arms. It usually extended to about mid-calf, and had slits in the bottom front and back, thus allowing the wearer to ride comfortably.

Templar Knights – members of a Catholic military order known for its skilled fighting units as well as its management of a large economic infrastructure throughout Christendom, including the organization of an early form of banking.

Tenso – a style of troubadour song, taking the form of a dialogue or debate between two parties.

Trobairitz – female troubadours of the 12th and 13th centuries, active from around 1170 to approximately 1260. Trobairitz composed music, wrote verses, and performed for the noble courts. Trobairitz were part of courtly society, as opposed to their lower-class counterparts, the joglaressas.

Troubadour – a composer and performer of lyric poetry during the High Middle Ages (1100–1350).

ACKNOWLEDGMENTS

Stephen Roxburgh, Ann Howard Creel, Nora Cohen, and Faith Free-woman have provided me with incisive and constructive critiques at various points in the writing of this book. I cannot adequately express my gratitude for their professional help and their words of support and encouragement. Working with Joni Firestone and the entire team at BHC Press has been a pleasure. My father Wolf Ulrich von Hassell would have enjoyed talking to me about the historical details of this book and plied me with excellent Sancerre wine all the while. In fact, my father, the most balanced, sane, rational think-ing person I ever knew, with endless resources of knowledge at his fingertips, a wonderful sense of humor, and an ability to discuss any given topic with detached intelligence and deep understanding, was my inspiration for the fictional elements of my historical character, Count Stephen I, first Count de Sancerre. As always, I am grateful for my son Ivan's support throughout the writing process.

ABOUT THE AUTHOR

Malve von Hassell was born in Italy and spent part of her childhood in Belgium and Germany before moving to the United States. She lives in Southampton, New York, close to the ocean and a bay beach where she meets flying sea robins and turtles on her morning walks with her rescue dog Loki. Aside from reading and playing chess with her son, her favorite activities are gardening, anything to do with horses, and dreaming of going on a horseback riding tour in Mongolia. She is a freelance writer, researcher, and translator. She has published a children's picture book, *Letters from the Tooth Fairy* (Mill City Press, 2012), written in response to her son's letters to the tooth fairy. *The Falconer's Apprentice* (namelos, 2015) was her first historical fiction novel for young readers. Her two most recent releases are *The Amber Crane*, a historical fiction novel set in Germany in the 17th century (Odyssey Books, 2020), and *Alina: A Song for the Telling* (BHC Press, 2020).

CPSIA information can be obtained
at www.ICGtesting.com
Printed in the USA
BVHW030301270720
584574BV00004B/22